A HANS LARSS[ON]

BOOK T[WO]

THE
TRADE

CHRIS THRALL

SERF
BOOKS

The Trade

First published in Great Britain by Serf Books Ltd in 2016.

www.serfbooks.com

ISBN: 978-0-9935439-1-3

A catalogue record for this book is available from the British Library.

Design by www.golden-rivet.co.uk

1 3 5 7 9 10 8 6 4 2

For Harry

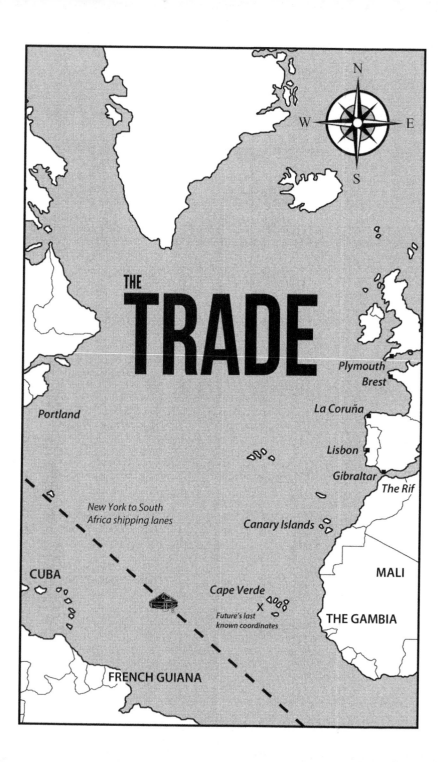

Ten miles off North Africa's Cape Verde islands, Hans Larsson prided himself on *Future*'s progress, the wind skimming the sleek-lined yacht across the wave tops at twelve knots. As the sea's invigorating spray landed on his tanned skin, the American reflected on the voyage so far.

It was eighteen months on from the murder of his wife and young son. Hans, a former Navy SEAL, had taken time off from running the Larsson Investigation Agency and his contract work for the secretive Concern organization to fulfill the family dream, taking his seven-year-old daughter Jessica on the yacht trip of a lifetime. Leaving Portland, Maine, they'd flown to England and bought the forty-one-foot *Future* in Plymouth, intending to sail back across the Atlantic via Europe, North Africa and the Caribbean.

So far the passage had provided the perfect opportunity for father and daughter to work through their loss and reinforce the deep bond between them. It had been an education and adventure to say the least, made all the more enjoyable by the bubbly Penny Masters, an experienced English skipper who'd agreed to crew for them on the crossing.

Having explored the historic port of Plymouth, Hans,

Jessica and Penny sailed *Future* across the English Channel, stopping in Europe, the Canaries and now Cape Verde. Immersed in a kaleidoscopic mix of Anglo, Latin, African and postcolonial culture, they'd sampled exotic food, explored the sights and enjoyed excellent fishing and scuba diving.

However, the trip was not without its challenges. A rogue storm slammed *Future* down in the Bay of Biscay, and a full-scale riot erupted all around them in Lisbon when the crew of a British aircraft carrier battled with the Portuguese police. Penny and Jessica had a close encounter with a bull shark while diving in Tenerife, and pirates had attempted to board *Future* off Cape Verde.

Penny had been a pillar of support throughout and an accomplished crew member. Hans knew he was in love and couldn't have felt happier, particularly as Penny and Jessica adored each other.

Now, as the fiery red sun lowered to the horizon, Hans brought the yacht around, the impending darkness not the only reason he looked forward to reaching port, for Penny was ashore attending to last-minute preparations for their Atlantic crossing.

Below deck, Jessica played with her beloved teddy in the sleeping quarters, clipping her safety line to the rail on their bunk.

"You always gotta clip on, Bear!" she told him.

Although knowing the man-overboard precaution was unnecessary inside the cabin, the little girl liked to demonstrate her seafaring skills to her companion – lessons drummed into her by her father.

"Good night, Bear." She tucked her furry friend under the covers and gave him a peck on his snout.

Washed off the deck of the *Tokyo Pride* during a storm, cargo container SIDU307007-9 had drifted around the North Atlantic for months, along with its consignment of high-tech televisions. Floating just below the surface, it was every sailor's worst nightmare, resulting in many a yacht crew having to evacuate to their life raft. SIDU307007-9 sat at 16° 15' north, 25° 40' west, directly in the path of *Future*.

At 1831 hours, Hans felt relaxed, content with the direction his boat and life were heading, all the time looking forward to dinner with Penny.

At 1832 hours, with a sickening crunch Hans' boat and life ripped apart, slamming him facefirst into the navigation console. He knew instinctively the yacht was about to sink.

"Jessie, get out! Get out now!"

The life raft's hydrostatic releases hissed and the bright-orange pod deployed. Hans dived inside the cabin, but a barrage of seawater washed him back into the cockpit.

Fighting for composure, he sucked in a lungful of air and thrust his body into the downturned hull, frantically trying to reach his daughter as the boat descended into the depths. Hans felt as though his chest would implode but continued into the blackness, rewarded to see his little girl swimming up to meet him.

That's it, Jessie! That's it!

Their hands clasped.

Hans experienced an immense sense of relief . . .

Well done, kid!

. . . then spotted Jessica's safety line clipped to the bunk, the sinking yacht ripping the little girl from his grasp, her desperate eyes fixed on his as the ocean devoured her.

Jessica felt the yank of the safety line and saw the horror on her father's face. She turned and began swimming back down, pulling herself along the line and kicking with all her might. Rather than waste time trying to unclip from the bunk's rail, she reminded herself to stay calm, as her father had taught her on countless scuba dives, and instead opened the locker under the bunk to retrieve her diving equipment. Hans always made sure they rinsed the kit in freshwater following a dive, refilling the tanks from the yacht's compressor and stowing the reassembled gear under their berths ready for deployment. To a girl who had completed her first open-water dive shortly after her fifth birthday and could hold her breath for almost two minutes, locating the air supply was a logical course of action.

In the gloom of the sinking cabin, Jessica grabbed her custom-made buoyancy vest as it attempted to float up past her into the open ocean, along with her teddy bear and other items of unsecured gear. Clutching the vest to her tiny chest, Jessica cranked open the air cylinder and flailed around looking for the mouthpiece, or regulator, which in the chaos had pulled free of the pocket she took care to store it in.

As she was not wearing a weight belt, the deflated

jacket had sufficient air inside to begin lifting her to the surface. Once again she willed herself to stay calm and began tracing the route of the regulator's hose from where it connected to the air cylinder, a process she could do blindfolded, since her father always made her set up her own equipment.

A touch of panic set in, but as Jessica contemplated ditching the kit and breaking for the surface, her hand contacted the round plastic regulator. She wasted no time clenching the mouthpiece's rubber teats between her teeth.

After blowing out to expel the water flooding the regulator, the little girl took several welcome breaths, unclipped herself from the bunk's rail and kicked for the companionway, squeezing a burst of air into the jacket as she did.

In her haste to exit the doomed craft, Jessica shot upwards, smashing her head into the companionway's surround. For a split second the painful shock saw her mind blank and her limbs go numb. It was all she could do to hold on to the equipment and remember to breathe.

By now *Future* was forty meters down and sinking fast – twice the depth Jessica had ever dove to, but she wasn't to know this. She thrust an arm out of the opening and eased herself into the open sea, praying none of the buckles or hoses would snag.

Once free of the cabin, Jessica knew it was imperative to ascend quickly. Too much time breathing air at depth would require a safety stop to rid her bloodstream of built-up nitrogen – impossible without a weight belt to achieve neutral buoyancy. She clamped down on the jacket's air-in button, fattening it like a car inner tube until she felt the overfill valves vibrate and heard the belch of escaping bubbles.

Rocketing to the surface, Jessica wondered if her ascent would ever end but knew her father would be there in the life raft to pick her up.

When her head burst through the increasing swell, she frantically scanned all around . . . to see blackness and nothing. The breeze had blown the life raft out of sight.

"Papa!" she screamed to no avail.

Ten miles out to sea, the little girl was alone, drifting in the dark on a vast ocean.

Clutching the buoyancy vest and air cylinder, she floated around in silence, trying to think what her father would encourage her to do. Hans had experienced a turbulent upbringing. As a result, he made sure to treat his daughter as an equal, empowering Jessica to make her own decisions and instilling a maturity way beyond her short years. He often praised her for being the kid who never cried, but tears rolled down her cheeks now.

"Get a grip, sweet pea!" she said, echoing her father's words. "Feel sorry for yourself, and sure as hell the world won't feel sorry for you!"

Her thinking helped – not enough to stem the fear but sufficient to see her struggle into the buoyancy vest, a safety drill she'd carried out numerous times in the icy water off Maine.

Wondering what had become of her dear teddy, "Get a grip, Bear!," she screamed across the void, then crossed her arms and settled back in the harness, exhausted but knowing her father would return.

Jessica awoke to the screech of a gull as it circled above, inspecting her floating figure as a potential source of food. The rising sun already burned with savage intensity, so she slipped out of her shorts and placed them over her head. Kicking around in a circle, she longed to catch sight of the life raft, but there was nothing, only rippling ocean and fragile sprays of white in an otherwise faultless sky.

The harness cut into Jessica's armpits, numbing her hands. She struggled to change position, wondering where Penny was. Surely she must know *Future* had sunk and be en route to pick them up.

An almighty thirst took hold. Jessica splashed seawater on her face but knew better than to drink it, because Papa said if you swallow seawater it makes you go mad. She was hungry too and thought about the tuna they had caught and barbecued on *Future* in the Canary Islands.

The noise of a diesel engine shook Jessica out of her muse. A black speck appeared on the horizon.

"Penny!" she screamed, knowing her friend was coming to the rescue and hoping her father was already safely on board.

The clank of the engine grew louder. Jessica grinned,

but as the ugly rusting hulk bore down on her, it looked like no ship she had seen before. She began to feel afraid. Something didn't feel right.

The vessel was about pass on by when a shout of "*Capitão!*" went up, and she slowed and came around. Thick black fumes spilled onto the water as two black faces stared down at the little girl bobbing in the swell.

Jessica read the faded nameplate on the rotting bow, *Rosa Negra*, and started to kick away.

- 5 -

One month later

Jens Greyling wiped the sleep from his eyes and reached for his coffee.

"*Dankie*," he grunted in Afrikaans, scanning the ocean ahead as dawn's fingers raked life into the oily black water.

The boy smiled. He'd been with the skipper long enough to know that behind this gruff morning exterior the appreciation was there.

Registered in Panama, the *Kimberley II* had plied the New York–South Africa shipping lanes for the past decade. At forty thousand tons fully laden, she was by no means a large freighter, and nearing her thirtieth year, the aging tub's days were numbered – something Jens would worry about when the time came. He'd taken over her command not long after his divorce eight years previous, and the old girl had proved a faithful companion – unlike the last one. The Filipino crew was his family, the boy the son he never had. The Rhodesian captain had woken up in a shack in the township one morning after a drunken knife fight to find Chamfar dressing his wounds. They'd been inseparable ever since.

Over the years Jens had put a moderate sum of money aside, and when his command of the *Kimberley*

II ended, he planned to take the boy and retire to Mozambique. The former Portuguese colony had recovered from years of war, and Jens knew the exact spot on Naherenge's endless powdery white beach where he would situate the fishing and dive center he planned to build amid the lush green palms.

The skipper massaged his temples, which throbbed in harmony with the *Kimberley II*'s powerful diesel engines, cane spirit being an unforgiving mistress.

"So, my friend, what are you going to do when we reach Kaapstad?" he asked his first mate.

"Girls, girls, girls!" Chamfar did the sexy dance and grinned fat white teeth.

"I guess I needn't have asked." Jens managed a chuckle, the sweet black coffee working its magic on his sore head.

Having departed Pier 6 at the Port Newark–Elizabeth Marine Terminal in New York three weeks earlier carrying vehicle parts, office equipment and petroleum products, they would cross the equator in four days' time and be two-thirds of the way to Cape Town.

On the boat deck Juan, the chief engineer, pulled a Voyager from a soft pack and shoved it between his lips, a morning ritual throughout his time at sea. Soon he would give the systems a thorough checking over, looking for tripped fuses, topping up water and oil reservoirs and replacing clogged filters, but not before drawing the coarse smoke deep into his lungs and letting the resultant waves of euphoria carry him across the shimmering wave tops to his home in the Philippines. Leaning against the rusty rail, he pictured his wife collecting his two boys from school, treating them to a ripe mango sprinkled with paprika on the walk to their village shack. He saw them once a year, flying home when the *Kimberley II* stopped for a month of routine maintenance in Cape Town.

The sun climbed ever higher into the unfolding azure. Juan flicked his butt over the rail and watched it tumble through the air into the ship's wake. He was about to leave the boat deck to attend to his first chore when something in the middle distance caught his attention.

It was an orange speck.

Juan screened his eyes from the sun and looked again. Nothing. Likely just light reflecting off the water and playing tricks.

Then there it was!

Definitely something orange, the color of distress, bobbing in and out of view with the rise and fall of the ocean.

Juan had seen his fair share of junk adrift on the sea over the years – cargo containers, fishing nets, steel and plastic drums, flotillas of ships' garbage, even a forty-foot-long inflatable swimming pool – but his instincts told him this was different.

Putting both hands up to block out the dazzling rays, Juan stared at the spot, waiting for the right combination of light and line of sight.

A brief flicker of orange and then . . . yes!

It was a life raft, cresting a wave and remaining in full view for what seemed an age though was probably less than a second. But it was definitely a life raft.

Juan's first thought was to duck inside the superstructure and run up the four flights of stairs to the bridge, where the binoculars were held, but he knew relocating the tiny craft could prove impossible, so keeping a fix on the life raft, he picked up the boat deck's intercom telephone.

"Captain, I can see an orange canopy one kilometer to starboard at three o'clock."

Jens Greyling jerked his head at the binoculars bracketed to the bulkhead, as he had done thousands of times before. The boy passed them to the skipper.

Using a figure-of-eight-pattern search – a throwback to his army training – Jens scanned the area Juan had pinpointed. Minutes ticked by, and he made several passes with the binoculars until – "*Ja!*" – he spotted the distant orange dot. "We got her."

Chamfar relayed the message to Juan, who began unlashing the webbing straps securing the *Kimberley II*'s rigid inflatable boat, or RIB, in preparation for a potential rescue.

Jens knew better than to take his eyes off the craft, which could disappear from view in a flash. Instead he barked orders at his first mate.

"Throttle back full and bring her hard to starboard." There was no way he could stop the ship on a dime, but an attempt to slow down while circling the tiny raft would be better than sailing miles away from it. "And wake the men and tell them to assemble on the boat deck."

As the boy reached for the telephone it rang, for, sensing the change of course and the engines winding down, the crew were already out of their bunks, and Carlos, the ship's cook, wanted a situation report.

In minutes Carlos and Virgilio, the deckhand, had kitted up in dry suits and life jackets and climbed into the RIB. While Juan operated the davit, swinging the inflatable boat outboard and lowering it gently over the side, the two of them fended with their hands to prevent it from smashing into the ship's iron hull.

The RIB settled upon the relatively calm sea. As Virgilio tripped the davit cable's quick release, Carlos throttled forward, and they surged into the white water streaming from the *Kimberley II*'s side.

Jens radioed directions to the two men, and minutes later Carlos blipped the engine in reverse, nudging the launch up against the beleaguered orange pod. Virgilio leant out and grabbed the exterior handline, but eyeing the sagging tubes and rust and algae smears on the sun-bleached canopy, the men could see the raft had collided with a ship, and they assumed its occupants must have drowned.

The raft's flimsy doorway flapped in the breeze. With his thumb and forefinger, Virgilio slowly peeled it back.

"Urrch!" Carlos retched on his empty stomach, the stench of death taking them by surprise.

Virgilio viewed the utter devastation inside. Rotting fish carcasses washed around in a stagnant pool, along with empty tin cans and a filthy, worn-out sleeping bag.

"Nothing," he concluded, then, holding his nose, thrust a hand into the putrid brown brine and plucked out a child's teddy bear. Turning to Carlos, he shook his head.

"Okay. We go." Carlos released his hold on the raft's handline and was about to restart the motor when they heard a long rasping wheeze.

Both men froze.

Virgilio looked tentatively to Carlos, then, crossing his

chest and muttering to Mother Mary in Tagalog, leant inside the flagging pod and lifted the flap of the sleeping bag.

"Mother of God!" His eyes widened.

"No." Carlos began shaking, and no more words would come.

From an emaciated and bearded face stared the eyes of a dying man.

Virgilio dropped the flap of the sleeping bag, his own eyes pleading with Carlos for direction. Both deeply superstitious, they were tempted to peel away and return to the *Kimberley II*, but here was a fellow mariner in the direst of need, and the law of the sea saw them put their own concerns aside and jump into action.

The man was in no fit state for them to transfer him to the launch. They would have to hoist him on deck in situ. Besides, if he died, the raft might hold clues as to his identity or the vessel he had abandoned.

Clipped to three anchor points on the launch was a triad of straps that attached to the davit's cable. In seconds Carlos had unclipped them and reattached the hook fasteners at equidistant points around the raft's exterior handline. Then they towed the stinking, sagging capsule back to the ship, radioing ahead with a sit-rep.

With the *Kimberley II* hove to, Jens joined Juan on the boat deck.

"Stretcher and medical kit," he hollered, slamming the davit's gear lever forward.

The life raft crimped inwards like a trawler's net, emptying out a torrent of filthy seawater as Jens maneuvered it up and over the rail. Juan dropped the stretcher and medical kit and rushed to release the webbing straps, then hauled the raft out of the way to make space for the launch, a dying stranger not a priority when two crew members remained at the mercy of the ocean.

With Carlos and Virgilio safely back on board, Jens ran over to help Juan, who had punctured the raft's tubes with a boatswain's knife and cut away the canopy to get to the survivor and lay him on the stretcher. Juan had taken a drip out of the medical pack but was struggling to find a vein in the man's wasted arms. When Jens knelt down beside his chief engineer, the stench wafting from the corpse-like figure forced him to turn his head away for a moment. He could tell the deep gash in the man's temple was gangrenous, and the infection had spread throughout his scrawny body.

"Give! Give!"

Jens took the saline pack from Juan. He knew the man's blood pressure was too low to get a vein up but had a better idea – another trick learned while fighting in the bush in Rhodesia.

"If we don't get fluid inside him fast, he will die. We'll shove it straight into his backside," the grizzled sea captain informed his crew with a lack of ceremony they'd long gotten used to.

Then he whipped out his sheath knife and lopped the hypodermic needle connection off the drip tube. Dignity not an option, they removed the man's soiled, shredded shorts and maneuvered him into a suitable position for Jens to insert the tube carrying the life-giving liquid.

"Okay, put two vials of antibiotics into his butt cheek, and keep the drip in place until it's empty," Jens ordered, then hefted himself back up to the bridge to send a distress call.

As the saline passed through the sensitive lining of the man's colon and into his bloodstream, the change in his condition startled them. The infected wound had swollen one eyelid shut, but the other, now lubricated with tears, began to flicker, the eye itself morphing from dry and drab, like that of a dead fish, into a bloodshot piercing blue. Color returned to his pallid skin, and he started to move, slowly at first but becoming increasingly agitated.

"Blanket!" Juan looked to Virgilio, who passed him one, but as Juan draped it over the rescued man, he thrust a hand out and grabbed his shirt.

"Jessica!" he rasped.

The three Filipinos jumped back in surprise.

"Jessica!" the man pleaded, his gaze unsteady as he tried to fix on Juan.

"Jessica?" Juan repeated, screwing up his eyes.

The man released his grip, and his arm fell backwards, pointing in the direction of the raft.

Virgilio walked over to the slashed-up craft and lifted out the teddy bear. "Docs he mean *this* one?"

Juan and Carlos looked at each other and shrugged. Virgilio held the bear up in front of the man's face. He let out a despondent gurgle and collapsed into unconsciousness.

Awaking in the Grande Verde's penthouse suite, Penny threw off the Italian linen on the emperor-size bed and padded barefoot across the marble tiles to the state-of-the-art kitchen. She hit the double espresso button on the fancy drinks maker and took the freshly ground cup of coffee out onto the veranda, sipping it gently while scanning the great ocean. Penny knew there was no chance of *Future* simply sailing back into port over a month after going missing but stuck to her morning ritual nonetheless to acknowledge the possibility of Hans and Jessica fighting for their lives in a life raft.

Penny had fallen for Hans the moment they met in the marina in England, making the decision to accept his offer to crew for them an easy one. Athletic, good looking, intelligent, thoughtful, nonjudgmental – the list went on – Hans possessed a deep understanding of the world and blazed a path through life guided by his own moral compass, circumventing intimidation, convention and others' self-serving rules. He made her laugh with his wry observations, self-effacing humor and subtle wit but occasionally flashed a more serious side, resulting from his tough childhood, horrors witnessed in the special forces and the murder of his wife and son.

Although an affectionate father, Hans was afraid of nothing and no one and would do whatever was necessary to protect those close to him. Penny witnessed this firsthand when two police officers tried to arrest them for no apparent reason during a riot in Portugal. Hans had gone easy on the men, resulting in a short stay in hospital for them, but a gang of pirates attempting to hijack *Future* offshore one night was not so fortunate.

Born to somewhat bohemian parents, Penny grew up on yachts and, other than practicing as a veterinary nurse for a year in London after graduation, had spent most of her life at sea. In recent times she'd made a comfortable living skippering rich folk to exotic locations around the globe and teaching them to scuba dive.

Because of the nomadic nature of the job, Penny hadn't been in a serious relationship before Hans, apart from a whirlwind romance with a playboy millionaire who'd hired her to captain his yacht around the Caribbean. Only, after parting company, Penny found out he was married with three children . . . *and* that she was pregnant. Alone with no support a long way from home, she'd opted for an abortion, a decision that still haunted her. It was impossible not to think of the adorable Jessica as the child she never had.

When Hans invited Penny to spend time with them in Portland, she knew it was time to leave the past behind and had looked forward to testing her land legs and finding work in a local sailing or scuba school.

In the penthouse's wet room, Penny turned the matrix of jets spurting from the gold-flecked charcoal tiles to full and stood amid the powerful spray. Another of her morning rituals, it was as if cleansing herself of the previous day's grime would somehow open the way for fresh fortune.

"Coffee?" Penny handed Phipps a mug.

"Thanks, honey."

The Concern's special operative set it down next to his laptop and took a welcome break, having been awake since 3:00 a.m. contacting vessels crossing the North Atlantic on a bearing intercepting the possible predicted drift of *Future*'s life raft.

They were on the floor below the penthouse in a guest suite originally used as a command center by the Concern, who'd flown a team of special operatives to Cape Verde following the yacht's disappearance. Hans – code name "Orion" – was one of the organization's foremost agents.

All they knew of the missing yacht were the coordinates, ten miles offshore, that Hans had radioed through to the local marina as he swung *Future* about to return to port. With no Mayday broadcast or a signal from *Future*'s emergency beacon picked up by satellite or aircraft, the coastguard believed the yacht must have collided with an object – possibly a whale or shipping container – and sank immediately.

"But there's still hope if they took to the raft," Phipps maintained.

Yet after overseeing an extensive air-and-sea search

involving multiple parties, the team's coordinator – Hans' handler, Innes Edridge, code name "Muttley" – had no choice but to ramp down the expensive operation, leaving only Phipps behind on Cape Verde to support Penny and liaise with the authorities and shipping.

A group of disenfranchised patriots and aggrieved special ops veterans formed the Concern after the Vietnam War, seeking to bring to justice individuals who had used the conflict for private gain. The list included politicians who spun the war so their cronies in the military-industrial complex made enormous profits, CIA operatives illicitly trading in weapons and drugs under the cover of the supply chain, and company directors and financiers doing business with both sides.

Operating below the radar of society and government, the Concern functioned on a need-to-know basis, recruiting highly skilled and accomplished individuals of all occupations – former special ops and intelligence types, medical professionals, airline owners, bankers, immigration and embassy officials, weapons specialists – through a system of sponsorship and rigorous background checks. The Concern had blossomed into a formidable force for good, its private contractors involved in all manner of operations, from exposing corporate wrongdoings and supporting humanitarian projects and persecuted political parties, to hostage rescue and generally sticking up for the dispossessed.

Proposed operations surfaced when a member of the Concern felt an individual or community needed support in the face of adversity or injustice. Funding came by way of financial donations from "enablers" – corporate directors looking to offset enormous profits to assuage their capitalist guilt. By playing John Wayne cum Mother Teresa from the comfort of an office chair, these folks got the honor of being in on one of the world's best-kept secrets and could take credit for its benevolent work.

Although not-for-profit, the group had a substantial investment portfolio and a network of agents spanning the globe. Hans held the position of special operative, as did Phipps, a former Navy SEAL buddy.

Hans hadn't divulged much information about the organization to Penny, nor his role in it. When *Future* went missing, she'd taken a calculated risk and contacted Innes Edridge – Muttley – knowing the elderly Scot worked in Goldman Sachs' Boston office.

Calm, methodical and with the clinical detachment required of true leadership, the former paratrooper, who went on to become colonel of the 22nd Special Air Service Regiment, quickly debriefed Penny, then put together a rapid-response team and accompanied them to Cape Verde to oversee the search operation. Through their contacts in the Concern, the team acquired the services of a leading public relations firm to raise awareness of the plight of the lost crew. Flyers went out to ports and marinas on both sides of the Atlantic for distribution to commercial shipping and yachts traversing an area where a think tank of experts from the fields of meteorology, oceanography and maritime rescue predicted the trade winds and currents would carry a life raft or a dismasted yacht. In addition to setting up searchforfuture.com, the PR firm targeted "missing" adverts to thousands of maritime-related webpages browsed by transatlantic crews.

At significant expense the Concern team hired every available skipper in the region. A veritable flotilla sailed for *Future*'s last-known position, along with a flight of twenty light aircraft, all coordinated by Phipps, who liaised with the Cape Verde coastguard and the crew of a Lynx helicopter dispatched from a British Royal Navy warship on exercise in the area.

Through a third party, the Concern's team offered a two-hundred-fifty-thousand-dollar reward for any information leading to Hans and Jessica's rescue, and a million for a rescue itself. The promotion attracted all manner of concerned parties to the searchforfuture.com website – amateur radio enthusiasts, skippers of yachts and cargo ships suggesting possible sightings, along with well-wishers with messages of support – but a fair amount of cranks and kooks too.

"Anything new?" Penny sat down next to Phipps, turning the laptop to view the hit counter on searchforfuture.com.

"The usual contributions," said Phipps, stretching his huge black arms above his head. "Another clairvoyant, a Brazilian guy, reckons they might be in the Philippines of all places."

From dawn until way past midnight, Phipps had worked tirelessly, sieving through possible sightings of the yacht, the life raft or debris, triaging them accordingly and communicating the information via satellite phone and offshore radio to shipping in the location to request support.

"It's not looking good, is it?" Penny ran a fingertip down her coffee cup, knowing she was stating the obvious.

"I'm not gonna lie. It's been a month now. If they did take to the life raft, that's quite some time to be adrift. But it has been done. And if there's one man who could survive . . ."

"I know." Penny managed an appreciative smile. "But that's *if* they took to the life raft."

The two of them fell silent, having discussed every permutation and outcome many times over, even the theory Hans might have sailed off with Jessica for reasons known only to him. Without evidence it was impossible to favor any one scenario. The Concern had invested a substantial amount of money into the search thus far, the bill for the penthouse alone reaching ninety thousand dollars. Penny worried that on the balance of probabilities they would pull the plug on the operation.

As if reading her mind, "Listen, Penny," said Phipps. "I'm going to ask Muttley for more time – another month. At least then we can be sure we've allowed for the maximum window . . ." His words trailed off as he realized how this sounded.

"Tony" – Penny used Phipps' Christian name – "I can't tell you how much I appreciate all you've done. Another month would be . . . I mean it would let me . . ." Penny fought back tears.

Phipps placed his hand on hers.

"And I don't have to stay here – the Grande Verde, I mean."

The Grande was the island group's most prestigious hotel, an impressive combination of pastel-cream stone, stainless steel and glass, tiered back against the hillside like an Aztec pyramid. Surrounded by lush green scrub and with a stunning ocean vista, the ultramodern retreat was popular with the rich and famous.

"I don't need an en suite cinema or a conference room," she continued. "Do you know what I'm saying?"

"Ha." Phipps smiled, having gotten used to the organization's no-expenses-spared approach. "Seems kinda weird, don't it?"

"Well, when you've shared bunks in a cramped cabin with strangers most of your life, waking up on a bed that's bigger than a yacht itself does seem a little excessive."

Phipps chuckled, relieved the mood had lightened. "Don't you worry about the Concern's finances, honey. With the money some of our funders make on a daily basis, you could buy fifty of these hotels and still have change."

Penny knew it to be true, also that the treatment she'd received was a token of the respect the organization had for Orion.

"Tony, can I ask you something?"

"How did I end up working for the Concern?"

"Yes."

"Whoa, where to begin? I loved being a Navy SEAL, everything about it – the tough training, being the best of the best, surrounded by a band of brothers who would willingly lay down their lives for each other. Got to see some serious stuff – some tough ol' fights. But after a while . . ." Phipps pulled down the screen of his laptop, as if shutting out the world to give himself the freedom to think.

"You began to question your motives?"

"You've been talking to Hans." Phipps grinned.

"He said a similar thing."

Phipps rubbed a fingertip over the laptop's silver logo. "I didn't think too deep about that stuff as a kid. Was just hooked by the lifestyle – the diving, the fitness, the travel, drinking beer with my buddies, and laying down as much firepower on an enemy as possible."

"But you started wondering who the enemy was."

"Penny, when you've been ordered to invade someone else's country by gutless suits in Washington and you've got a twelve-year-old boy armed with a Kalashnikov standing side by side with his father, his uncles, his brothers, doing what anybody would do, defending their homeland . . ."

Penny saw the same dark look come over Phipps' face she'd seen on Hans' when he talked about this. She was about to change subject, but Phipps continued.

"When you join the military, it don't matter who you are – high school or graduate – you might know all kinda stuff, but you ain't been on the planet long enough to put the jigsaw together, to see things in the context of time. Everything seems black and white, good versus evil, and God bless America."

"And now we've got the Internet."

"Exactly. You'd have to be some kinda idiot to have that information at your fingertips and not realize something ain't right. You know, when they opened the first McDonald's in Kabul, folks back home actually cheered." Phipps took a gulp of his coffee and slowly shook his head.

"So you got out?"

"I got out before I did something in combat I would live to regret. It's one thing to take a life when you're young and naïve and believe you're doing the right thing, but . . ."

"So you saw the Concern as a way of putting things right?"

"Not exactly. When I left the navy, I worked in investment – hedge funds, real estate, corporate finance, that kinda thing. Married my girlfriend, commuted two hours back and forth every day wearing a suit, 'did lunch,' even took up golf."

"Something tells me that life didn't suit you." Penny smiled.

"It wasn't so much the life. I enjoyed spending more time with my girl." Phipps pulled out his wallet and slid a snap across the desk. "That's Jainee, and my boy, Anthony Jr. Hell, my golf swing sure improved, and I could handle the work. But I got to thinking, is this all there is?"

"Missed the excitement?"

"Yeah, but mostly the camaraderie. What is it the French call that shit?"

"Esprit de corps."

"Yeah, esprit de corps."

"I can relate to that. It's the same in sailing. You cross a huge ocean, battle waves as big as mountains, knowing your life is in the hands of the people around you. You bond as a team and everyone plays their part, because whether you're still alive in the morning depends on it. Then you get back on terra firma, having stared death in the face, and friends say, 'Oh, that's interesting,' then start talking about their new handbag or where they're planning to go on holiday next year."

"Purses, vacations, the next Lexus, Republican-

Democrat bullshit, whether the Knicks will make the play-offs . . ." Phipps gave a despondent shrug. "But do you know the worst of it?"

"Go on."

"In the military, folks act with integrity and honor. If you're in a tight spot, your buddies close ranks and get you the hell out of there. If there's an obstacle, you go over it. A bullshit rule, you bend it. But in civilian life so many people are just gutless cowards. They close ranks all right – not to help you, but against you. Obeying the rules to protect their petty promotions and greedy salaries, all to pay a mortgage on a life they don't even own."

Phipps fell silent. Penny took the opportunity to refill their mugs. When she sat back down, the huge African American had a grin on his face.

"You know, we had a fire in our building. Only a small fire, but the alarm went off, and we had to leave our office on the third floor and take the stairs down to the street. There's this one guy in a wheelchair parked on the landing. Everyone's rushing past him like he was invisible. So I shout to my boss to help me carry the guy down. And he says, 'No! Safety and health policy! We leave him here and let the fire department deal with him.'"

"Really?"

"Yeah, in case we inadvertently hurt him and he sued the company!"

Penny raised her eyes.

"And the crazy thing was the guy was happy to go along with it. He'd rather risk burning to death than break the goddamn rules!"

"That pretty much answers my question," said Penny. "I can see the appeal of working for the Concern."

"The Concern's about doing the right thing. Something exciting that you can feel good about—"

The phone on the desk rang. Phipps held up an apologetic hand and answered it.

"Phipps . . . Okay . . . yeah . . . yeah." His hand clenched the receiver, his face deadpan as he spoke in brief, clipped tones.

Penny could tell it was the coastguard's office and leant forward as a feeling of dread came over her.

Phipps scribbled down a long number and the name "Kimberley II." Ending the call, he looked Penny in the eye. "Hans has been picked up."

"A-a-and?"

"She didn't make it."

Lieutenant Dave "Bungy" Williams flew the Lynx Mark 8 helicopter low over the emerald-green water of the North Atlantic as he radioed the bridge of HMS *Fortitude*, "Flight, this is one-seven-seven, over," his upper-middle-class English accent unwavering and professional.

"Go ahead, one-seven-seven."

"We have visual on the cargo ship, over."

"Proceed with caution, one-seven-seven. We await a sit-rep, over."

"Roger that, out."

HMS *Fortitude*, a Type 23 frigate, had been on a joint training exercise with the Cape Verde coastguard. Upon receiving the news of Hans' rescue, Phipps wasted no time in contacting its captain to request a casualty evacuation. The ship steamed toward the *Kimberley II* to get within the operating range of its Lynx helicopter. Hans would remain aboard the British warship until the ship's doctor was satisfied his condition had stabilized enough for the chopper to transfer him to Cape Verde's Agostinho Neto Hospital.

Despite having spoken to the captain of the *Kimberley II* by satphone, Bungy Williams circled the aging vessel twice, as per procedure, checking for any landing hazards before making his final approach, flaring the high-tech bird gracefully to set her down on the designated shipping containers highlighted with a crudely painted white H.

The aircrewman leapt out and skipped across the stack of freight to where Carlos and Juan crouched next to Hans' stretcher, doing their best to shield him from the downwash from the rotor blades. After a brief conversation the Filipinos helped load the injured man onto the Lynx.

"Wait, wait!" Carlos yelled above the din. "You better take this." He pulled the teddy bear found in the life raft from his overalls.

With a shrug, the crewman threw it into the hold and clambered in himself, and the chopper was away.

Meanwhile, in Boston, Muttley had organized an experienced medical team, who would fly out to Cape Verde on the Concern's Learjet and provide urgent treatment before returning Hans to a hospital in the US. Naturally, Penny and Phipps insisted they accompany him on the flight.

On the deck of the *Kimberley II*, Jens and his boy Chamfar watched the helicopter depart until it was a speck on the delicate blue backdrop. With the reward money shared among the crew, this would be Jens' last voyage on the faithful old barge.

He put an arm around the first mate's shoulders. "So how do you think the fishing is in Mozambique, my friend?"

"I think it is very good, Captain," the boy replied with his ever-cheeky grin.

9

"**H**ey sailor," Penny held Hans' hand as he opened his eyes.

"Miss Masters I presume." He feigned a smile.

They were in a private ward in Boston's exclusive Ross Medical Center, where Hans had spent a week in an induced coma following surgical debridement to remove gangrenous tissue from the side of his head. The surgeons left the gaping wound open at first to allow the site time to self-heal, closing it when reinfection was no longer a threat, leaving a jagged red welt only a skin graft would fix. Hans came out of the coma four days ago, but it was only now he was lucid that the various intravenous feeds of drugs, fluids and nutrients had been removed.

"Feeling better?" Penny knew it was a ridiculous question, but there was not a lot else she could say.

Hans squeezed her hand and stared into the distance. Their thoughts locked. It was all Penny could do not to dissolve into a sobbing mess. With painkillers flooding Hans' bloodstream, the full extent of Jessica's loss had yet to hit home, and she prayed she could do something to ease his pain when it did.

"I . . . I can't believe she's gone." Hans' good eye fixated on the teddy bear sat on the table by his bed.

"Let me move this," she offered.

"No!" Hans rasped, placing his hand on her arm. "No."

Moments passed in silence, the agonizing reality suspending them in a meaningless black void.

"I thought I had her, Penny."

"You don't need to talk about it now—"

"No, I need to." Hans turned to face her. "She was swimming up to me as *Future* sank. I grabbed her hand . . . but the safety line . . . It was clipped to the bunk . . . 'You always gotta clip on your safety line, Bear,' she used to say. But I never thought she'd clip on inside the cabin."

"Hans, you weren't to know. How could you?"

"I thought she was in the life raft with me. I could see she wasn't herself, but I thought she was in the raft."

Hans reached for the bear. Penny passed it to him, and he clutched it to his chest.

"I thought you were with me, sweet pea."

He drifted into unconsciousness.

10

Dr. Simon Preece, Boston's leading trauma specialist, removed his glasses and slid them into the breast pocket of his immaculate white coat.

"He's been through a lot, Penny. Way beyond what a person should ever have to take, to be truthful. Another day or two at sea, and we wouldn't be having this conversation."

Sitting on a green leather chesterfield in the doctor's spacious office, a room that could easily have passed for an executive suite at the nearby Ritz-Carlton, Penny wished they weren't having this conversation.

"I'm sorry. I haven't offered you a drink." Preece stood up. "Tea, coffee, soda – or perhaps something stronger?"

"Oh!"

The doctor smiled. "I'm not a big believer in drinking tea at a time like this."

"A beer perhaps," Penny tendered, feeling it couldn't have come at a better time.

"Of course."

Preece walked over to an oak panel and pulled it open to reveal a well-stocked refrigerator. He took out a Budweiser for Penny and a Perrier for himself.

"Glass?"

"No, no. It's fine." Penny cracked the tab on the can.

Preece winked – which would have seemed odd from any other doctor – and eased into his sumptuous swivel chair, picking a stray fiber off his pant leg and brushing down his lapels before continuing.

"Hans has experienced what is known medically as brief psychotic disorder, sometimes called reactive psychosis. It's brought about by trauma and extreme stress, such as the loss of a loved one or an accident or assault – basically, an extremely disturbing event."

"Jeez," Penny muttered, staring down at the expensive Persian rug.

"I'm sorry, Penny, is this too much? We can talk about it later—"

"No, no. It all makes sense. Hans' wife and son were killed last year, but he doesn't talk about it."

Preece kept quiet. As a long-standing operative for the Concern, he was well aware of the circumstances surrounding the horrific double murder.

"And to witness Jessica drown . . ."

The doctor pushed a box of Kleenex across the desktop. "And then there's the physical trauma. He took quite a thump to the face."

"So does this explain why he thought Jessica was in the life raft all the time? Like his mind simply refused to accept the truth and blanked it out?"

"Not so much blanked it out, like denial, for example. It's more that his mind took on a parallel reality."

"Which would explain the delusions."

"The delusions, the hallucinations – but!" Preece widened his eyes and beamed. "It's called *brief* psychotic disorder for a reason, and it would appear he's over the worst of it and making a full recovery."

"And the infection?" Penny realized she had unknowingly finished her beer and was crumpling the can.

"The infection's under control. With a little help from antibiotics, the human body is a wonderful thing. But spending some time in the hyperbaric chamber will speed his recovery – get a little oxygen into his tissues – and some cosmetic surgery, a skin graft, wouldn't go amiss, if he wants to retain his good looks that is!"

"I never thought the words 'Hans,' 'Larsson,' and 'cosmetics' would ever be in the same sentence, Doctor," Penny joked, and they both chuckled.

"Another beer?"

He needn't have asked.

"**A**re you sure you want to do this?" Penny asked as the Learjet came in to land at Cape Verde's São Pedro airport.

A month into his recovery, Hans couldn't let Jessica's body lie at the bottom of the ocean any longer, despite the doctor's advice to rest a good deal more. Fingering the crude scar on his temple, he gave a slow but decisive nod.

Regular flights to Cape Verde took twenty-four hours, with two transfers, then a further hop from the main island of Santiago to the smaller São Vicente, ten miles off which the sunken yacht lay. Hans would have had no problem taking this cheaper option, but Muttley insisted upon the Learjet and booking them in at the Grande Verde.

As they exited the plane and climbed down the stairs to the tarmac, the hot Atlantic air brought a rush of memories and emotions back to Hans. Suddenly feeling queasy, he grabbed Penny's arm, fearing his legs would give way. Fortunately, an airport car was there to drive them to the terminal, where Karen Shapiro, the US ambassador, waited behind the sliding entrance doors to greet them.

"Hans, Penny, I wish our meeting could be under

better circumstances," said the tall and attractive African American, who dressed island style in a T-shirt, denim miniskirt and flip-flops and spoke in a Southern drawl.

"It's thoughtful of you to come," Hans replied, knowing Karen lived in the capital, Praia, on the island of Santiago, a two-hour flight away.

Penny nodded a polite agreement.

After shaking hands, Karen led them straight through immigration, bypassing the kiosks and throwing a smile of acknowledgment to one particular official, and out to one of the Grande Verde's limousines.

"Guys, I wanted to say a quick hi and give you an update on the search for *Future*, but if you'd rather settle in and get some sleep I can grab a room and meet you tomorr—"

"Now's fine," Hans seized the opportunity. "If that's okay?"

"Of course," Karen replied, and then introduced them to the driver, who ushered them into the car.

"Phew, what a relief!" said Penny, fanning the cold air around her face.

"Kinda gets you, don't it?" said Karen.

Hans appreciated the ambassador's personable approach and could tell her laid-back persona belied a tough woman who'd fought hard to achieve all she had. It was good to have her on side.

Karen slid open the refrigerated drinks cabinet set into the Mercedes' lunar-gray velour and, without asking, handed Hans and Penny ice-cold cans of beer. Hans' admiration for the woman went up a notch, and Penny's thoughts flicked to the gentle Dr. Preece.

"It's Strela, brewed here in the islands."

Karen was about to add that they'd probably tasted it before but thought it best not to remind them.

Preliminaries over, she gave them an update on the search, choosing her words carefully, since she knew it wasn't recovering the wreckage itself that was at stake. Hans had specifically requested that, when found, the yacht and the memories it contained remained on the seabed. The idea of salvaging, repairing and selling *Future* on filled him with dread, since the thought of a new owner sailing her gleefully around the yachting community would keep the nightmare alive.

"Hans, as you know the satellite images your . . . *contacts* provided have been obstructed by the weather. We're in what's known locally as the *tempo de brisas.* The—"

"Time of the breeze," Penny chipped in.

"Ah! *Fala português,*" Karen complimented her.

"*Falo, um pouco,*" she replied modestly.

"I'm sure you speak a lot more than I do, honey!" Karen let out a self-effacing chuckle before continuing. "And as we're not looking to raise the yacht, there's no point bringing in a salvage rig and crew from Dakar. So, as I said on the phone, I've put one of our local guys on it. You'll like Silvestre. He's quite a character and something of a celebrity around these parts for his treasure-hunting escapades—"

"But *can* he find the yach—?" Hans checked himself, realizing he may have sounded rude. "Sorry, Karen, I didn't mean to blurt all over you. But is this guy any good?"

"More than good, Hans." Karen reached into her bag. "Have a look at this." She handed them a folder containing an underwater photograph Silvestre snapped with his boat's umbilical camera that morning.

There, unmistakably, in a picture taken deep in the ocean's murky depths was a gilt-lettered wooden plaque screwed to the hull of a yacht: *Future*.

12

The Mercedes purred along the coast, the ruffled waters of the Atlantic stretching as far as the eye could see on one side of the road, orange desert dotted with white terra-cotta-roofed homes on the other. As the far-distant hills shimmered in the afternoon heat, a mixture of shock, relief and emotion held Hans and Penny in a trance. Under the circumstances it was the best news they could have hoped for.

"I'm sorry. I didn't want to show you this right at the airport . . ." Karen's voice trailed off as Hans and Penny continued to stare in silence at the image of *Future*'s nameplate.

After a time Hans lifted his head and exhaled deeply. "How far down?"

"She's lying on a sandbar about fifty or sixty meters."

"And . . . ?"

"No, Hans, both Silvestre and I thought it best to wait until you arrived before a dive's carried out. I've arranged for you to visit the site tomorrow. Obviously, Silvestre's got all the dive gear, so we can begin the repatriation there and then if that's your wish."

"Yes, of course." Hans pressed the tips of his fingers together, resting them against his lips as he rocked gently back and forth.

"How did Silvestre find the site, Karen?" Penny asked.

"I'm no expert, but from what I understand he took the last set of coordinates Hans radioed through to the marina and, factoring in the wind at the time, extrapolated a return bearing. He's been scanning the seabed with sonar for weeks, factoring in the drift, but yesterday we had a stroke of luck. A fishing boat spotted a float, and it turned out to be *Future*'s how do you say, man . . . ?"

"Man-overboard line." Penny referred to the two-hundred-foot-long floating rope streamed aft as a safety precaution when a sailor is alone on deck – also known as the last-chance line for obvious reasons. As with the fenders, life jackets and cockpit cushions, Hans had painted the yacht's name on the fluorescent polystyrene float attached to the end of the nylon rope.

"And . . ." Penny was about to say something when she noticed Hans looking overcome.

He leant forward and put his arm around the two women, and as they hugged, tears ran down all their cheeks.

"Thank you, Karen," Hans whispered, wiping his eyes.

"It's nothing. You can thank Silvestre."

The driver turned off the road, headed up the Grande Verde's palm-lined boulevard and pulled to a stop at the hotel's entrance, fronted by a magnificent modern-art fountain in gray and tan stone.

Branca, the Grande Verde's concierge, waited to greet them.

"*Amiga*! Good to see you again." She threw her arms around Penny, drawing back to look her affectionately in the eye. "Anything I can do, you ask, okay?"

Karen said good-bye and climbed into the car to return to the airport for her flight back to Praia, a hundred miles south. She handed Hans her business card.

"Good luck tomorrow, and call me anytime day or night, you understand?"

"Yes, thank you." Hans pursed his lips and nodded.

Then, casually gripping the neck of her T-shirt with two fingers, Karen said, "And give my regards to Innes when you speak to him. I owe that man."

Hans, thinking fondly of his handler, Muttley, scratched his eyebrow with two fingers. "I certainly will."

Branca showed them to their suite, a somewhat more modest affair than the penthouse but impressive nonetheless, with a stunning ocean view. The porter dropped off their bags, and Hans tipped him while Penny grabbed a couple of beers from the fridge.

"Well, Karen was really nice." She handed him a can.

"And sympathetic to the Concern's cause."

"Huh? How do you know that?"

"Did you see the way she grabbed her shirt with two fingers?"

"No, I didn't notice it."

"You wouldn't. No one on the outside would."

"Are you saying . . . ?"

"It's a hand sign – shows membership or affiliation." Hans emptied his beer. "You didn't notice me return the signal by scratching my eyebrow?"

"But what if you hadn't been a member?"

"Like I said, I wouldn't have noticed it."

"Ah, I see."

"I knew she was on our team anyway. Muttley

mentioned it a while back."

"It's still a cool little trick." Penny wondered how many more surprises Hans would spring on her. His life was far from boring. "Another beer?"

"Why not."

Penny got up to fetch the drinks, but when she returned to the bedroom, Hans was fast asleep, snoring on the bed.

- 13 -

Hans and Penny enjoyed an en suite breakfast, after which they entered the extravagant lobby to find an elderly man with white hair and stubble, deep tan lines etched into his olive skin, looking out of place on one of the burnished-leather couches surrounding the hotel's koi carp pool. He stood up immediately, took off his well-worn green baseball cap and screwed it in his hands as he walked toward them. It was a moment of reckoning for Hans.

"Silvestre."

He shook his firm hand.

"Senhor Hans, it is my great pleasure," he replied in a Portuguese accent. "And . . . ?"

"This is Penny."

Silvestre took her hand. His smiling hazel eyes projected a kind and humble nature.

They sat down, and Hans called the waiter over to order coffee. "So, Silvestre, how long have you been in the islands?"

"Oh, a good ten years now. I grew up in Angola. My parents owned a cashew nut plantation there."

"Luanda?" Penny asked.

"Ah, you know Angola, Miss Penny?"

"Only the capital. I skipper yachts, and we've stopped

there a couple of times on the way to the Cape."

"The Cape! That's tough sailing. I am proud to have you on my crew."

"Thank you."

"We once had it good in our beautiful land, and then came the uprising. First we lost the colony, and then there was civil war – so many bombs, so much bloodshed. Our farm was destroyed, and my parents returned to the mother country. I stayed awhile, but it was not the same Angola."

"How did you get into treasure hunting?" Hans took his coffee from the waiter and set it down on an ornate ebony drinks table.

"When I first learn to scuba dive, I know right away I love it – like a fish, huh?" Silvestre grinned and made a finning motion with his palm. "So I go to work for a salvage company off the Eastern Cape – so many commercial vessels sinking in those treacherous seas. Hans, you too are diver Miss Karen tells me."

"Ha, I've done some. But it's Penny who's the instructor."

"Ah, so good." Silvestre reached into his faded denim jacket and pulled out a hip flask. "Rum. It's also good, no?"

He passed the flask to Penny, who poured a shot into her and Hans' cups.

"Eventually I have enough money to buy a small boat and start searching in my own time. At first just small finds – broken porcelain from trading ships coming from China, wine bottles and musket shot, this kind of stuff – but then I discover coins, lots of coins – gold, silver – from a Dutch East Indiaman sunk off Port

Elizabeth. Not enough to get rich but enough to buy a bigger boat and search full-time. Over the years I work my way up the coast, and Cape Verde – ahh! A Portuguese island, it's like home for me, no? So I decide to stay a while."

- 14 -

The *Outcast*'s twelve-liter diesel thundered beneath their feet, propelling the bouncing boat at breakneck speed across the choppy green swell, her turbocharged screw churning through the water to spew a raging white plume high into the air at the bow.

As fresh salty air filled Hans' nostrils, he experienced a cruel twist of emotion. It felt good to be back on the sea, particularly after a month spent festering in a hospital bed, but having to recover Jessica's body after it had lain on the seabed for weeks, all manner of creatures gnawing away at her bloated decomposing flesh, was the hardest thing he'd ever had to do.

Ever the bullish character, Hans asked Silvestre if he could descend onto the wreck of *Future*, but the treasure hunter and Penny wouldn't hear of it.

"Hans, you must remember her the way she was," said Penny. "Silvestre will place her in the body bag, and that's all you need to see."

Penny had serious concerns but hadn't mentioned them to Hans. She could tell he was making an effort to stay strong in order to return his little girl's body to the States for a proper good-bye – but what would happen after that? To lose his wife and son and now his remaining daughter – how much could the man take?

48

She knew their relationship was not reason enough for him to go on living.

A large orange buoy bobbed in the distance, and the crew made final preparations for the dive. Silvestre and a young mestizo named Marcos would drop the fifty meters down to the wreck, while Samson, a muscle-bound black African from the Ivory Coast, remained on board as surface cover. He would communicate with the divers via walkie-talkie and have a second set of equipment to hand should they require assistance.

Being over forty meters meant it was a technical dive, so Silvestre and Marcos would breathe a trimix gas – a combination of oxygen, helium and nitrogen – to increase their bottom time and reduce the risk of nitrogen narcosis and decompression sickness. However, the narrowness of *Future*'s companionway made it impossible to enter the hull wearing the additional gas cylinders required for safety, which would hang off the men's equipment harnesses like weights in a grandfather clock. It meant Silvestre had to swap to a fresh cylinder upon reaching the hull and unclip the others before proceeding inside, giving him approximately eight minutes to make his way through the saloon and into the sleeping quarters to retrieve Jessica's body.

"Are you sure?" Hans frowned.

"*Mais ou menos*," the Angolan said, shrugging, and the American knew not to press the issue.

Samson dropped anchor over the wreck, while Silvestre and Marcos kitted up and did equipment checks. Then they stepped off the back of the boat and, after a final set of checks, gave each other the thumbs-down and sank below the surface.

Hans and Penny sat in silence listening to the communications exchanged over the radio in Creole. A tense twenty minutes passed. Then without warning a bright-yellow airbag burst to the surface. The two of them jumped up in anticipation of the moment of dread, but Samson waved a dismissive hand – "No, nothing" – and began fishing for the airbag with a boat hook.

Hans helped lift the flotation device aboard, surprised to find his scuba gear, which he'd stored under a bunk, clipped beneath it.

The divers ascended, making carefully calculated decompression stops. Hans and Penny watched bubbles from the men's exhalations boiling on the surface, until two neoprene hoods broke through the swell.

Samson lowered the step-on lifting platform at the stern and winched Silvestre on board. Then he steadied the skipper's heavily laden self and walked him backwards in his clumsy fins to sit on one of the benches along the sides of the deck.

As Samson lowered the lift's aluminum footplate to collect Marco, Silvestre peeled off his mask and rubbed his face.

"She's not there," he said, looking into the American's eyes as seawater poured from the pockets in his equipment.

"But . . . did . . . you . . . ?" Hans was lost for words, shaking his head in a daze.

"Yes, Hans, I check everywhere. I check the bunk rail like you said, but *nothing*. No safety line clipping on to it, and only the one set of scuba gear, not two like you thought."

Hans put his head in his hands, racking his brain as he tried to take in the information. How could she not be there? There was no way the safety line could snap or unclip itself, nor could the locker under the bunk containing her dive kit open on its own accord – it was fastened by a bolt that clamped shut.

"She . . . must have gotten out," he muttered. "She must have gone for the scuba gear."

The thought of his brave little girl staying calm, as he had always taught her, only to swim free of the sinking yacht and find herself clinging to the equipment, adrift in the dark on the ocean, was too much to take. As he began to sob, Penny put her arm around him, and Silvestre nodded to Samson to fetch the rum.

- 15 -

One month earlier

Jessica awoke from a deep sleep following the night spent drifting on the ocean. She'd dreamt a bizarre repeating dream in which bad men were trying to capture her and Papa was too busy sailing the yacht to stop them. When she opened her eyes, the horror of the last twenty-four hours brought reality crashing home.

In the feeble glow from a flickering bulb, she ripped off the coarse gray blanket covering her and shook it, hoping and expecting to see Bear drop out so she wouldn't be alone. Since the death of Mom and JJ, Bear had been her faithful companion, and to have him here now would have lessened the fear and homesickness she felt.

Bear was gone, and Jessica remembered the last time she saw him was when the seawater flooded into *Future*'s cabin and washed him away. As her eyes welled up, she took a deep breath and shook herself.

"Get a grip, funny face!" she said, echoing her father's favorite reprimand. "Sobs are for slobs!"

Jessica's thinking helped, spurring her into action. She scanned her surroundings but could only vaguely remember having been in such a place before, when she was much younger.

Where is it?

It reminded her a little of the cellar beneath their home in Maine – only the walls were built from large, crumbling yellow blocks covered in damp mold and smelled like their kitchen did when Papa juiced vegetables after his morning run.

The door was a modern internal type, smaller than whatever had been the original and hemmed in with a rough-shorn timber surround. Jessica wasted no time trying the handle, easing it downwards and pulling the door toward her – *Damn!* It only opened an inch. Someone had bolted it from the outside.

There were no windows in the room, and the same aging yellow stonework formed the ceiling, so old that stalactites had formed. She sat back down on the lumpy white mattress, its black pinstripes barely visible beneath unsightly stains and grime.

Barefoot and wearing shorts and the T-shirt she had draped over her head when the men plucked her from the sea, Jessica shivered in her miserable dank prison. She wrapped herself in the blanket just as someone started to undo the padlock.

Jessica stared at the door, fearful and confused, hoping it was her father, who would pick her up in a bear hug, and everything would come good.

The man entering the room had a bald head and goatee beard and was definitely not her father.

"Ah, Maria," he announced in an accent that wasn't American.

"I'm *not* Maria," she snapped with a slight tremble.

"Yes, you are," said the man. "Sweet little Maria is

going to behave and make us a lot of money."

"I'm not," she spat, her eyes throwing daggers.

"Ha! Why not?"

"Because my papa's gonna come and get me."

"Is he?"

"Yeah, and he's gonna kick your ass!"

"So your father is a fighter?" the man grunted.

"My papa is a *detective* and he was a *Navy SEAL* and he's not afraid of *anything*."

"Your father is dead, *Maria*. He died when your boat sank, so we will find you a new family."

He gave her a twisted smile and turned to leave.

Jessica leapt off the bed and kicked him as hard as she could in the back of his leg.

"Ouch!"

The man spun around with a look of shock in his docile eyes, then backhanded her across the face.

Jessica flew across the room and cracked her head on the bed's wooden frame, flopping onto the cold stone floor. She lay there paralyzed by shock as the coppery taste of blood filled her mouth and she passed into unconsciousness.

- 16 -

Back at the marina, Hans thanked Silvestre and his crew for their efforts. Muttley had insisted the Concern would pay for the Angolan's services, but after exchanging business cards, Hans pressed a fat envelope into the old man's hand. With Penny's help, he carried the scuba gear along the floating pontoon, passing the variety of craft nosing up against it, which ranged from aging wooden yachts to the latest million-dollar cruisers. Sitting in the cockpit enjoying a late lunch in the sunshine, the German crew of *Edelweiss* threw smiles and hellos and gave thumbs-ups upon seeing the dive gear, the scene and sentiment far removed from Hans and Penny's living nightmare.

At the marina office they stopped to say hello to Baba, the larger-than-life Senegalese manager who had helped Penny when *Future* went missing. Upon hearing the result of the search, he grasped their hands as tears welled in his kind brown eyes.

"Anything I can do, Miss Penny, Mr. Hans, please let me know."

The street outside the marina was typical of Cape Verde, flanked by two-story colonial builds painted in vivid pastel colors, most with spindly wooden balconies, giving the impression of a frontier town. In this quiet part of Mindelo, São Vicente's port city, pickup trucks carrying trade goods and people-packed Toyota minibuses cruised by. There were surprisingly few cars, though, and those they saw were mostly Japanese models, their bodywork faring well in the dry climate.

Hans was lost in thought in the afternoon heat, and as Penny hailed a cab he found himself staring at a Fulani woman sitting at a table in an open-fronted restaurant across the street.

The Fulani were Africa's largest ethnic group. Centuries of conquest and migration had resulted in them occupying vast expanses of land in a longitudinal belt south of the Sahara. In keeping with the nomadic tribe's tradition, the woman wore a flowing yellow-and-lime-patterned robe and head scarf, a mesh of colorful coral necklaces, gold hoop earrings, a nose ring and brass anklets, with cowrie shells and silver coins attached to her long braided hair. She had blackened her lips with indigo ink, sported henna tattoo sleeves on her hands, wrists, feet and ankles, and had tribal scarification around her eyes and mouth. Even at a distance she projected a palpable aura of grace, strength and unadulterated femininity.

But it wasn't the Fulani's appearance capturing Hans' attention. Something seemed odd. Perhaps that she sat on her own or appeared to be aware of his gaze, glancing at him several times, nervousness or shyness evident in her dark-brown eyes. Hans was about to say something to Penny when a cab pulled up and his attention switched to helping the driver load the dive gear into the trunk.

On the drive to the hotel, Penny made polite but

subdued conversation with the cabbie, who'd immediately sensed the couple's anguish and ceased with the tourist banter. After a time "*São os pais da menina*?" he whispered, asking if they were the parents of the little girl.

Penny said yes to keep it simple and asked how he knew.

The driver explained that the islanders had followed the search for *Future*'s crew on the news and felt terrible about the tragedy. The TV station had run a bulletin following Hans' rescue by the *Kimberley II* and another announcing his return to Cape Verde to recover Jessica's body with the help of Silvestre, the islands' very own treasure hunter.

"But the senhor, he look different to the one on the televisão," the driver queried.

"Oh." Penny shrugged but chose not to elucidate, for coordinating the media around the search, the team from the Concern purposely concealed Hans' and Jessica's identities. "We don't want our special operative's picture flashed around the world," Muttley had said. "It's a life raft or a drifting yacht we want to draw attention to, not the faces of the people inside."

"And . . . no is lucky today?" the driver asked softly.

"No, no luck," Penny muttered, gazing out over the ocean she had spent a lifetime upon but not feeling the usual longing to return.

She wished there was something she could do to relieve Hans' agony, compartmentalizing her own grief for his sake. With Jessica's body still missing, closure was impossible, and even if they had recovered her today, Hans' mental state was a serious worry.

Arriving at the Grande Verde, Penny fished in her daypack for her pocketbook, but the driver refused payment. After unloading the scuba kit, he shook their hands, offering condolences while bowing his head.

Penny sat down on the suite's vast leather couch and put her arm around Hans. "What now, honey?"

"I don't know. It feels wrong to go home." Hans massaged his eye sockets, then turned to her, seeking direction.

"Then we don't," Penny said promptly. "Let's take a trip. Anywhere, but let's get off this island."

"I know it's crazy, but do you mind if we stay awhile? I just . . ." Hans couldn't explain his feelings.

"Hans, take all the time you need. But let's get out of the hotel tonight. I hear the seafood's top-notch down at the front, and I'm paying."

After a shower and a change of clothes, Hans and Penny drank a few beers in the room and then went down to the lobby, where Branca had one of the hotel's cars ready to take them downtown. Their driver was Paulo, a young mestizo, who had driven Penny to the Grande Verde the night *Future* disappeared.

As Paulo drove out of the hotel's grounds, he pushed a button on the satnav set into the Mercedes' center console, and a Portuguese soap opera replaced the electronic map on the screen. The young man had no problem keeping half an eye on the TV show as he sped along the ocean road, weaving with ease around vehicles in their path. Hans and Penny looked at each other and smiled, so amused at Paulo's relaxed driving style they failed to notice the taxicab that had tailed them from the hotel.

Paulo dropped them at Mindelo's beachfront by a row of open-air restaurants lining the promenade. They opted for Casa Frutos do Mar and seated themselves at the only table not taken by locals and tourists indulging in the exotic food fare on offer.

"Wow, this is nice," said Penny, taking in the view over the brightly painted fishing boats beached above the high-tide mark on the postcard-yellow sand. "Perfect place to watch the sun set."

"And have a liddle drink." Hans mimicked their dear departed Dutch friend Marcel, making Penny smile, then caught the waiter's attention.

A bottle of red wine arrived, and Hans filled their glasses.

"What are you going to order?" Penny asked, scanning the menu.

"I'm not sure. You'd think after a month in a life raft I'd be sick of fish."

"Oh, Hans! I'm so sorry." Clutching a hand to her mouth, Penny looked mortified. "When I suggested seafood, I didn't think. We can go somewhere else."

"Don't be silly. This is a *slightly* better setting than what I'm used to – the restaurant doesn't bob up and down, and the food won't try to escape."

Penny smiled but fell silent, staring at her wine.

"You're wondering what it was like being adrift," Hans tendered.

"If you don't want to talk about it—"

"No, it's fine. I just don't know where to start."

Penny reached for his hand across the table.

Hans took a gulp of wine. "When *Future* went down, there was an almighty storm. I thought we – I mean, I – was done for. The waves kept pummeling the raft, and I had to bail like a maniac to stay afloat. I've never been so relieved to see the sunrise. When the emergency rations ran out, I managed to put together some fishing gear – even used some of your jewelry-making wire to make a trace."

"You had my jewelry box?"

"It floated up when *Future* sank and pretty much

saved my life. The fishing got real good after a couple of weeks, since an ecosystem grew beneath the raft – barnacles, seaweed, and then these minnows hatching outta nowhere. I started to catch a few dorados. Just eating them raw was better than any steak in a restaurant. Then the sharks came, bumping the raft all night. Big whitetips, and those guys don't mess around. Hell, when you're out there alone, it's pretty terrifying."

Penny shuddered.

"But sharks weren't the biggest problem. I snagged a fishhook on one of the raft's inflation tubes just below the waterline. Started sinking right away. Took two days swimming in shark-infested water to fix the damn leak and then get the raft pumped back up."

"Did you see any ships?"

"I saw 'em all right – damn used up all the flares on the first one that passed. They just didn't see me, though. Another ship ran us down in the middle of the night."

Penny caught the word "us" but didn't say anything.

"Making water was the toughest challenge. You know that hand-cranked desalinator I bought in Plymouth?"

"From Old Bill in the chandlery?"

"Yeah, but it was missing from the emergency ditch kit, along with the radio and rescue beacon. I think Jessie had been playing with them and didn't put them back in the bag. All I had was this solar still that came with the raft – like a Second World War contraption that floated on the sea and produced about a cup a day. It wasn't much, but enough."

Now it was Hans' turn to fall silent. After a time he let out a morose chuckle. "I can't believe I thought she was there with me the whole time . . . and it was that goddamn bear."

Penny squeezed his hand. "Dr. Preece talked to me about that in Boston. He said the trauma you went through brought on—"

"Reactive psychosis. I know. You just never think that kinda illness is gonna affect you." Hans shook his head slowly and emptied his glass.

"Do you remember anything about the rescue?" Penny reached for the bottle.

"No. I was out of it by that stage. I only remember waking up in the hospital—"

A middle-aged white guy approached their table. He'd been walking through the crowded forecourt, handing out leaflets.

"Can I give you one of these, mate?" he asked in an English accent.

"Sure," Hans replied, assuming it was a flyer for a nightclub or a music event – though the guy looked a little too respectable to be hustling for a buck. What Hans saw instead made him jump to his feet.

Headed "Missing," the leaflet featured the face of a girl about Jessica's age, the text in English and Portuguese explaining that Holly had gone missing from this beach a week ago.

"Oh, buddy. Please, please take a seat!" Hans pulled out a chair.

"Thanks," said the Englishman, the black bags beneath his eyes speaking for him. "I've been passing these out all day. I'm Mike Davenport by the way."

"I'm Hans, and this is Penny. You're on holiday, Mike, I take it."

"That was the plan. We flew into Praia and spent a

couple of days exploring the city before taking the ferry up here to enjoy the beaches. But it all went *so* wrong. She was building a sandcastle no more than five meters away from where my wife and I were sunbathing. When I looked up, she was gone."

"What have the police said?" asked Penny.

"They said several kids go missing from the island every year, but usually migrants whose parents arrive here illegally, so it doesn't get reported."

"Oh God!" Mike's head dropped into his hands as he fought back tears.

In Hans' work for the Concern he'd been involved in several such cases. Cape Verde was both a source country and a hub for human trafficking – known in law enforcement circles as "the Trade." Ruthless criminal networks targeted economic migrants and impoverished locals, duping them into drug-smuggling operations, domestic and industrial servitude and the sex trade, trafficking them as far as the Americas, Europe and the Middle East.

The fate of some of the children was particularly depraved, kidnapped to supply sophisticated pedophile rings. Politicians, senators, prime ministers, the rich and famous, even royalty were allegedly involved, but with the power, money and connections to cover their tracks, the links were hard to prove.

As the sun lowered to the horizon, setting the sky ablaze with a sprawling palette of pinks, yellows, grays and silver blue, Hans ordered Mike a beer and told him about Jessica.

"Oh, guys, I didn't mean to add to your grief. I-I—"

"It's not a problem, Mike." Hans gripped the

desperate man's shoulder. "Listen. Go back to your wife and get some rest. Penny and I will hand out the rest of these leaflets."

"Are you sure?" Mike's mouth fell open.

Hans took a business card from his wallet and slid it across the table.

"More than sure," said Penny, knowing it would do them both good to focus on something else for a while.

- 18 -

Postponing their meal, Hans and Penny began making their way along the beachfront restaurants, stopping to speak with diners and handing leaflets to passersby. Most were only too happy to listen, Hans explaining the situation to the English speakers, Penny the Portuguese, but an overweight German man with a puffy sunburnt face, busy tucking into plates piled with shellfish and guzzling wine, dismissed them with a patronizing wave – "No, we don't buy anything!" – before turning to his friends and roaring with laughter.

The American's blood boiled, and he clenched his fist. Penny slapped a leaflet down on the red-and-white-checked tablecloth and steered him sharply away.

Later they chatted with an amicable Swiss couple enjoying swordfish steak in the last eatery on the front, only Hans stopped midsentence, staring through the darkness to the nearby main road.

"Honey, are you—?" Penny began.

Hans held up his hand, for standing under a streetlamp on the far side of the road was the Fulani woman he had seen earlier in the day.

"Penny, wait here, or I'll see you back at the hotel."

Hans was off on his toes, much to Penny and the Swiss couple's surprise, but by the time he'd crossed the street the woman had disappeared. He stood looking all around, knowing it couldn't be coincidence and had something to do with Jessica. He was about to walk back to the restaurant when a taxicab glided by and he happened to glance through its rear-side window to see the woman was inside. She turned her face away, attempting to hide in her colorful shawl.

Hans watched as the car drove into the distance, then turned and flagged the next cab down.

"Hotel, sir?" the young islander asked.

"No. Just follow that car." Hans realized how absurd this must have sounded.

"Okay, boss." The driver screeched away as if he had been waiting for those words all his life.

"But keep your distance, hey?" Hans took out his cell phone to send Penny a brief text explaining his departure.

"Distance is my middle name, boss!" The driver grinned in the rearview mirror.

They drove out of the center and were soon in a maze of backstreets, the area shabbier, the buildings increasingly run-down.

"Where are we?" Hans asked.

"Lombo – the old town. You want girls, drugs?"

"I want you to follow that cab, but keep back, okay?"

"Okay, boss." The young Cape Verdean kept a discreet distance, letting the other cab drift almost out of sight, before speeding up and jumping red lights to keep on its tail.

"Cab's stopping, sir."

"Okay, I'm getting out." Hans shoved a bunch of notes into the guy's hand, then ran along the sidewalk, keeping in the shadows, closing on the spot where the woman got out. He stood scanning the adjacent building up and down and saw a light come on in a second-floor room.

The front door was locked. Hans made up his mind to smash it down if necessary, but increasing pressure from his shoulder forced it open.

In the darkness Hans smelled the odor of garlic and chicken stock mingling with soiled diapers and cigarette smoke. He edged his way up a flight of creaking wooden stairs toward the spot where light shone beneath an apartment door.

There was no door handle, only a small brass padlock hanging open on a latch. Hans threw caution to the wind and pushed the door with his fingertips.

The Fulani stood in the center of the small room, as if expecting him. A mattress lay on the floor, the only other furnishings an open wardrobe, stuffed with brightly colored garments, a chest of drawers and a table and two chairs. Stacked neatly next to a camping cooker and a box of food were pots, pans, crockery and cutlery.

"Mr. Larsson," the woman stated impassively, her dark eyes unblinking.

"Yes," Hans replied, thinking, bizarrely, what a pride this woman took in her appearance considering the humble abode she lived in. "You were expecting me?"

The Fulani nodded at a chair and walked serenely to the still-ajar door, peeking into the corridor before wedging it shut with a length of wood. "I saw the news report saying you had returned to the island and Mr. Silvestre would be taking you out to your boat."

"Is that why you were at the marina?"

"The marina, and I followed you from your hotel

tonight. I wanted to speak to you earlier, but . . ." The Fulani looked away.

Hans noticed her hand trembling as it rested on the tabletop. For the briefest moment he admired the intricate henna artwork coiled in an ensemble of bangles and sprawling along her slender wrists to greet her immaculate, black-polished fingernails.

"Your daughter, she is alive," the Fulani announced without ceremony.

Hans' existence blurred.

He slumped onto the chair, stunned and unable to absorb the information. For a man known for his composure in adverse circumstances, he fought to regain it, managing to stammer, "H-h-how?"

"Wait." The woman retrieved a small black bottle and two mismatched glasses from her kitchen goods, then joined him at the table.

Hans could tell she was stalling but let her, despite his frantic mind demanding that he cut to the chase.

"You must understand, if they find out they will kill me." She poured a generous shot of dark-treacle-like spirit into a chipped glass and pushed it across the tabletop.

"Who?" Hans made an effort not to sound forceful.

"*Os traficantes,*" she muttered, and filled her own glass.

Even with his limited knowledge of Portuguese, Hans recognized the name of the people she alluded to, "the traffickers," their vile commercial operation known to law enforcement agencies around the globe as "the Trade."

Hans downed the drink, its foul herbal taste hardly

registering in his adrenaline-fueled mind. "You must tell me."

"I work shifts in a factory processing fish near to the port. Many of the women marry to the fishermen. There is much gossip. One night I hear a conversation – a worker telling a friend that her husband's boat picked up a young girl floating far out to sea. She is wearing – how you say, *mergulho*?"

"Scuba gear?"

"Yes, this is the one."

"Do you know the fisherman or the name of his boat?"

"The man will not help you. Like his wife, he is a greedy, ignorant fool who could never be trusted with the information you seek. But the boat is called *Rosa Negra*. The captain, Alvarez, is a very bad man."

"Where have they taken her?"

"I don't know." The Fulani broke eye contact.

"Please." Hans was about to place his hand on the woman's arm but, remembering the cultural divide, thought better of it. "Can you find out?"

"I have a friend, an old Fulani. She has been on the island many years and knows such things. I will visit her tomorrow."

"Listen, here's my card. Do you have a phone?"

The Fulani shook her head.

"In that case, if you learn anything please use a pay phone or someone's cell and make a reverse-charge call or try and get me at my hotel, the Grande Verde. If I don't hear from you, I'll meet you here tomorrow night. Is that okay?"

"I think to meet me is better. After 8:00 p.m., when I finish my shift."

"Sure, and I can pay you for your trouble." Hans reached into the pocket of his sport coat.

The Fulani stood up, walked across the dimly lit room, took a photograph from the dressing table and handed it to him. Hans stared at the picture of a little girl, recognizing the eyes of her mother.

"Her name is Binda. No money can replace her, Mr. Larsson. Do you understand what I'm saying?"

Hans nodded as the pieces of the puzzle fell into the place.

"But you must be careful. These are people with powerful connections." She set the photograph back on the dresser, her fingers lingering on the fading image.

"What's your name?" Hans got up to leave.

"Djenabou," she replied as a tear rolled down her cheek.

19

"**I**ncoming!"

Private First Class Duffy of the 405th Parachute Infantry Regiment, US 82nd Airborne Division, threw a grenade into the enemy bunker situated in a bombed-out post office on the outskirts of 1944 Berlin.

He didn't know why he was shouting, since his entire platoon was dead.

Climbing out from behind a mound of rubble, Duffy ran toward the German position in stilted moves, firing his Thompson submachine gun from the hip, spraying lead in the general direction of the screams emanating from the fire and stinking smoke billowing from the sandbagged shopfront.

From experience he knew there would be at least one SS trooper to finish off with a burst of the tommy gun before completing the mission.

The screams reduced to agonized moans and whimpers as Duffy edged his way around the building seeking a firing point. His grenade had blown away a good few sandbags, and he crept into the gap, ready to bid good night to the remaining swine.

The convulsing body of an enemy combatant entered his field of vision.

Duffy leveled his submachine gun and – *click*.

Damn! Out of ammo!

He scanned his dead comrades' webbing pouches, looking for more bullets, spotting a flashing orange box with an *A* on it hovering a foot above his late lieutenant's lifeless form.

Move to the A*! Resupply your ammo!*

With three fresh clips, Duffy crawled back into position. He set his sights on a dying German, squeezed the trigger and—

Jonah's cell phone rang. He interrupted his Xbox game of *Operation Berlin* to see Sylvester Stallone's image on the screen.

"Orion!" He used Hans' code name. "I thought you were like *dead*, dude, in some yacht accident and shit?"

"Odysseus, my dear nerd, I can assure you I'm very much alive."

"Oh, *cooool*! I tried to call your cell before, but nada."

"Yeah, that one took a little dive. You still playin' those crummy war games?"

"I'm still playin' 'em, Orion, and I'm still smoking the *weeeeeeeed*!"

Jonah took a long toke of his doobie, blowing out a yellowy-brown plume in defiance of his fellow agent's fatherly lectures.

Jonah, code name "Odysseus," lived in a converted Greyhound bus in a trailer park in LA. His Aspergic savant made him one of life's interesting characters, a computer genius who'd hacked into NASA's database at thirteen and retrieved highly classified information from the Apollo program. His subsequent arrest made mainstream news and, despite his learning disability, resulted in a stint in a juvenile correctional facility. Nonplussed, he'd used his skills upon release to expose a huge pensions and shares fraud committed by Weltertech Corps, his evidence in court putting several fat-cat criminals behind bars.

Jonah knew his way around computers blindfolded. Under the screen name "Glaxo," he ran one of the biggest torrent operations on the planet, providing free movie, music and software downloads to over a billion people worldwide. Having learned from the mistakes of his youth, he could also hack into any computer network in existence *and* cover his tracks – a talent of particular interest to the Concern, hence his recruitment and subsequent code name Odysseus, the genius behind the Trojan horse.

"Odysseus, I need an address."

"Shoot, dude." Jonah reached for a two-liter bottle of Cherry Coca-Cola sitting among the smoking paraphernalia cluttering his custom-built desk. He took several noisy slugs, oblivious to accepted social graces.

"It's the captain of a boat, the *Rosa Negra*, registered in Cape Verde. Name's Alvarez."

"Dude, go to the Fisheries Commission. That shit will be registered there."

"It's three o'clock in the morning here, fartface. I need the info now."

"I'm on it."

Eight minutes later Hans' cell phone rang.

"Orion, I got your address. It's public knowledge, you know? I also scanned the CIA database and police records. There's nothing on this guy."

"That figures. Gimme the address."

"Forty-eight Rua de Avis, Porto Alto, Mindelo. Anything else?"

"Yeah, I love you, you nerd."

"I love you too, Orion."

Hans resisted the urge to tear around to Alvarez's address and find out where his daughter was – using any means necessary. It was two months since Jessica's kidnapping, and the odds of her still being in the fisherman's possession were slim. Besides, an impromptu visit would warn the traffickers further up the chain and could result in dire consequences. Hans needed advice from Muttley, so he took a cab back to the hotel, calling Penny en route to let her know he was okay.

20

As Jessica came around on the filthy stone floor, she felt someone dabbing the back of her head with a wet cloth.

"Ouch!" She opened her eyes, expecting to see her father.

"Hello, Maria."

The awful reality hit home once again. Instinctively, Jessica lashed out with the right hook her papa taught her. The man jerked backwards, clutching a bleeding nose as his eyes watered. He raised his hand and would have given anything to belt the little pissant around the room, only he remembered his boss's orders: *Do not mark this one, for she will fetch us a high price in Europe or the East.*

The man grabbed Jessica's hair and yanked her to her feet. Then, smothering her mouth and nose, he began to suffocate her. Jessica panicked, fighting for breath and flailing with her fists. The man held the little girl at arm's length, mocking her with a sadistic grin, staring into her tiny blue eyes with his menacing bloodshot ones.

Jessica's body convulsed and she peed herself. The man released his hold and let her drop to the floor.

She scurried backwards until she came up against the solid-wooden bedframe, where she sat, shocked, but managing to scowl.

"Maria." The man's voice deepened as he hovered

over her. "We can do this easy or hard."

"Didn't hurt." She screwed up her lips and gave him a look of utter hatred.

The man lurched across the cell and, taking a firm grip of Jessica's hair, went to pull her shorts down, his sick urge taking control. Again he remembered his boss's words – *Do* not *be tempted with this one. She must be intact, for we cannot be sure who will buy her* – and went back to wiping the blood from the gash in the back of her head.

Jessica tried to think of her beloved Bear and her father, but her mind was too afraid and confused to focus. She prayed with her whole being for this horrible experience to end.

As the man finished wrapping a crepe bandage around her head, securing it in place with a safety pin, he heard Jessica mutter something.

"What did you say, Maria?"

"I said my papa's gonna kill you, you *prick*!"

The man felt the almighty impulse to pick the impudent little pissant up by the ankles and smash her head against the cell wall, and not to stop smashing until her skull caved in and her brains spread across the stonework in a satisfying spray of dark-green and yellow globules. But he had been by his boss's side for twenty-five years and would be lost without his protection and guidance. He couldn't go against his word.

There was a time in that war-torn place when he did as he pleased with the innocents, where the only authority was that of the other man, who was equally if not more sick than he was. But that time had passed, and now the game had rules, and if he dared break them, the Trade would suffer, as would he.

"Strip!" he ordered.

She looked at him, puzzled.

"I said strip!" he bellowed. "Take off your clothes!"

"No!"

Jessica was horrified. Her parents had always warned her that this type of behavior was wrong and she must refuse at all costs, despite the threats made.

The man thrust his hands out and began to suffocate her again. Jessica's legs gave way, and he let her go.

The man lifted his foot and placed it inches from her head. "I give you one more chance." He shook with anger. "Or I smash in your head, you little pissant."

Everything became a blur to Jessica. Without realizing, she began to sob and, sitting up, pulled off her shorts and filthy T-shirt. Huddling naked on the floor, she continued to cry and slipped deeper into shock from the acute embarrassment.

The man picked up her clothes, grunted and left the room.

21

"**H**ans!" Penny cast her laptop aside and leapt off the sofa. "What happened?"

"Sorry, honey. I couldn't really talk in the cab. Things just got serious." He held Penny's shoulders and looked into her eyes. "She's alive – but she's been kidnapped."

"Wh-wh—?" Penny burst into tears, Hans holding her in silence as droplets rolled down his own cheeks.

"Take a seat. There's a lot to tell you. But first I need a drink."

Hans went into the kitchen area and pulled a bottle of rum from the fridge. He poured the amber spirit into cut-crystal tumblers and took a big gulp before continuing. "There was a woman at the seafront watching us, an African, who I saw at the marina. I knew it couldn't be coincidence, so I followed her to her home. She told me Jessica was picked up floating in her scuba gear by local fishermen and sold on to people traffickers."

Penny listened without interruption, horrified as the truth was unveiled. "But, Hans, you have to go to the police, surely."

"It's not that simple, honey. It's not like they can arrest the boat captain on hearsay. And if he's not taken into custody, he'll warn the traffickers we're onto them and . . ." Hans shook his head. The ramifications didn't bear thinking about. He downed his rum and refilled the glass.

"But we must do something. What about speaking to Karen? As the US ambassador—?"

"No, I need to speak to Muttley again," Hans replied, having given his controller an update on the search earlier in the day.

Hans checked his watch. It would be 10:00 p.m. in Boston. He took out his cell phone and stabbed at the keypad.

"Orion, dear boy," Innes Edridge answered in his stately Scottish tone.

"Muttley, the game's changed."

"I figured that," said Muttley, knowing the special operative wouldn't call at this late hour for nothing.

Hans filled him in on the details in the short-and-to-the-point manner the organization favored.

"The way I see it is this, Orion: with no clear evidence, the most the police will do is knock on our friend Alvarez's door and ask for a cozy chat. At which point he'll slam it in their face and immediately warn his paymasters."

"But what about Arachne?" He referred to Karen by her call sign. "Can't she pull some strings?"

"Hans, even as US ambassador she has little sway over the way the locals do things. This isn't Baghdad, you understand?"

"Of course."

"In addition, this, errhum, 'trading' business is Cape Verde's dirty little secret – hell, it's half the world's bloody secret. You'll be blocked every way you turn trying to get to the truth. We know from our own intel this stuff goes all the way to undesirables in Washington."

"That figures."

"Besides our symp in immigration and one or two others, Carter doesn't have any influence in the territory."

"Carter," or the name of any former US president, was a code word Concern operatives used for the organization during unprotected communications. "Symps" were useful individuals sympathetic to the cause.

"While we've been speaking, I've run a sweep on this guy Alvarez, and I can't find any information linking him to a higher chain. He doesn't even have a bank account."

Hans smiled. Muttley could carry out a casual phone conversation while tapping on a computer keyboard and conducting a call on another line without you even realizing.

"So unless you hear anything more from me by seven in the morning your time, my advice is to liaise with Arachne to make a plan and pick up the necessary toys and a get-out-of-jail-free card, then go around to this guy's house and beat the information out of him. Don't hold back, Orion. You have nothing to lose but a lot to gain. He's a lowlife who can't exactly go to the police and report you roughing him up. Once you get what you need, I would recommend buying him a lollipop to prevent him talking, you understand?"

Hans did understand. "Lollipop" meant a termination.

"Orion, be discreet, but if anything comes of it we'll

get you and your good woman out of there."

"Thanks, M."

"And O."

"Sir?"

"Give that bastard one from me."

22

Penny awoke in bed alone feeling a pang of alarm. "Hans?"

"Here," came a shout from the living room.

She pulled on a bathrobe, stepped into flip-flops and entered the front room to find Hans, coffee in hand, staring at his notebook computer.

"I was worried."

"Sorry, Penny, I've been up a couple of hours getting some work done."

Penny looked at her watch – 6:00 a.m., meaning Hans had less than two hours' sleep.

"How's the head?" he asked, kissing her on the cheek.

"Nothing a double espresso won't fix. What are you doing?" Joining him on the couch, she peered at the official-looking data on the notebook's compact screen.

"Checking the CIA database for anything on Alvarez."

"What! You've hacked into it?"

"Not exactly hacked. The CIA uploads amended files every twenty-four hours onto an external server to back up their database. By placing the electronic equivalent of a filter in the upload process, we effectively take an image stream of the data for our own use."

"How do you bypass their security protocol?"

"We don't. We're not hacking into the system, just

accessing data from the inside, and bar a clever little box on a fiber-optic cable buried under six feet of concrete in Langley, the tap's impossible to uncover."

"Aren't you worried about using the hotel's Wi-Fi? I mean, can't people trace your movements?"

"There's ways to prevent it, like browser software and proxy servers, but I'm not using the hotel's Wi-Fi." Hans held up his cell phone, connected to the notebook by a cable. "I'm using my cell phone provider, Bluebird. It's a budget company that buys network downtime from Velafon and uses their coverage."

"And let me guess. Bluebird is owned by the Concern."

"Ha! You didn't hear that from me, but yes. Bluebird provides a regular phone service as a front and source of income – but as an operative, your comms are automatically scrambled. It's not fail-safe, though near enough, hence why we still use codespeak."

"And there was me thinking you just enjoy playing James Bond."

"Well, there is that."

Penny got up to make coffee. Hans took a break from his research, sliding open the door to the balcony and stepping out into the warm morning air. As the island's ever-present breeze fluttered the palm fronds lining the Grande Verde's immaculate boulevard, he found himself staring at the shimmering ocean beyond.

The sea had always been a part of Hans, one of the few stables in his turbulent upbringing. His late grandfather, a US Marine Corps veteran, bought him an aging wooden daysailer for his twelfth birthday, and Hans spent more time at sea in her exploring the coastal inlets around Misty Port than he did at home or school. It came as no surprise to anyone when he joined the navy at seventeen to serve as a radar operator on board USS *Nimitz*, nor when his thirst for adventure saw him transfer to the elite Navy SEALs. Iraq, Kuwait, Afghanistan – Hans had seen his fair share of desert, but it was the open ocean where he felt most at home.

Only now, fixating on the wave crests glistening like diamonds on their endless surge from the horizon, all he could see was Jessica's face, the yacht dragging her into the deep, her desperate eyes fixed on his, on the man who said he would never let her down . . .

"Coffee, hon?" Penny shook him out of his muse, and then, sensing his thoughts, added, "You will find her, Hans."

"I know." He feigned a smile.

Changing the subject, "Hans, can you tell me more about the Concern?" she asked.

"There's not a lot more to tell. After Vietnam a group of pissed-off vets and flag-wavers got together to bring a few of the bad guys to justice – the warmongers and profiteers. A couple of office chairs decided to throw some cash behind the project, and it grew from there. We try to keep it under wraps, not for any wrongdoing – although the rules do get bent occasionally – but to keep us out of the media, hence the code names. The operatives are figures from Greek mythology, and cartoon characters for the handlers."

"So the US ambassador, Karen – 'Arachne.' Wasn't she transformed into a spider?"

"By Athena, for blasphemy. If you think 'Black Widow' – Karen's husband was killed in the embassy bombing in Nairobi. The handlers allocate you a moniker that's a little left field and easy for others to remember."

"Right."

"Tell me the time."

"Sorry?" Penny glanced at Hans' Rolex, thinking she'd misunderstood something.

Hans grinned. "It's our version of Cold War spyspeak. If someone's checking your authenticity, they'll order you to give them the time rather than ask politely. So you reply with 'It's four o' four' or 'six o' six' or 'two twenty-two' – any alliteration with the right hour but the wrong minutes. Then you apologize, as if you've made a mistake, and give the correct time."

"Hmm, neat. But who manages the organization?"

"The Alþingi – it's an ancient Icelandic word meaning parliament – made up of a hundred and ninety-three representatives, known as *goðar*, who are the senior handlers in each country. Technically each country, as not all have a senior handler, and some have more than one. Every year they meet at a secret location somewhere in the world for a gathering known as the Þingvellir, where the senior council, the Lögrétta, made up of seven individuals to represent the seven continents, presides over the issues on the agenda. Heading up the Lögrétta is the chief of the Concern, the Lögsögumaður – the law speaker, or Logso for short."

"I see." As Penny sipped her coffee, it was as if the endless procession of waves symbolized the million questions flowing through her mind. "And the Lögrétta – do you ever get to meet them?"

"In my lowly role I don't get to know who they are. I

don't think Muttley does either – if so, he keeps one helluva secret. Some say they're the Concern's founding members. Others that they're voted in by the Alþingi and rotated every so often to avoid the power going to their heads."

"So in theory the Logso could be the president of the United States."

"Ha!" The irony made Hans chuckle. "It could be, but judging by the amount of bombs he drops on behalf of the corporate brat pack, I doubt it."

"Do you know how many people work for the Concern?"

"Technically none – with the exception of the Lögrétta and a core of administrative staff, plus a few vital bods, like techies and consultants, held on retainers. The rest of the network is made up of sleeper agents – SOs, handlers, enablers, and symps."

"Explain."

"SOs, 'special operatives,' are people like me – folks with specialist trades who get tasked with the risky stuff. Handlers, like Muttley, who you've met, oversee us on operations. Enablers are the corporate types who back us with funding or services – like the airline owner who provided the Learjet we flew in on. Symps are people sympathetic to the cause who can't offer significant financial support but who have other services of value, like Karen for example. There's no hierarchy to speak of – in fact, we're kinda communist in that respect – and everyone plays a crucial part. We all undergo the same initiation and provide our services for a token fee plus expenses, and that stops division and hubris and corruption."

"Wasn't it Lord Acton who said power corrupts and absolute power corrupts absolutely?" said Penny, recalling her student days.

"Exactly."

"And the initiation? Trouser leg rolled up, stand on one foot, drink the blood of a bat?" she joked.

"Ha, we're not the Illuminati! It's actually quite simple. You meet with your sponsor and handler somewhere private – mine was in the pool shed in our backyard. You hold a pebble, meant to represent the Lögberg – what the Icelanders called the Law Rock, which was the speaker's platform at their Þingvellirs – and recite the ten pillars of the Concern's constitution from the Jónsbók, or 'law book.'"

"Like?"

"Like, I promise to always make myself available, as far as reasonably possible, should anyone acting in the capacity of the Concern request my services – blah, blah, blah."

"No death before dishonor then?"

"No, just the pledges you'd expect from a weird bunch of covert do-gooders, followed by the symbolic burning of a scroll listing an operative's seven requisite qualities."

"Such as?"

"Courage, loyalty, selflessness, sense of humor in adversity – that kinda thing."

"Now who do I know that possesses them?"

"I don't know – it's not that guy from room service, is it?"

- 23 -

At exactly 7:00 a.m. Hans' cell phone rang. It was Muttley, calling to say he hadn't managed to pull any additional intel on Captain Alvarez and to proceed with the plan, adding that he'd briefed Karen, and she was expecting Hans' visit.

Hans called the ambassador to let her know his flight's arrival time, leaving Penny in the hotel and taking a car to the airport. From there a scheduled island-hopper flight landed him in Praia on the island of Santiago in a little under two hours.

Although only a hundred miles closer to the equator, Hans felt the increase in temperature and flapped his shirt as he walked through the arrivals hall.

A middle-aged Latino dressed in a cream sports coat and designer jeans approached.

"Mr. Larsson?"

"That's me."

"Enrique Ramos." He beamed and thrust a hand out. "Miss Shapiro sent me to collect you."

Enrique led Hans to a modest beige Ford sitting innocuously in the parking lot. "It's one of our runarounds. I have orders not to draw attention to ourselves, huh?"

"Good thinking," Hans replied, and hopped in the

passenger seat.

"You're looking a lot healthier than when I last saw you, Mr. Larsson."

"Really?"

"I was at the airport when the British Navy helicopter brought you in. You had us worried. No one expected you to make it."

"Thank you, Enrique, and call me Hans."

Enrique drove into the city, the difference between the two islands immediately apparent to Hans. The traffic moved with a sense of purpose along wider streets, lined with taller, five-story builds best described as "functionalist postcolonial" – less lurid pastels and solid concrete design as opposed to Mindelo's rickety authenticity – with banks, cell phone companies, bathroom and furniture showrooms and other outlets pandering to the growing economy leasing the ground floors.

"So how do you end up in the Foreign Service?" Hans asked.

"My parents were Nicaraguan immigrants to the US, so after graduating in foreign relations from Harvard, I went back to Central America and worked in international development. Fifteen years ago I joined the Foreign Service and have been on the island for ten."

He pulled into a private parking space in front of a surprisingly nondescript townhouse. The only clue as to the goings-on inside was the American flag flying from a pole jutting out at a forty-five-degree angle from the premise's dirty cream walls. Below it was a circular plaque featuring the US coat of arms.

Two US Marines, looking out of place at the building's

shoddy aluminum-framed door, sprung to attention. Enrique ushered Hans inside and into an antiquated elevator to travel the three floors to Karen's office, where he left them in private.

"Hans, good to see you!"

She stepped out from behind a somewhat flimsy wooden desk – complete with bald eagle figurine nonetheless – crossing the stock red-pile carpet to greet him. A gold-tasseled Old Glory hung wearily in a corner of the compact office.

After a hug Karen pulled a chair across for Hans and slumped in her leather-backed one as she cut to the point.

"So, it's a lot better news than we coulda hoped for, but still far from good. This guy Alvarez is just one of the many scumbags feeding the trade for human life in these parts – but tell me about this Fulani woman. We have nothing on her."

"You won't. I'm pretty sure she's an illegal, but she's gone out of her way to make contact, and she's risking her life by getting us more intel."

"Are you sure it's genuine – or is she after a handout?" Karen tilted her head, skepticism clear in her eyes.

"No, this isn't about money or a work permit."

"And you don't think it could be a trap set up by the Trade?"

"For her this is personal. You can see it in her eyes."

"What's your rationale for approaching Alvarez?"

"We've nothing else, Karen. The guy's got no record, no bank account, no known criminal associates. On the face of things he's a simple fisherman. There's no way to trace where the hell Jessica is – other than putting a tail on him. But that could take months to turn up a connection. Besides, how do we know this isn't just a one-off, like opportunistic?"

"Agreed. It's not every day a poor fisherman comes across a windfall floating in sea – sorry, Hans, I—"

"It's okay. But you see my point?"

"Sure. That's why I've arranged for you to have this." Karen pushed a black-covered diplomatic passport across the table. "You're now officially contracted to the embassy in your capacity as private investigator."

"Pleased to be of service." Hans flipped open the crisp document to see a working visa stamp on the first blank page. "Was it hard to get authorization?"

"No, it's within my remit to employ temporary staff – both local and domestic – but I had to run it by the State Department and the foreign office here. Luckily, Cape Verde's prime minster is in the US' pocket. He's just signed a foreign aid agreement with Washington that requires cooperation in certain areas – crimes involving US citizens being one of them – so he's eager to impress."

"The mighty dollar."

"The Trojan horse – but be discreet. This isn't a license to kill – except in self-defense. You're cleared to consular level on special mission status, meaning you can still be arrested if you cross the line but can't be sent to prison."

"Lucky me."

"I'm guessing you'll need a 'toy.'"

"Some backup wouldn't go amiss."

"Then you'll need these." She handed over a gun permit and a diplomatic pouch to transit a weapon and ammunition through the airport.

She buzzed the receptionist. "Catarina, can you ask Enrique to join us?"

"Is he on the level?" Hans raised an eyebrow.

"He's most definitely a patriot – but it's no secret around here he's with the agency." Karen gripped her neckline with two fingers. "So, we keep our thing quiet, huh?"

"What happens in Vegas . . ." Hans smiled, recalling whose database he'd accessed earlier.

After a brief explanation of events, "Enrique, can you take Hans to the armory and give him what he needs?" Karen asked, and then said good-bye.

Enrique took Hans down to the basement in the elevator, where a short corridor led to a formidable steel door. He typed in a code and pushed it open, flicking a light switch to reveal a fair-sized vault with a locking rack bolted to the wall to secure thirty M16s.

"For the Marines," Enrique explained. "A detachment of thirty's barracked down the road."

"I'll stick with a pistol," Hans joked, spying ten military-issue handguns below the rifles.

"Karen put a Beretta M9 down on the gun permit."

"M9's fine," said Hans – a similar model to his sidearm back home.

Enrique opened a padlock and slid back a retaining bar to release the weapon, double-checking its serial number against the paperwork. Then he spun the dial on a walk-in safe and stepped inside.

"Hollow point or regular?" He nodded to shelves of neatly stacked ammo.

"Regular's fine. A couple of boxes."

"Less of a cleanup job, huh?" Enrique winked, both knowing the damage a hollow point did to its victim. "Wanna fire a couple off on the range?"

"You have one?" Hans looked surprised, as the building wasn't exactly huge.

"Under the trap." Enrique pointed at a metal hatch set into the concrete floor.

"No, I'll be fine," Hans replied, casting an eye over the sizable collection of ordnance in the safe – plastic explosive, detonators, grenades, Claymores and rocket launchers. "Quite an arsenal you've got here."

"US soil, so we can defend it by any means. But if you ask me it's not enough. Remember Benghazi."

"Right."

Enrique handed Hans a weapon-cleaning kit, oil, a shoulder holster and four fifteen-round clips. "And you'll be needing comms. Cell coverage can be hit and miss around here." He pulled out two walkie-talkies, earpieces and a charger. "Anything else?"

"A set of eyes please," said Hans, nodding to a Leupold Mark 4 sniper's spotting scope. "And I'll take one of these." He lifted a bulletproof vest from a pile.

"Safety first, huh?" Enrique grinned.

- 24 -

The cell door burst open, and the angry man walked in.

Jessica sat cowering on the filthy mattress, wrapped in the rough gray blanket to preserve her modesty. She trembled but tried not to show it.

The man threw a tub of wet wipes at her and dumped sandals and clean clothes on the bed, but not out of compassion, his orders as always to maintain the captive's marketability. Then he left the room, leaving the door ajar.

Jessica was up in a flash and dashing across the floor to peer through the gap. Looking up and down the narrow stone corridor, she saw that hers was one of a series of rooms.

Seize the moment and move like there's no tomorrow! Hans' fatherly guidance echoed in her mind, and she knew it was time to escape.

She rushed over and grabbed her new attire – a pair of shorts and an ugly pink T-shirt with a transfer of Hello Kitty holding a balloon on it. Her parents never bought her pink crap.

Without wasting time dressing, she ran to the door and . . .

She heard the sound of approaching footsteps in the corridor.

Jessica threw the clothes down, leapt back on the bed

and pulled the blanket back around her. The man appeared in the doorway carrying two buckets, one – filled with water – inside the other, and a plastic basin containing a plate of food, a plastic beaker and a roll of toilet tissue. He stopped abruptly, his eyes flicking to the sandal lying at his feet.

As his mind almost registered the escape attempt, the quick-thinking little girl hurled the other sandal at him.

"And you can take that one too!" she screamed, folding her arms and sticking her bottom lip out.

Her cover-up worked. The man shook his head and set the stuff down. He picked up the footwear and threw it at Jessica, mindful not to hit her in the face, then placed the beaker and plate of food on the bed.

"For washing." He held up the basin and set it down by the wall. "Toilet." He dropped the roll of tissue into the empty bucket.

He pulled a toothbrush and a tube of toothpaste from his suit jacket pocket and dropped them on the floor, then rummaged in another pocket for a strip of pills. He popped one and handed it to Jessica.

"*Vitamina* – eat!"

The man took up the beaker, filled it with water and handed it to her.

Hesitantly, she put it in her mouth and swallowed, so parched the pill stuck in her throat. It tasted foul, making her gag.

"Drink!" the man ordered, and for once she did what he said.

Then he stood there, contemplating whether to feed his urges and make her dress in front of him. But, deciding he'd had enough of the little pissant for one day, he turned around and left the room, this time shutting the door behind him and slamming the bolt home and padlocking it.

Not having eaten for two days, Jessica snatched up the plate. It looked like the kind of leftover food she got the day after her parents threw a dinner party or cooked something special on a Saturday night. The meat was dark brown and covered in an orange-flavored sauce. Jessica didn't know what it was, but it tasted like chicken. She wolfed it down and began scooping up the small boiled potatoes garnished with fresh parsley and the sugar snap peas and baby carrots, shoving them into her mouth as fast as humanly possible.

Jessica cast the plate aside and began to get dressed. She pulled on the ugly T-shirt and the blue shorts but suddenly felt dizzy, gripping the bed to steady herself. She became increasingly light-headed and the room started to spin. Jessica stared at the floor, unable to work out if it was above, below or beside her, and then her legs buckled and she collapsed.

25

Hans packed the gear from the embassy into a khaki gym bag and placed the pistol and ammo in the diplomatic pouch. He asked Enrique to drop him off at a hardware store, saying he would make his own way to the airport.

Peering through the store window, Hans checked there were no CCTV cameras installed before proceeding inside. Even with the diplomatic pass it was best to err on the side of caution and leave as small a trail as possible.

Figuring Cape Verde would be a little short on leather gloves, he added a light pair of rubber industrial ones to his collection, a roll of duct tape, a foot-long jimmy, Maglite and a black balaclava – the type worn by metalworkers.

At the airport he entered the security channel reserved for diplomats and aircrew, showing his passport and gun permit to the official, who asked him to place his bag and diplomatic pouch on the X-ray machine, explaining the pistol and ammunition would go in the plane's hold.

Before boarding, Hans made a call to Penny, having agreed she would speak to Baba, the kindly Senegalese manager at Mindelo's Porto Grande Marina, and ask him about Alvarez.

"How'd you get on, hon?"

"Hans, I was about to call. Baba says he knows Alvarez, and the *Rosa Negra*'s berthed at the industrial port next to the marina. He showed me her through his binoculars."

"You mean she's not put to sea?" Hans frowned and began massaging his forehead.

"That's why I was about to call – according to Baba, it's unusual. He says these guys go out three-six-five in all weather. Do you think something's up?"

"I don't know. Where are you now?"

"I'm in Salgadeiras, the café bar, keeping an eye on the boat."

"I'll see you there in two hours."

Back on São Vicente, Hans headed for the airport's Hertz desk. Karen had offered to ship an embassy car to him the next day, but Hans didn't want to draw attention to himself in an official vehicle, plus he needed wheels right away.

Browsing the laminated brochure, he ignored the flashy high-end models, opting for a compact Daihatsu Terios jeep in modest gray. It was small enough to negotiate the island's narrow backstreets and hectic traffic, capable of going off-road, and blended in with the hundreds of other 4x4s buzzing about. Hans left his driving license and credit card details and drove toward the marina.

26

"Any change?"

Hans joined Penny in Salgadeiras, the cabana-style café bar she'd sat in every day for a month watching out over the ocean when *Future* went missing.

"See for yourself." Penny pointed across the harbor to a rusting tub moored against the dock wall.

"No one's approached her?"

"Not a soul. Is it worth making more inquiries – with the fisheries department or in the fish market?"

"No, it will only cause a stir. I gotta pay this guy a visit anyway."

"Do you think the Fulani woman could have talked?"

"She was making inquiries into Jessica's whereabouts, and it's possible Alvarez got wind. When I see her tonight, I'll ask."

"Could Jessica be on the boat?"

"I'm pretty sure Jessie changed hands weeks ago. Alvarez wouldn't have kidnapped her without the contacts to sell her on. Plus the boat's been at sea every day. It would be impractical to keep her on board – Alvarez knows the fisheries inspector could pay a visit any time, or a dockworker might see or hear something suspicious."

"I've asked Baba to tell his staff to watch out for any

movement."

"Good thinking."

Hans hadn't eaten since breakfast, and it was now midafternoon. "Fancy some food?" He pulled a menu from the condiments rack.

"The cachupa rica is good," said Penny. "Slow-boiled stew with pumpkin, sweet potato, and fish or chicken. And try the local red, bottled from grapes grown in a volcanic crater on Fogo."

"What's this *perceves*?"

"Sea fingers – purply-brown things. You crack off the skin to get at the meat. Looks like squid."

"But what are they?"

"Gooseneck barnacles. They're a popular dish."

Hans thoughts flicked to his time in the life raft, where eating these creatures prevented him starving to death.

"Er, I think I'll give them a miss. The capucha rica sounds good."

As their food arrived and Hans finished updating Penny on the morning's events, his cell phone rang – Jonah in LA.

"Odysseus, what you got for me?"

"I've got a picture of our man Alvarez. It took some trawling, but I found an archive article in the *Cape Verde Chronicle*. The guy led some protest against the Fisheries Department a few years back. I'll text it over – or do you want high-def?"

"No, low-res is fine, so long as I can get a positive ID."

"So are you gonna put one right between his eyes?"

"Ha! That's for me to know and for you not to." Even considering Jonah's Asperger's syndrome, Hans never knew if the kid was joking or serious. "Say, what's the time over there?" he asked.

"Seven in the morning. I've been on this all night."

"And I bet you've been smoking the weed all night too."

"I've been *smoking* it, Orion!"

27

In preparation for the evening, Hans laid his newly acquired equipment on the hotel bed. Penny watched as he disassembled and cleaned the Beretta, pulling the barrel through with a lightly oiled rag before putting it back together. Then he adjusted the shoulder holster for size, slid in the pistol and tried it on underneath a dark-blue sports coat. Satisfied with the weapon's concealment, he loaded the four clips with rounds, having wiped each one first with a cloth to remove any grime and fingerprints. He put the rubber gloves, flashlight, jimmy and duct tape into Penny's daypack, along with a contrasting change of clothes, and pocketed his diplomatic passport, gun license, wallet and keys. After switching his cell phone to vibrate, Hans took a cold shower, emptying his mind of all thought and focusing solely on his breathing – a mindfulness technique to purge his body of anxiety. Revitalized by the spray, he dressed in dark colors but dismissed the bulletproof vest.

Finally, Hans gave Penny a rundown on the walkie-talkies. Cell coverage was good on this part of the island, but he didn't want to take any chances.

"Penny, if I'm on the radio, it's fine to go ahead and speak because I'll have the earpiece in, but I won't be wearing it the rest of the time, since I don't want to draw attention to myself. So if you need to get hold of me, use your cell. If I can't answer, leave a voice mail or send a text."

"How long's this going to take?"

"Depends on how cooperative this guy's gonna be."

"Are you visiting the Fulani first?"

"I figure. She might have information that short-circuits the need to see this creep. If I'm out of contact for more than two hours, get ahold of Karen, and failing that, Muttley."

Hans typed the Fulani's address into the Daihatsu's satnav and began following directions given by Mr. T – of A-Team notoriety. Hans smiled. Whoever rented this jeep last sure had a sense of humor.

Driving the coast road in the dark, he turned on the car radio and scrolled through endless channels of hyperexcited DJs, call-ins conducted in Portuguese and Creole, and anonymous pop music. Hitting the button again, Hans heard an English voice reading the news on an expat station. He listened to an interview with a professor from the local university, who explained in simplified terms the increased ferocity in ultraviolet rays, backing up the recent health service recommendation that locals and tourists should apply a minimum of factor 40 sun cream.

Hans was about to change channels when the newsreader announced, "Following the abduction of five-year-old Holly Davenport from Praia Beach, the mayor of Mindelo, Videl Gonzales, has offered a reward of ten thousand US dollars from his personal savings to anyone offering information leading to her safe return. The mayor, noted for his contributions to children's charities, wants to reiterate this is a one-off occurrence that should not deter tourists from visiting the region."

A one-off occurrence, Hans mused. *And what about all the missing local kids that go unreported?*

Hans had decided not to mention anything to Holly's father at this stage in the investigation. Overcome with emotion, Mike would only see the smaller picture, and there would be no way of stopping him informing the authorities. With no firm evidence to make arrests, it would warn the traffickers Hans was onto them. He changed the channel and listened to a chat show in Creole – the eclectic mix of Iberian, West African languages and slang spoken by the islanders – and although Hans only understood the odd word, the laid-back patter soothed his nerves.

Taking the slip road to head into town, Hans felt sure a car was tailing him. He made a random series of turns to be certain, the headlights remaining in his rearview mirror until he got close to the Fulani's home. He considered forcing his assailant to a stop and pulling out the M9 to extract some answers, but to keep the odds in his favor he came up with another plan.

Tapping the gas station icon on the satnav brought up two red nozzles on the digitalized map. Hans selected the one nearest to his location and heard, "Rerouting, you crazy fool!" followed by, "At the junction, go straight over. Destination is a hundred yards on the right, sucka!"

Hans laid the M9 on the passenger seat, unlocked his cell phone and set the video camera to record. Then, as the forecourt lights of the gas station came into view, he wound down the window and pulled up at the pump nearest the highway, using the Daihatsu's door pillar to conceal the phone from view.

Taken by surprise, the driver of the other car, a silver Mercedes with tinted windows, braked at first and then sped off down the road.

"Amateur," Hans muttered.

He'd figured his pursuer wouldn't risk a confrontation in a public place, particularly one well lit with surveillance cameras installed, and now, unbeknown to the tail, he had the car and its license plate on film.

He gave Penny a quick update over the radio, then pulled back onto the road, spinning the jeep around and heading in the direction he came from. Sure that he'd lost the Mercedes, he rerouted the satnav.

After a command of "Turn right, sucka!" and "Destination is on the left, fool!," Hans drove past the Fulani's building and parked up in a side street. He placed the daypack out of sight in the Daihatsu's trunk and hurried toward the property.

At this hour the streets were deserted, bar the odd scraggy feline on the hunt for a rodent dinner. Hans reached the front door unnoticed and, recognizing the name Djenabou scrawled in spidery handwriting, pressed the corresponding buzzer.

No answer. Hans left it a few seconds and tried again . . . to no avail. Remembering Djenabou worked until 8:00 p.m., he checked his Rolex – 7:45 p.m., which explained why no light shone from her second-floor room.

The occupant of the silver Mercedes watched him from a distance.

Rather than hang around, Hans returned to the jeep and headed for Alvarez's place, not far away in the adjacent district.

Again he parked discreetly, taking the daypack with him. In this part of town, Porto Alta, the housing consisted of a maze of crumbling brick bungalows surrounded by sagging picket-wire fence, weathered and undulating like the decking of an antiquated roller coaster. Hans smelled the stench of sewage and heard soulful *morna* folk music blaring into the night, along with raucous laughter as adults smoked weed and got drunk and yelled at kids playing in the yards.

The fence around Alvarez's humble abode had all but collapsed. Hans stepped over it and circled the ramshackle property, peering through windows, looking for any sign of life but seeing none. He found an open sash and paused to put his gloves on and cock the M9. After clicking the safety catch off, he cracked his wrists and ankle joints, a cat burglar's trick to prevent any giveaway noise, and slipped inside.

Hans crouched on the bare wooden floor, letting his eyes adjust to the dark. He craned for the slightest sound, ignoring the miasma of cigarette smoke, body odor, stale urine and filth pervading his nostrils. His night vision kicked in to reveal a bedroom, though not one any self-respecting human would sleep in. He opened the door to find the bungalow empty, pulling the rough sackcloth drapes across all the windows before switching on the Maglite.

Starting with a chest of drawers in the bedroom, Hans began a systematic search, looking for anything linking Alvarez to his little girl's disappearance or a connection to the traffickers. He lifted the filthy mattress on the floor to find an adult magazine, an empty wallet and a pewter necklace with a peace sign pendant, but nothing else.

He moved to the kitchen. Painted in hideous pink gloss, bubbling and peeling like a bad virus, it housed a grease-caked two-ring stove and blue gas canister, on which sat a blackened frying pan and a half-full pot of rice, both still warm. A rough-hewn set of shelves displayed tinned goods, a jar of instant coffee and a bag of white sugar, a chipped cup and a plate and a heavily stained Nescafé mug holding cheap and tarnished cutlery. Beer bottles piled up against a cut-down oil drum overflowing with trash in the corner.

Hans played the beam of his flashlight around the living room. A couch with patches of stuffing bursting out of it faced a small black-and-white television set. On an improvised coffee table, consisting of four plastic beer crates with a sheet of wood on top and a nautical flag for a tablecloth, sat an untouched plate of rice, fish and beans, and an unopened bottle of beer. Alvarez had abandoned this place in a hurry.

A two-foot-long crucifix hung on the wall above a shelf of bric-a-brac and a photograph of a demure young woman. Hans peered at it, wondering what part this innocent played in Alvarez's past. For a moment he felt pity for the fisherman, understanding the utter poverty that had shaped his destiny, but the thought of the crime Alvarez had committed against his daughter sobered Hans' mind, for even in such desperate circumstances human beings have the power of free will and are accountable for their actions.

In amongst the clutter on the shelf was a voucher to claim two-for-one drinks in a local bar. Hans slipped it into a jacket pocket, along with the beer bottle, and climbed back out of the window he'd entered.

A dilapidated shack the size of a home garage sat in the backyard, likely, Hans figured, where Alvarez kept equipment from his boat. He slid back the bolt on the door and stepped inside. There were no windows in the shack, so Hans could play the beam of the flashlight about without worry of drawing attention.

Strewn about the floor were piles of fishing nets, nylon fenders, a rotting wooden tender, engine parts, hauling machinery and electrical equipment. In the corner was a tall metal cabinet, the type used to stock stationery in offices. Hans opened the door to see the cabinet divided down the middle. The left side contained shelves of rusting tools and an assortment of bearings, nuts, bolts and other fixings, plus a pair of ripped flip-flops. The other side was empty, bar what looked like a pile of faded life jackets.

A glint of chrome caught Hans' eye. He lifted a life jacket and froze, heart stopping dead in his chest.

There, slung in the bottom of the cabinet, was Jessica's scuba gear.

28

Hans raced back to the jeep. He needed to speak to the Fulani, figuring the Mercedes tailing him and Alvarez's impromptu disappearance had something to do with her inquiries, desperate to hear if she had information on Jessica's whereabouts. He brought Djenabou's address up on the satnav and drove toward her home, aided by B. A. Baracus' dulcet tones.

As a precaution, Hans parked two streets from the woman's building, changed into his lighter-colored clothes and shoved the Beretta into his waistband.

He keyed the radio: "Penny."

"Hans, are you okay?"

"Fine, but Alvarez took off, and I had someone on my tail."

"Oh God."

"Listen, I'm going to see the Fulani. I want you to call down to the front desk and tell them under no circumstances to give out your room number or let anyone up to the suite. Tell them to say you're out and to take a message. Don't answer the door to anyone, and turn off the lights as a precaution. I should be back within the hour."

Hans slid the jimmy inside his jeans, where it hung conveniently by its hook. Rather than approach the front entrance, he made his way down the back alley, knowing Djenabou lived in the fourth building from the end of the block.

A battered wooden fence ran either side of the alley. Hans took out the jimmy, prized off a couple of slats and squeezed through into the building's backyard.

A dog barked a couple of doors down, setting chickens off in someone's henhouse. Hans ignored the raucous birds, scooting across the dirt and climbing onto the roof of a shed to get to Djenabou's window. Her drapes were drawn, but no light shone through them, giving Hans cause to worry. Djenabou would have long since finished her shift at the fish factory and knew Hans was coming to the apartment.

The sash lock was across, so Hans put on his gloves, inserted his knife through the gap and knocked the small brass lever off the locking plate. He held back the drapes and hopped inside.

The coppery smell of blood told him the Fulani was dead.

In the beam of the Maglite, Hans saw she lay on her front, with an arm stretching toward one of the room's cracked plaster walls. He secured the drapes and stepped over her lifeless figure to flick the light switch.

Whoever committed the murder had clicked shut the padlock on the outside of the door. Hans rammed a chair under the interior handle for added security.

He rolled Djenabou over to find her throat cut and the front of her kaftan drenched in blood – the work of an amateur or a sadistic individual who enjoyed watching their victims suffer, as, judging by the hideous red sprays from floor to ceiling, her death had been a slow one. Yet the Fulani had refused to die in vain, for written on the wall in sticky dark blood was a name.

Logan? Hans pondered, then squinted at the squiggle-like mark. It looked like the letter *w* or an animal claw, or perhaps it represented something else altogether. He put his cell phone to use again, taking several snaps of Djenabou's desperate last message and capturing a slow sweep of the room on video.

On the table were two glasses and the bottle of bitter spirit Hans had shared with the African the previous night, giving him the impression she must have known her assailant or that his approach had been friendly. Holding the glasses up to the light, Hans was relieved to see both had fingerprints on them. He found a plastic carrier bag in the Fulani's kitchen space and placed them inside and then, using a third, smaller glass, took an imprint of the woman's bloody dabs for later comparison.

After a last check all around, Hans used a rag from Djenabou's dishwashing bowl to wipe the lettering off the wall. He took the photograph of little Binda from the dresser and placed it in her mother's hand. Then, after pausing to give a moment of respect for this courageous woman, Hans turned off the light and left the way he had entered.

29

Awaking on the cold stone floor, Jessica had a pounding headache, and her thirst raged. The last time she felt like this was when she drank mojito with Marcel, the kind Dutch sailor they had met on the yacht trip. Her papa did say it would make her sick as a pig, but she'd gone ahead and downed a glass anyway. She knew this feeling was something to do with the pill the Mouthwash Man gave her. She'd named him Mouthwash Man because his breath smelled like mouthwash, the same smell as the stuff that her papa defrosted the car windshield with in winter.

Jessica dipped the beaker into the bucket and gulped the water down, then refilled it and drank another. As she satiated her thirst, the little girl's mouth filled with horrible metallic-tasting saliva, and she threw up. Knowing Mouthwash Man wouldn't be happy, she began scooping up the sick and dumping it in the toilet bucket. After carefully rinsing her hands so as not to spoil the drinking water, she crawled back under the blanket and fell asleep.

She was right. When Mouthwash Man entered the cell, carrying a whiteboard and a bowl of food, he was far from pleased to see the mess in the bucket.

"What's your name?" he demanded.

"Jessica Kerry Larsson," she said, scowling.

"*What's your name?*"

"Maria," she acquiesced, opting to play it safe until her papa arrived and beat this man to a pulp.

"Very good." He nodded and then cleaned her face with a wet wipe. He placed the whiteboard against the cell wall, grabbed Jessica's hair and dragged her in front of it. "Look happy," he ordered, taking a camera from his pocket.

Jessica feigned a smile, and the man snapped several shots.

"When is your birthday?" he demanded.

"The eleventh of November," she replied.

"Okay, say, 'My name is Maria Dennis, and I was born on the eleventh of November.'"

Jessica did as told to prevent the man getting angry. He made her repeat it ten times, then scooped a beakerful of water, handed it to her and took out the bottle of tablets. She placed the opiate in her mouth and, as the man screwed the lid, maneuvered it under her tongue and pretended to wash it down.

Mouthwash Man grunted and left the cell.

- 30 -

Hans eased open the door of the hotel room to find Penny asleep on the couch. Careful not to disturb her, he grabbed a beer from the enormous refrigerator in the kitchen area and returned to the living room, content to sit there watching her sleep, feeling a sense of deep gratitude as a host of memories washed over him.

He recalled their chance meeting in the marina in Plymouth as he and Jessica prepared *Future* for the transatlantic crossing, how she'd hit it off immediately with his little girl and hadn't hesitated to accept his offer to crew for them. He thought about the inner demons she suffered because of the abortion she'd had following the fling with the cheating millionaire – her trauma worsened when a fortune-teller she'd visited for a bit of fun on a friend's bachelorette party "saw" the termination and declared the baby would have been a girl.

Watching the gentle rise and fall of her chest, Hans experienced a sense of closeness to this beautiful woman, one he hadn't expected to feel again, not since losing Kerry. Penny came into their lives when he and Jessica still didn't know which way was up, not expecting anything in return and bringing her ever-caring and effervescent persona. He would get Jessica back for all of their sakes or die trying.

Needing something stronger, Hans went to the kitchen and fetched the half-empty bottle of rum. When he returned, Penny stirred.

"Hans, are you okay?"

"I'm fine, but the Fulani is dead."

"No!"

Hans got another glass and filled Penny in on the details, including the bloody message and the mysterious Mercedes.

"Why would someone kill her, and who would be following you?"

"I'm not sure. Something doesn't figure, but . . ."

"Did you get the license plate?"

"I'm hoping I got better than that." Hans took out his cell phone and downloaded the video he had captured to his notebook computer.

"Here goes nothing." He double-clicked the file icon.

The result wasn't what he'd hoped, the car flashing past in the blink of an eye.

"Damn!"

Hans replayed the video in a series of pauses, but even reduced to its original frame size, the image was grainy at best, the registration number blurred by the car's speed and its license plate light. The driver remained shielded from view by the car's tinted windows.

"No good?" Penny frowned.

"Not brilliant. Car's an E-Class Mercedes – a popular choice for the movers and shakers on the island . . ." Hans' words trailed off, and he stared into nothing.

"What is it, hon?"

"I've seen this car before. I just can't think where."
Hans stroked his stubbled chin. "And can you see on top
of the license plate there's a logo of some kind?"

Penny fixated on the small yellow blur. "Could it be
territorial, like where the car's registered?"

"I don't think so. We have that at home – you know,
like this plate's from Alaska or such and such. But I
haven't seen it here."

"Guess we'll have to keep our eyes open and see if we
can spot this type of plate." Penny shrugged.

"We could try Google Images." Hans opened a web
browser, but a search turned up nothing of interest.
"We'll have to make inquiries with the police and
whoever produces the license plates here," he concluded.

"And the name Djenabou wrote? Are you sure it was
for you?"

"Who else could it be for?"

"Right, and you think Alvarez killed her."

"Sure looks that way."

Hans downloaded the image file from his cell phone
and brought the haunting message up on the notebook's
screen.

"What is that, Hans? Lo . . . gan, Logan?"

"I think so."

"But what about this clawlike thing?" Penny studied
the bloody symbol.

"Hell if I know. I'll email it to Jonah. See what he can
come up with."

Penny's cell phone rang – Baba on late shift at the
marina. "Miss Penny, the fishing boat is sailing."

"We'll be right there!"

Hans grabbed the keys to the jeep and they rushed to

the elevator, arriving at the marina's office fifteen minutes later to find Baba, the huge Senegalese, with binoculars in hand.

"What's happening?" the American asked, panting.

"She put to sea a moment ago. Here." Baba passed the glasses.

"How many aboard?" Hans asked as he watched the *Rosa Negra* rounding the port's protective wall with her running lights off. "Did they have a child with them?"

"I didn't see." Baba held up his pink palms. "I only heard her engine start up and saw a couple of guys throwing off the mooring lines."

"Do you think Jessie could be with them, Hans?" Penny cast her eye over the pile of the Holly Davenport "missing" leaflets the marina's staff had been handing out to yacht crews.

"There's a slim possibility, or Alvarez could just be making a discreet getaway."

"Where would he be going?"

"One of the other islands." Hans looked to Baba. "Or possibly the North African coast."

Baba nodded. "It's only three hundred miles. He'll have more than enough fuel on board."

"Hans, he's the only link we have to Jessie." Penny clutched his arm.

"I know. Baba, can we request the coastguard intercepts him with their patrol craft?"

"We can, Hans, but they only operate a standby crew. By the time they put to sea, the *Rosa Negra* will be one of many blots on the radar screen."

"In that case I need to borrow your launch."

The marina owned a small speedboat, mostly used to

rescue inexperienced skippers who drifted too near to the shore and couldn't start their motors.

"It's yours." Baba pulled the launch's engine cutout key from a peg and gave it to Hans.

"And get on the radio and request other boats keep watch for the trawler."

Baba was already on it.

"Penny, you drive. I need you to get me alongside."

The two of them rushed along the pontoon and untied the launch. Penny inserted the cutout key into its socket on the launch's console and clipped the end of the leash to a belt loop on her shorts. In seconds they roared out of the marina, the city's lights reflecting off the *Rosa Negra*'s superstructure, giving away her position in the pitch-black night.

Outside of the harbor's protective lee, the swell kicked up, drenching them in spray. The little craft pitched violently, launching off breakers and slamming down on the shimmering ocean, threatening to somersault. Penny eased back the throttle.

"No!" Hans shouted above the noise of the outboard engine, redistributing his weight to keep the bow up. "Give her all she's got!"

Penny thrust the throttle forward, the two of them instinctively bending their knees each time the launch went airborne off a crest. Just as it seemed they'd catch up with the *Rosa Negra*, she picked up speed, her huge bulk indifferent to the challenging conditions.

"He's seen us!" Hans yelled, spotting Alvarez's silhouette in the pilothouse's rear-facing window.

"She's no match, Hans," Penny screamed back as they entered the larger boat's wake, intuition telling her they would outrun the trawler.

Hans cocked and reholstered the pistol and shifted across the launch. "Okay, I'm gonna board her—"

The *Rosa Negra* exploded into a million burning pieces.

Hans slammed back against Penny, knocking her into the sea, a huge fireball engulfing them as shrapnel from the trawler's hull began raining down.

Fortunately, the cutout key did its job, and the launch slowed to a stop. As Hans dragged Penny back aboard, his thoughts turned to Jessica. He prayed she hadn't been on the doomed vessel.

"Are you okay?" he asked, holding up the flap of his jacket to shield them from the heat.

"I'm fine." Penny spat out seawater and restarted the outboard.

Without another word, she twisted the throttle and chugged through the debris field toward the site of the explosion.

Two dead crew members floated faceup side by side amongst the flotsam, giving the impression the dead men were holding hands.

Hans reached down into the oily scum and grabbed the body of a third, rolling it over to reveal Alvarez, with half the flesh stripped from his skull, resulting in a hideous death grin. He thrust the corpse away in disgust, knowing the captain had the easy way out.

There were no other human remains, so Penny spun the launch around and headed back to the marina.

- 31 -

Back at the hotel, while Penny took a shower Hans powered up his notebook and began typing out a timeline of events, adding in brackets the unanswered questions each incident threw up. He knew his liaison with the island's police force was long overdue, and he wanted to have the upper hand when they met.

Penny emerged from the bedroom in jogging bottoms, a T-shirt and flip-flops, toweling her damp locks.

"What are you thinking?"

"I'm thinking someone – possibly this Logan character in Djenabou's message – is trying to cover up any links to Jessica's kidnapping now that he knows I'm after him."

"But why not just take you out?"

"He could easily have done that as I drove down the coast road to meet Djenabou tonight. Instead he used me to get to her, to eradicate her, and to spook Alvarez into doing a runner before blowing him to kingdom come."

"I-I—"

"I'm confused too. We can assume that whoever it is knew Djenabou had been making inquiries and was gonna spill the beans but didn't know where she lived, hence the tail."

"But you said you'd lost them." Penny slumped on the couch beside him.

"I thought I had, but somehow they managed to stay one step ahead." Hans poured Penny a shot of rum. "And they were watching our movements tonight," he continued.

"How do you know that?"

"The explosives planted on the *Rosa Negra* must have been radio-controlled – as opposed to a timer – or the boat might have blown up in the harbor. And they detonated them before we could reach her, saving us from going up in smoke and causing an international incident."

"So someone was watching the boat leave the harbor tonight." Penny downed her rum and poured two more shots.

"I just can't figure who."

"Are we in danger? Here at the hotel?"

"No, what with all the media interest around *Future*'s sinking and me returning to the island, they would draw attention to themselves by going after us."

Penny yawned and checked her watch. "Hans, it's almost three. We should get some sleep."

Hans threw back the covers on the huge bed and answered his cell phone.

"Odysseus, what you got for me?"

"Orion, check your email, dude."

Hans nudged Penny, then flashed up his notebook in the living room and hit a message titled "Bingo!" Jonah had prepared a full PDF report on Logan, with details procured from various sources.

"I'm reading."

Eddy Logan was a low-level British criminal from South-East London. He owned a bar in Praia called Chico's, bought following a four-year jail term in the UK for money laundering. Logan had served in the British Army, seeing action in Iraq, but received a dishonorable discharge for "conduct unbecoming of a soldier."

Hans scrutinized a paragraph detailing how Logan got off a charge for child abduction two years previous.

"Odysseus, this is gold."

"Orion, that claw thing in the woman's message — look at the guy's Facebook profile."

Hans scrolled to the end of the report to see a shot of Logan, a bald musclehead with a goatee beard, fists clenched doing a bodybuilding pose for the camera. Creeping above the neckline of his T-shirt were the claws of a full-torso dragon tattoo.

"Odysseus, you're ace."

"I know."

"Listen, get me everything you can on this guy – phone records, bank statements, emails. I need a picture of his movements, particularly the last two months."

He ended the call.

"Hans, what's happening?" Penny joined him in the living room.

"Jonah's found our man. Here."

As Penny read the file, everything fell into place – the name and claw symbol drawn in blood, Logan's military and criminal record, and the child abduction.

"What do we do?"

"If this guy's based in Praia, then I need to be on Santiago."

"You?" Penny threw a sideways look.

"Hon, you have to leave Cape Verde. Four people are dead, and there's no telling what Logan will do next."

"Then I suggest you find a place on Santiago where he can't find us, because I'm staying."

Hans knew there was no point arguing.

- 33 -

Jessica endured the same routine for weeks, waking up afraid in the dimly lit chamber, not knowing whether it was day or night, forced to repeat the name Maria Dennis and her assigned birthday. The only way to tell the approximate time was by the meals Mouthwash Man brought her, and although she was afraid of him, eating was the only thing she had to look forward to. Breakfast would be fresh buttered bread with ham, cheese or jam, initially with a mug of bitter black coffee, but as she couldn't stomach it, the man brought orange juice instead. Lunch was always a bowl of potato and kale soup with chunks of chorizo floating in it. Dinner would be meat, fish or poultry, with vegetables, her favorite being salted cod baked with pumpkin, onions, tomatoes and olives.

Every day Jessica tried to hide the horrible pill under her tongue and spit it out after the angry man left. She wasn't sure what the medication was for but remembered her father and Penny discussing something written in a travel guide about not leaving drinks unattended in bars because bad men could put pills in them and make you ill, and then steal all your belongings or make you do stuff against your will. She thought it must be to do with this and made sure to act woozy on the days she avoided swallowing it.

"Daily routine, runner bean!" was another of her father's aphorisms. Hans began each day by jumping out of bed at 6:00 a.m. and waking the household up with a bloodcurdling Tarzan bellow, drinking a pint of water and then going for a ten-mile run along the coast. "Structure holds your life together when things are bad," he would say, so Jessica stuck to this approach now, and, following breakfast and before going to sleep at night, she did push-ups like she did with her papa and then ran around the tiny cell twenty times, increasing to fifty as the days went by.

After the morning exercise she occupied her mind with singing songs, telling jokes to Bear as if he were there with her, reciting riddles and repeating the names of the kids in her class at school. Other times she ran through the preparations for a scuba dive – strapping the air cylinder to the buoyancy jacket, connecting the hoses, loading her mask, fins, wetsuit and diving knife into a kitbag and stowing it in her papa's truck for the trip down to the beach. Then kitting up and going through the prechecks – buoyancy vest, weights, quick releases and air – before wading into the water, putting on her fins and doing a final check. She loved diving with her father and could recall the details of all thirty recorded in her logbook, such as time, depth, temperature, leftover air and the marine life she saw.

"Jab, jab, hook, straight, uppercut!"

Jessica danced around the cell shadowboxing an imaginary opponent, in this instance her friend Stevie Worth from the Little Dragons Muay Thai School in Portland.

"Front kick, straight, jab, jab!" she puffed, then –

"Ooph-ooph!" – took a couple of shots to the head.

"Is that all you got?" she mocked Stevie, although her pa would not have been happy if she ever said that in the ring.

The more Jessica visualized the sparring session, the realer it got, to the point where she could see and feel the gymnasium, the boxing ring and equipment, even picturing the orange shorts Stevie wore and the bright-red padding protecting him from her punches and kicks.

She was proud of her own shorts, electric-blue silk embroidered with Thai script down the right leg, ones JJ gave her as a Christmas present.

"Jab, jab, uppercut, elbow smash, push kick . . . spinning back kick!" Jessica polished off little Stevie and turned to face three more contenders. "If you wan' it, come an' get it!"

- 34 -

Penny ordered a breakfast of bagels with smoked salmon and scrambled egg, which they ate while packing. Afterwards, Hans flicked through the channels on the suite's widescreen television to find a local news report. A shot of the quayside cordoned off with blue-and-white police tape and packed with emergency vehicles filled the screen. In the background the coastguard patrol vessel and a police diving unit circled the scene of the explosion.

"What are they saying?" Hans asked.

Penny dumped her rucksack on the couch and listened as a female reporter spoke in rapid-fire Portuguese to the camera.

"She says a fishing boat caught fire and sank as it left harbor last night. The three crew members are in hospital with burns and that this should serve as a reminder to local fishermen to pay attention to maintenance issues and safety equipment."

"Well, they've played that down," Hans mused.

"Do you think Logan has friends in high places?"

"It's possible, or it might be the media has been told to keep a lid on it for the sake of tourism."

"Will the police have spoken to Baba?" Penny felt uneasy at the thought of them interrogating their kind friend.

"I'm sure they'll get around to it."

"And you told him it was okay to tell them about us?"

"I had to. The explosion woke up every crew in the marina, and they're bound to have seen us out there in the launch."

"Do you think the police will want to speak to us?"

"Depends on whether they buy Baba's story that we borrowed the launch for a spot of night fishing." He shrugged and turned his palms up. "I guess we'll cross that bridge when we come to it."

Hans called Karen's cell phone en route to the airport. "We're shifting to Praia and need somewhere to stay that's quiet."

"Come to the embassy. I've got just the place."

A little before 7:00 a.m. Hans and Penny returned the jeep's keys to the Hertz desk, but as they were about to leave the office, Hans grabbed Penny's arm.

"I *knew* I'd seen it somewhere!"

"Seen what?" She followed his gaze to see a poster of an E-Class Mercedes, the rental agency's executive model.

"That's the car," he whispered. "The one I got on film."

"Which explains the yellow tag on the license plate," Penny whispered back. "It's the Hertz logo."

"Logan or one of his thugs must have rented it here when he flew in from Praia. It's the only Hertz outlet on the island."

"Can you ask who?" Penny looked over to the agent serving behind the counter.

"I don't want to draw attention. I'll call Jonah. He'll

find out for us."

Hans and Penny boarded the island hopper and took up their seats. Soon after takeoff, the flight attendant approached.

"Mr. Larsson?"

"Ma'am?"

"We've had a call from the police. They wish to speak to you when we land in Praia."

"Did they say why?"

"I was only told to give you the message."

A police car was waiting on the tarmac as the plane touched down. Out stepped a short, fat local man dressed in black dress pants and a Hawaiian shirt, which looked as if it would burst open at any second. He walked over and introduced himself as Barbosa Amado, the chief inspector of the Judicial Police.

"Mr. Larsson." He pumped Hans' arm up and down. "Miss Masters." Penny received the same treatment. "The hotel said you were on your way to Praia. Would you come with me please?"

"What's this about?" asked Hans, stepping into the vehicle and noting from the nervous look on Amado's bloated face that he felt way out of his depth.

"Inside, inside." The chief inspector waved a finger in the direction of the terminal, as if this bypassed the need for an explanation.

The car dropped them at the arrivals building, Amado ushering them up a flight of stairs into a nondescript office. A slim Italian-looking man, midforties with graying black hair, stood waiting to greet them, sweating profusely in his dark wool suit.

"Mr. Larsson, Miss Masters, this is Inspector

Leonardo Mucci from Interpol's Praia office."

Mucci pulled out a handkerchief and wiped his palms before shaking hands.

"Inspector Mucci is coordinating the joint operation with Scotland Yard into the British girl's disappearance," Amado continued. "You know of Holly Davenport?"

"We're aware of her, yes," said Hans.

"Forgive me, but you returned to the islands to recover the body of your daughter, er, Jessica."

"Correct."

With Mucci keeping quiet in the background and Amado's lack of eye contact, Hans knew this was a fishing exercise.

"But you have no luck, huh?"

"It's a big ocean out there."

"Exactly. And I understand you have recently acquired a diplomatic passport."

"I'm doing a little work for the embassy, yes."

"Detective work, huh?" Amado's eyes kept flicking down at the desktop.

"That's my job," Hans replied, his stare unwavering.

"Would that explain what you were doing in Mindelo harbor last night when the fishing boat – er, what was her name?"

"I don't know," Hans replied deadpan. "What *was* her name?"

"Ah yes, the *Rosa Negra*. She was blown up while you were out, erm, 'fishing.'"

"Blown up?" Hans raised an eyebrow. "I thought it was a fire?"

"Yes, a fire, of course."

"And are you suggesting I had something to do with

it?"

"Not at all Mr. Larsson—"

"Call me Hans."

"Hans, you understand my predicament. You didn't find your daughter, and next you're chasing a local fisherman and *boom!*"

"Chief Inspector Amado, my sole aim is to explore every possibility of recovering my daughter's body. You have my word if in the course of my investigation I come across any information that links to Holly Davenport's abduction I will let you know."

"I trust you will do." Amado took a business card from his breast pocket and passed it to Hans. "And if I can be of assistance to you in any way, don't hesitate."

"Of course," said Hans, reciprocating the gesture.

Hans rented another jeep at Nelson Mandela Airport, and they drove through the traffic packing the faux-colonial streets. Before arriving at the embassy, Hans pulled over and took out his cell phone. He wanted an update from Mike Davenport before meeting Karen.

"Mike, Hans Larsson."

"Hans, how are you?"

From his tone alone, Hans could tell there had been no developments and he was putting on a brave face.

"I'm fine, Mike. Just ringing to see if there's been any news."

"Acht! The police keep saying they're coming up with leads, but they're only blowing smoke. We're being kept in the dark. They've splashed Holly's photo everywhere, but I can't help thinking they're gambling on something random turning up. They've assigned some bumbling inspector to the case, real Colombo type but without the brains."

Hans smiled.

"My wife Carrie's returned to the UK to raise media and political interest and funds for a private investigation. I'm in a hotel in Praia so I can be near the police headquarters and not have to keep flying back and forth between the islands. Anyway, enough about me.

Did you have any luck finding your daughter's body?"

"No. No, we didn't, Mike. We've decided to stay awhile to try to get some closure, so we'll be in Praia too. If there are any developments, anything we can do to help, or you just fancy a couple of beers, please get in touch."

"I will do, Hans. I appreciate your call."

Hans filled Penny in on the details of the conversation as he drove toward the embassy.

"Are you sure it's not best to tell the police what we know? I mean, widen the net so to speak." Penny felt uneasy.

"Did you see the increase in security at the airport?"

"Keeping an eye out for Holly. I saw some of those 'missing' leaflets at the marina too."

"Exactly. Scotland Yard – with a little help from Interpol – will have put pressure on the island's police to prevent her being taken out of the country. That's why Holly's photo is all over the news."

"I'm listening."

"It doesn't make sense at this stage to put the heat on Logan. Small-island police are inept at the best of times. They'll be keeping Scotland Yard's officers at arm's length and blundering through the investigation themselves. You remember that little girl's disappearance from a swimming pool changing room when we were in the Canaries?"

"Anita someone."

"That's her. It was twenty-four hours before the police bothered to seal off the crime scene. By that time every Tom, Dick and Harry had crawled over it and contaminated the forensic evidence. Then after forty-eight hours they alerted the media, but not Interpol."

"Strewth!"

"*Sh*yeah. If Jessica's being kept in the islands until the Holly Davenport situation dies down, our best bet is not to let Logan know we're onto him."

"What's the plan?"

"Carry out surveillance, make subtle inquiries and see if Jonah turns up any more intel. If we draw a blank, then I'll give Inspector Amado a call and level with him."

- 36 -

"**H**ans, Penny, good to see you."

Karen welcomed them into the office and buzzed her secretary for coffee. They made small talk until the drinks arrived and the secretary left the room.

"I see Senhor Alvarez went up in smoke." The ambassador pressed her lips together as she passed Hans a cup.

"Nothing to do with me, Karen. The Fulani was murdered too."

"Gosh!" said Karen, genuinely surprised. "There was no mention of that on the news or the bureaucratic grapevine."

"At this point in time I think it's only us and the killer who are aware of it," Hans concluded.

"I see. Any leads?"

"Does the name Eddy Logan mean anything to you?"

"British gangster comes to mind." Karen pulled a pained expression.

Hans filled her in on the details and showed her the horrifying message in the photo.

"I've met him at a couple of functions around town," said Karen. "Likes to come across as a Mr. Playboy Businessman, but he didn't make all that cash he flashes around selling cocktails out of a bar in Praia."

"More like selling children." Hans looked stern. "I'm waiting on further intel to come back from Odysseus. In the meantime it's good ol'-fashioned surveillance."

"Is it worth liaising with the island's police?"

"Funnily enough, we met Chief Inspector Amado at the airport. He was waiting to speak to us with a suit from Interpol, asking why we were down at the harbor last night. They're looking into Holly Davenport's abduction. But I figured showing our cards at this stage would do more harm than good."

"What about asking Muttley to fly a team in?"

"I thought about that, but other than a name there's not an awful lot to go on, and I can cover for the time being."

"In that case I suggest we bring Enrique in on this. He's been with the embassy ten years, knows the scene here inside out, and with his CIA connection and contacts in law enforcement I can't see it would do any harm."

"Agreed, but remember we have intel on Logan we can't divulge to Enrique, for obvious reasons." Hans tapped two innocuous fingers against the face of his Rolex.

Karen dialed Enrique's extension and asked him to join them. While they waited, Karen gave Hans a door key and wrote down an address.

"This is my private retreat." She looked up, smiling. "It's on the coast not far from here. I rented it to get out of the city at weekends, only I've been too busy to go there, so hardly anyone knows it's mine. It might need a vacuum, and take some supplies, since the cupboards are pretty bare, but you're welcome to stay as long as you need."

Enrique entered the room. Having met Penny when the Royal Naval chopper flew Hans in to the airport, the American-born Nicaraguan cracked a broad grin.

"*Minha amiga*, so nice to see you again!"

They hugged like old friends, and Enrique pecked her on both cheeks.

Karen got straight to the point. "Enrique, we have it from a reliable source that Alvarez, the captain of the boat that . . . caught fire and sank last night, picked up Jessica after their yacht went down."

"Reliable source, Karen?"

"A Fulani woman, a migrant. She also came up with the name Logan, who we think is Eddy Logan."

"Ah, our playboy millionaire money launderer."

"Well, it looks like he doesn't just rinse cash."

"That doesn't surprise me. How can I help, Hans?"

"Karen tells me you have connections in certain places."

"It's not something I broadcast, but yes."

"Any end-user info you can pull on this guy would be a start."

By "end user," Hans inferred someone cleared to access the global intelligence community's databases.

"Any local knowledge would be a help too – associates, movements and such."

"Sure." Enrique scribbled notes on a pad.

"I appreciate you must be busy, but if you can put some time into this I'd appreciate it."

"Four people are dead, Hans. I'll make time. Anything else?"

"Yeah, there is. Where can I buy a decent camera?"

"**T**he Canon E74S is perfect for your needs, *senhor*," the shop assistant informed Hans, handing over the state-of-the-art camera. "It's lightweight, compact, has an eighteen-megapixel full-frame sensor and comes with a powerful seventeen-to-forty-millimeter zoom. The battery is lithium, so it will take about twelve thousand pictures before going flat."

Hans had heard enough and, feeling the effects of spending a month in a life raft, was keen to get out of the busy shopping mall. He pulled out his wallet and paid the equivalent of $2,200 by credit card.

"Shall we go and find Karen's villa?" Penny asked, sensing Hans' unease.

"First we need a post office. I've gotta send these prints to Muttley and get them run through the lab." Hans had sealed the three glasses he'd removed from Djenabou's place and the beer can from Alvarez's in separate ziplock bags.

"Can't Enrique request the police here do it? Wouldn't it be quicker?"

"I don't want the island police to have any dots to join up – not at this stage."

There was a post office on the same street. He scribbled a note to Muttley explaining that one glass was a sample of the Fulani's prints, and the beer can Alvarez's, asking him to check if the other glasses held Alvarez's or Logan's prints or some unknown's. He placed them in a padded envelope and posted it priority airmail.

On the drive to the villa Penny was unusually quiet.

"Honey, are you okay?"

"I'm fine," she replied, staring at the dashboard.

"Penny . . ." Hans placed his hand on hers. "I've been through some pretty tough scrapes in my life. I'm not afraid of these guys, and I'll do whatever is necessary to get my daughter back. If anything happens to her, I'll take every single one of them down and . . ." Hans' knuckles whitened on the steering wheel. "Listen, I'm trying to say that I'm all in. There's no going back. But I don't expect you to come on the journey."

"Hans, why are you saying this?"

"It's just . . . I can see this thing's bothering you. Hell, why should you get dragged into it? And—"

"Hans!" she could see where this was going. "I've loved you and Jessie since the moment I was lucky enough to set eyes on you. I will follow you to the end of the earth to help get her back. I'm not worried. I'm . . . I'm . . ." She burst into tears.

"Honey, what's up?" Hans pulled the jeep over.

Penny threw her arms around his neck. "Hans, I hate seeing you like this . . . and to be like this, to know Jessie's out there somewhere. You've been through so much and yet you bulldoze on through, remaining strong and so fucking professional. I can't imagine what you're going through. I wish I could do more. I wish this was over – u-hut-huh-huh . . ."

"Baby, we're gonna get her back – for you, for me, for us. Then we'll take a year out and do nothing except be together and relax and have fun."

"Hans. I-I-I—"

"I know, I know."

- 38 -

One afternoon Jessica was in the middle of putting an evil overlord to bed with a jump kick when she heard footsteps in the corridor. She scrambled back under the blanket and pretended to be comatose from the morning's pill. However, Mouthwash Man never entered the cell and unbolted the next one along.

"In!" she heard him yell, and the door slammed.

Lying there puzzled, Jessica heard a little girl's cries coming through a ventilation grate set into the bottom of the dividing wall. She got up off the bed to investigate and crouched by the vent, where the tears sounded louder and more real.

"Hey!" she whispered, and the crying ceased. "I'm down here!"

The bed in the next room creaked, and someone tiptoed across the floor. Peering through the vent, Jessica saw a silhouette appear.

"What's your name?" she asked the stranger.

"My name is called Holly," the girl replied with a sob.

"My name is Jessica Larsson and I'm seven years old – but I might be eight now, I'm not sure."

"I'm five, and I want my mummy and daddy," Holly whimpered.

"Don't worry. My daddy's coming to get me and he's a detective and he was a Navy SEAL and he's not afraid of

141

anything. If you want, we can take you with us and go and find your mommy and daddy."

"Uh-huh."

"Holly, you talk funny. Are you an American?"

"I don't know. What's a Mercan?"

"It's someone that comes from the States."

"What's a states?"

"It's a country a long way away. Which country are you from?"

"I'm from Little Hamstead."

"Oh. Where's that?"

"It's in Devon."

"I've been to Devon! It's in England! Me and Papa went to Plymouth and we bought a boat called *Future* and we were gonna sail her home to Portland but it got sunk. Have you got a boat too?"

"No," Holly whispered. "We haven't got any water in Little Hamstead."

"Do you know about Sir Francis Drake? He lived in Devon."

"Ut-uh."

"He was the queen's favorite sailor and he had a big boat called a galleon and he sailed around the world and he found new people who lived in a jungle. And you'll never guess what."

"What?"

"His boat had a lot of guns on board and he needed about *one* hundred men to help sail her."

"Who's that man?"

"What man?"

"The bad man who put me in his car and brought me to here."

"Oh, I call him Mouthwash, because he stinks like mouthwash. Did the pirates give you to him?"

"What pirates?"

"The pirates who pulled you out of the sea."

"I wasn't in the sea. I was on the beach and a woman said I had to go with her because Daddy wanted her to buy me an ice cream."

"Did you get one?"

"No."

"Why not?"

"Because she told me mummy and daddy were going to die and it would be my fault if I didn't get in the car with that man."

"Acht, he's a real jerk! He'll try to make you eat some pills, but you gotta spit them out when he's not looking or they make you drunk like mojito and then you'll be sick."

"I want my mummy."

Holly started to cry again.

"Hey, get a grip!" Jessica sensed she had a job on her hands with this one. "Sobs are for slobs!"

Holly tried to stifle her tears.

"Hey, what comes down but never goes up?"

"Huh?"

"It's a riddle. You have to tell me the answer. What comes down but never goes up?"

"I don't know."

"The rain! Because the rain can only come down and can never go back up!"

"Uh-huh."

"Knock, knock."

"Who's there?"

"Major."

"Major who?"

"Major answer the door – hee-hee!"

Holly giggled.

"Look, go and get your blanket and I'll get mine and we can sleep down here. Then I can talk to you if you get scared."

"But how long do I have to stay here?"

"Erm, not long. My papa's probably gonna come tomorrow and then him and Penny will look after us."

"Okay, I'll get my blanket."

"I'll get mine too."

39

Karen's holiday home, a white-walled bungalow with terra-cotta roof tiles, sat right on the edge of the sea five miles from the city. It nestled in a secluded spot between greeny-black basalt cliffs topped with sparse dry scrub.

"Look at this!" Penny stepped out of the jeep and breathed in the fresh, salty air accompanying a stunning vista.

"Now *that's* what I call blue!" Hans crossed the flagstoned patio and hopped up onto the parapet to see waves lapping the rocky shore ten feet below.

"I'd say turquoise," Penny remarked, gazing out over a lagoon sheltered by rolling headland. "Do you think that's the boat Karen mentioned?"

An orange plastic skiff moored to a buoy bobbed contentedly a few yards out.

"Looks like it. She said the outboard's in the shed, if you fancy a spin," Hans said, grinning.

"Have we got time?"

"There's not a lot else to do while we wait for Jonah and Enrique to come back to us with anything. Besides, it will give me time to think, and we can unpack later."

Hans took out his wallet and cell phone and laid them on the wall. Then he peeled off his polo shirt.

"What are you—?"

"Geronimo!" He launched into a spectacular backflip, still grinning as he entered the inviting water with hardly a splash.

"*Mr.* Larsson!" Penny looked down, laughing. "And how am I supposed to follow that?"

"You could start by digging out that motor," Hans yelled, shaking water from his hair.

"Aye aye, skipper!" Penny threw a mock salute and went to fetch it.

Hans duck-dived and in a few powerful strokes emerged by the boat and climbed on board in one fluid movement. He untied the painter and rowed ashore, then helped carry the five-horsepower motor down the steep steps carved into the rock, which led from the house to the water's edge.

Penny took the tiller, and they cruised out of the lagoon, the sunlight sparkling on the water doing wonders for their mood. After a circuit of the bay, she cut the motor and lay down opposite Hans on the plastic-molded seating.

Hans had stripped to his boxer shorts, revealing ugly red welts where the life raft had rubbed his joints raw, resulting in huge infected ulcers.

"Your wounds have healed well," Penny complimented him.

"Yeah, I can't say I miss that foul stench. Kinda felt for the staff in the hospital. But this still gives me a lot of pain." He fingered the jagged scar running down his temple. "The doc said there'd be nerve damage."

"He said you needed cosmetic surgery too, but I told him fat chance of that!"

"Saved me telling him."

They lay there, basking in the late-afternoon heat and listening to the waves splashing the hull.

"It was good to see Enrique again," Penny piped up. "He was a pillar of support when you were rescued."

"He's a good guy – not your typical CIA type."

"How do you figure?"

"I was surprised he didn't push me to file a missing persons report. You know, to do things by the book and get the backing of the agency on this."

"I guess he bows to your and Karen's better judgment."

"Seems so. The last thing we need right now is a meddling bureaucrat. Did you see him scribbling stuff down in a notebook?"

"I don't remember it. Why do you ask?"

"Because being CIA, he knows exactly what information we would need about Logan. He didn't have to write it down."

"Perhaps he was nervous – like big intelligence fish in a small pond needing to get things right to impress the ambassador."

"That could be."

"Why did you ask him to access the CIA's databases when you can do that yourself?"

"Because it's what any good private detective would request. He doesn't know about the Concern, remember."

"I see."

"There's something else I've been thinking too." Hans shifted onto an elbow.

"Go on."

"I'm gonna call Silvestre and get him to drop me on

the wreck of the *Rosa Negra*."

"You think it might hold some clues?" Penny turned her head to face him, shielding her eyes from the sun with a hand.

"A little forensic work might turn something up."

"Do you think the police have done a search?"

"More than likely, but the authorities seem intent on putting it down to an accident, so even if the cops do figure out what caused the explosion, it's not information they're gonna share – and certainly not with us."

"Are you fit to dive . . . ?"

Penny realized it was a stupid question before the words left her mouth, her remit as scuba instructor thinking for her. In view of the former Navy SEAL's single-mindedness, not to mention the thousands of technical dives he had successfully logged, they'd be no way of stopping him.

"Wanna see fit?" Hans sat up and stretched. "Race you to the seabed!"

Penny looked over the side, and even though the boat had drifted to within forty yards of the rocks, she reckoned it was still a good thirty feet down.

"Okay, but last one to the bottom fires up the barbecue!"

She stripped off her T-shirt and shorts and, without warning, dived over the side. Hans laughed and leapt after her, catching up easily and teasing Penny by turning on his back to pull stupid faces as they descended. Both were as at home in the water as a couple of dolphins.

Upon reaching the coarse black volcanic sand making

up the seabed, they swam along hand in hand, until Hans pointed to a scattering of rocks and headed for them. Penny followed, vision blurred by the salt water, wondering what Hans had spotted, her curiosity turning to surprise when he picked up a melon-sized boulder and handed it to her.

Despite the increased density of the seawater, Penny struggled to keep on her feet while holding the hefty rock. Hans lifted a boulder for himself and began running along the seabed into the darkening blue.

Penny's body craved oxygen, her lungs feeling as if they were about to implode. She managed five steps before a pang of anxiety sent her shooting to the surface, where she trod water while waiting for Hans.

A good thirty seconds later he'd yet to appear, and Penny began to worry. She swam back to the boat and was about to climb on board when she heard "Whoop! Whoop!" over her shoulder, turning to see her favorite idiot clambering onto the rocky shore.

"I don't suppose you could pick us up?" he joked, then dove back into the sea and swam front crawl to the boat.

Penny smiled. There was a barbeque to light.

40

Karen's villa couldn't have enjoyed a more idyllic setting. Hans and Penny lay on sun loungers on the terrace, charcoal smoke wafting over them, witnessing a fiery spray sear across the sky as the sun burned into the horizon. It should have been paradise, but a dark cloud hung over the two of them.

"It was her idea, you know." Hans sat up and rested his chin on his hands while gazing at the myriad of colors making up majestic backdrop. "The yacht trip, I mean."

"Really?"

"We were gonna do a double crossing of the Atlantic originally, as a family, but when Kerry and JJ died that idea seemed doomed. I didn't feel like crossing the goddamn street, let alone an ocean."

"What changed?"

"Jessie asked me one day, when are we gonna sail to England and back like we planned? It hadn't even occurred to me she would still wanna do it. She'd even started mapping our itinerary and showed me a book called *Secrets of the Caribbean* she'd borrowed from the school library. She'd bookmarked all the touristy things she thought would be interesting – beautiful waterfalls in Jamaica and cave tubing through underground rivers in Belize."

"Pretty smart for a seven-year-old."

"Yeah, it was – although she was only six at the time. You know the backpacking trip I told you about, the one we went on in Peru?"

"Uh-huh."

Kerry and I let the kids decide everything – what to eat, where to visit, which hostels to stay in. Gave them a little help, of course."

"In modern parlance they call that inclusion. It never ceases to amaze me when parents bring kids into the world and then drag them around like unwanted accessories."

"We even walked the Inca Trail. You know, up to Machu Picchu, the ancient settlement high in the mountains."

"What, all of you?"

"No, JJ stayed in Cusco with his mom – he was too young."

"Hans, that's like twenty miles!"

"Twenty-six, hence why no tour company would take us. They said the minimum age was twelve due to the arduous route and challenging conditions. So we went on our own – me, Jessie, and Bear."

"No!"

"Apparently, it's forbidden – to go without guides – but we just hiked on through, overtaking the tour groups, and they had all their gear carried by porters. We slept in a little two-man tent every night and cooked up backpacker broth under the stars."

"Backpacker broth?"

"It was a recipe Kerry came up with to keep it simple

for the kids. Fry up vegetables from the market and then add an instant soup mix or a pack of noodles – delicious after a day's hike."

"Sounds like sea rations. When you're cold, wet and hungry, any combo tastes amazing."

"The *whole* experience was amazing. We trekked through cloud forest and jungle, crossed wild rivers and climbed mountains. Jessie never complained, not once. Insisted on carrying her bag the whole way and was good with the map too."

"How was Machu Picchu? I've only ever seen pictures."

"Unbelievable. One of those places that looks surreal in photos but is ten times as impressive when you see it for yourself. We climbed the last mountain, which went up and up and up, and then came over the brow – wow! – to find a complete Inca settlement, all the stonework rebuilt, in the most surprising setting you could ever imagine."

"In what way?"

"It's so high in the sky it's totally hidden from the valley beneath – hence why the Spanish conquistadors never discovered it when they plundered the Inca gold – and all around you is rolling jungle and rivers so far below they look like tiny gray lines."

"It's on my to-do list."

"And you know the best thing?"

"Go on."

"We wanted to watch the sunrise from inside the site. Like, wake up in our tent and *there* it is! But they kicked everyone out at 5:00 p.m. So Jessie and I climbed to the highest point, up these ancient rock steps carving through the crags, and then we waited until the evening to see if we would be asked to leave."

"And no one did?"

"Not a soul. We sat there on the peak with the most incredible view over the whole of the settlement, the forest sloping off thousands of feet all around us. The sun went down and the insects chirped up, and we're sitting there in the exact same spot the ancients did before modern civilization existed. Hell, being there with Jessie I wouldn't have wanted to be anywhere else at any other time in history."

"Did you pitch camp?"

"We crashed out the sleeping bags and slept right where we were. In the morning we woke up to watch the sunrise, and Jessie says, 'Aw, look, Papa. It's a little snake.' And right there curled up on her sleeping bag is a fer-de-lance."

"Aren't they extremely dangerous?" Penny shuddered as she pictured the scene in her head.

"Third most poisonous snake in South America, but it didn't bother Jessie one bit!"

They chuckled and drifted off into their own thoughts.

After a long silence, "Hans," Penny said quietly, her face tense as she looked him in the eye, "where could she be?"

"Oh." Hans lifted his broad shoulders, pulling a face that said the question was never far from his mind. "I'm guessing in a halfway house somewhere in the islands."

"How can you be sure?"

"Because I know how the Trade works. There's a massive global market in trafficked children. Thousands go missing every year, mainly between tier-three countries."

"Tier three?"

"Nations whose governments don't comply with internationally agreed standards to prevent people trafficking – Saudi Arabia, Kuwait, Cuba, for example. The kids are forced into labor, slavery, like sweatshops and begging syndicates, but some end up in prostitution rings or brothels or sold to pedophile gangs."

Penny winced.

"Then there's the sham adoption rings. Third World kids are bought from poor and often illiterate parents, or plucked from homelessness, and placed in phony orphanages alongside genuine orphans. The child's given a false identity, and officials are bribed to ignore the illegality and speed up the international adoption procedure – pretty appealing to wannabe parents faced with all the red tape and bureaucracy that's standard in the West."

"This . . . this . . ." Penny struggled to find words.

"Some kids are stolen to order – which is probably what happened to Holly Davenport. Blond hair, blue eyes and young enough to be brainwashed into a new identity, she'd be the ideal child for an amoral European couple looking to adopt – or some sicko's fantasy."

"But who arranges all this, and how do they get away with it?"

"It starts with an agent, who works on behalf of the end buyer. They're part of long-established underground networks and know how to cover their tracks. They can spot websites providing 'domestic services' and 'cheap labor' that are actually a cover for human trafficking, and they communicate via secure forums that require certain browser certificates, special computer settings and recognized IP addresses."

"How can you be sure Jessie hasn't already been sold abroad?"

"Because even for children stolen to order it takes weeks to get the necessary documentation together – forged passport, new birth certificate, adoption paperwork – and then there's the brainwashing the kids undergo before being transited. Jessie's kidnapping was opportunistic. Alvarez plucked her from the water to make a quick buck. So the whole process wouldn't even begin before they found a buyer. Plus, with her European looks the traffickers will be after a hefty paycheck, which requires time to find the right buyer."

"I guess it's not as if she'd be sold into some sweatshop in a developing country. She'd stand out like a sore thumb."

"That's why the traffickers will look for a buyer in the West."

"God these people are sick."

"In their minds they're just predatory capitalists, no different to corporate criminals or the warmongering politicians most folks vote for every four years."

41

While Penny placed vegetable-and-snapper kebabs on the glowing red embers, Hans called Silvestre to ask his advice on diving on the *Rosa Negra*.

"Senhor Hans, it is no problem, but best we do it alone and after dark, no?"

"Understood," Hans replied, knowing their interest in the wreck needed shielding from prying eyes, arranging a flight to São Vicente to meet the treasure hunter the next day. He was about to ask Penny how the kebabs were doing when his cell phone rang. It was a number he didn't recognize.

"Hans, it's Enrique. I have the information we spoke of. Do you want to meet up tomorrow, or I can come to you now?"

"If you could come now, it would be appreciated." Hans didn't want to waste any more time.

Within ten minutes the throaty rev of a sports car's engine filled the villa's driveway. Enrique stepped out of a vintage silver Porsche, dressed casually in three-quarter-length cargo pants, leather flip-flops and an Armani shirt.

"Hey, Hans." He beamed and held up an expensive bottle of wine.

"Thanks for coming this late, Enrique. You hungry?"

"Always hungry!" the CIA man replied, giving Hans a hearty hug. "Where's Penny?"

"All shall be revealed." Hans smiled and ushered him through to the patio.

"Penny!" Enrique embraced her with Latino affection. "Food, food, food!"

They sat around a picnic bench to eat, and Enrique briefed them on what he knew.

"Logan served four years in jail for money laundering, but under a new provision in UK law, the Proceeds of Crime Act, he agreed to pay back the money he had made in order to receive an early parole, only—"

"He didn't pay back a cent," said Hans.

"Exactly." Enrique took a gulp of wine. "And due to the fickle nature of the legislation, he was able to relocate to Cape Verde, meaning it would take up too much time and money to chase him for the debt. It seems everyone on the island knows he's got his fingers in a lot of pies, but there's been no firm evidence to prove it."

"Has there been *any* evidence?" Penny asked.

"There was a child abduction allegation leveled against him a couple of years back by the Cape Verde police after the coastguard stopped him leaving the harbor in his million-dollar speedboat and found a local kid aboard. Logan claimed the kid was wandering along the marina and he offered to take him for a ride. Said he loves kids, and where's the law against that? In the kid's mind he was going on a boat ride, so Logan got off scot-free."

"Anything else?" Hans asked.

"He runs a bar called Chico's that's a known hangout for – how shall we say – undesirables? And because he has no criminal record here, he's been able to obtain a shotgun and a pistol license. Is that enough to go on for the time being?"

"Yeah." Hans stared at his kebab. "I think it is, Enrique, thanks."

Then as an afterthought he added, "Do you happen to know if the police got any forensics off the wreck of the *Rosa Negra*? I'm planning a little dive tomorrow night."

"To protect tourism, the police will likely guard their findings, but I'll look into it for you."

42

When Hans' plane landed in São Vicente late the next afternoon, Silvestre was at the airport to meet him.

"Senhor Hans, good to see you."

Silvestre shook hands firmly and then led Hans to the taxi rank, from where they took a cab east along the coast road to Mindelo.

"So you've brought the boat from Santo Antão," said Hans, knowing the Portuguese lived on the archipelago's westernmost island, less than an hour's cruise across the São Vicente Channel.

"Yes, the boat is here." Silvestre took out his faithful hip flask and passed it to the American. "I have left her in a quiet place, no? Not even my crew knows I am here."

"Good thinking," said Hans. "And how's life on Santo Antão?"

"*Tranquilo.* I buy a small place in the hills above Porto Novo with my wife twenty years ago. When she passed, I decide to stay. It's a rugged island, not so much for the tourists, huh? And many more shipwrecks to find." Silvestre shrugged and took a slug of rum.

"You never remarried?"

"No, Hans, only to the rum."

"Family, children?"

"We have a little girl, Francesca, but the cholera

came . . ." The old man fell silent a moment, staring at the flask as if it contained all his memories. "Maybe some cousins in Portugal still alive, I don't know. I have no contact for many years."

Hans' respect for the treasure hunter deepened, and his reasons for helping search for Jessica became clearer.

"*Aqui, por favor,*" Silvestre told the cabdriver as they neared the port area.

He led Hans down an alley running through shanty housing and on to a small garbage-strewn cove. A young lad sat on a rubber dinghy on the sand skimming pebbles across the scum-laden wave tops. Silvestre took a few escudos from his wallet and handed them to the boy, who grinned black teeth and scarpered. Hans climbed into the inflatable, and Silvestre pulled on the oars and headed for his boat, *Outcast*, anchored discreetly a few hundred yards out.

Once on board they hauled in the tender, and Silvestre fired up the twelve-liter diesel and motored into the channel, the plan being to approach Mindelo Marina in a wide arc under the cover of darkness. Silvestre would remain with the boat a quarter of a mile offshore while Hans swam on the surface to the location of the sunken trawler.

In a pile on deck sat a wetsuit, scuba gear and a steel tank with a yellow-and-green-striped band around it signifying enriched air nitrox, which would extend Hans' bottom time and reduce the need for a lengthy decompression stop. The American began a systematic check of the equipment, looking for signs of wear and familiarizing himself with its idiosyncrasies, such as the position of the air inlet and outlet buttons on the wing-design buoyancy harness and how to operate the weight belt's quick-release buckle, should he need to ditch it in the event of an emergency.

As darkness fell Silvestre synchronized his watch with the time on Hans' dive computer. They would communicate over the radio built into the full-face scuba mask and aim to keep the dive to ninety minutes, with an additional thirty added on for the swim. If a problem arose, Hans would surface and make his way out to the boat by following a back bearing on his compass, since the *Outcast* would not be under running lights, or signal three times with his flashlight if he was in difficulty and needed picking up.

Under the glow of a waning moon, Silvestre maneuvered the dive boat into position as Hans kitted up. He considered clipping an emergency cylinder of nitrox to his harness but dismissed the idea, figuring it would prove too cumbersome should he need to enter the hull of the *Rosa Negra* and that it would hang down and kick up silt, ruining visibility when he inspected the seabed for evidence.

After strapping a hefty diver's knife to his left forearm and putting on his fins, he sprayed an antifogging agent inside the mask and took a compass bearing on the lights of the marina. Good to go, he shook hands with the old man and stepped off the dive lift's aluminum footplate at the back of the boat. Following a radio check to test comms, Hans pulled the mask back down around his neck and began finning toward the wreck.

Due to exertion and the insulating effect of the neoprene, Hans found himself getting hot. He stopped kicking on several occasions to pull open the wetsuit's neck and let seawater in to circulate and cool him down. The swim was tougher than he expected, his muscles weak and his joints aching from the month spent in the life raft. He imagined Penny shaking her head in disapproval, knowing in reality she would be the last person to suggest he didn't dive. He smiled and finned harder.

Looming twenty yards distant was the orange buoy the police had left to mark the position of the *Rosa Negra*. As Hans felt a sense of relief, the noise of an outboard motor and distant laughter reverberating off the water caught his attention. A crackle came over the radio's earpiece in the mask dangling around his neck. Hans spun around to see a yacht crew returning to the marina in high spirits, having drunk a Sundowner or two. Wishing to remain out of sight, he clamped the mask over his face and released air from his buoyancy jacket, allowing him to slip under the surface as the yacht passed overhead.

"Hans, *Outcast*, over." Silvestre sounded stressed.

"*Outcast*, I'm okay. Descending now, over."

Hans left it several seconds before turning on his flashlight and finning to locate the marker buoy's tether. He followed the line down, pumping small bursts of air into his buoyancy wing to compensate for the increase in pressure and steady his descent.

The *Rosa Negra* lay on her side at a forty-five-degree angle in sixty feet of water. Visibility wasn't great, but Hans could see the length of the forlorn vessel's hull and the ragged hole where the explosion tore through its sheet metal. The wheelhouse was gone, exposing what remained of the mess deck and galley. Whoever planted the explosives certainly knew what they were doing, taking out the crew and holing the boat below the waterline to sink the evidence.

Hans reached for a pair of tweezers clipped to his harness on a recoiling lanyard spool. Silvestre had also provided a plastic container the size of a lunch box with a slit in its lid lined with fine brushes to use as an evidence collector for small objects and fine particles. Hans had it secured around his waist like a fanny pack. He picked several flakes of burnt paint from around the hole in the hull and pressed them through the slit into the container, which had now filled with water. The brushes prevented the flakes from washing out of the box. Hans then began a systematic search in increasing clockwise circles around the *Rosa Negra*, using gentle frog kicks so as not to disturb the sand and sediment on the sea bottom. Silvestre and Hans had considered using an underwater metal detector but eventually rejected the idea, since thousands of pieces of shrapnel littered the seabed for up to a hundred yards all around.

By Hans' fifth circuit of the hull he hadn't found anything of significance. He paused to check his dive computer for the umpteenth time and radio the information through to Silvestre.

There was no answer.

"*Outcast . . . Outcast*," he tried again. "Will commence one more circuit of the vessel and surface, over."

Still no response.

It was out of character for Silvestre, and Hans wondered if his position had been compromised – perhaps by the coastguard – and he'd had to move the boat.

On the final circuit Hans spotted a fingernail-sized piece of aluminum lying on the sand. On closer inspection it looked to be a fragment from a small cylinder. Hans knew what it was immediately – the end of a detonator casing.

Pleased with his find, Hans secured the casing in the evidence box and checked his computer. He had just enough nitrox left for the required decompression stop and began his ascent, yet still no response from Silvestre on the radio.

Hovering several feet below the surface for the safety stop, Hans sensed the throb of a powerful boat engine and wondered why Silvestre had closed in to pick him up when the plan was Hans would swim back out to sea. He could tell by the reduced flow of nitrox from his regulator that it had all but run out and was glad when the three-minute decompression period was up.

Breaking the surface, Hans heard the roar of a boat engine and turned in time to see a gleaming white prow bearing down on him.

Wha—?

He had a problem – the paintwork on the *Outcast* was navy blue.

Hans exhaled sharply and with a frantic stroke of his arms sank below the surface, releasing a burst of air from his buoyancy wing to speed his descent. The draw of the propeller sucked him upwards as the boat thundered overhead, and Hans ducked his head to prevent it chopping through his skull.

Now the nitrox ran out, and he fought not to panic, dropping the regulator from his mouth and swapping to the air outlet hose on the buoyancy wing. By depressing the valve, he could suck air from the wing itself. It bought him some time, but the loss of buoyancy saw him slowly sinking.

He needed a plan and fast. It was imperative he took on his attacker right now rather than attempt a swim to the *Outcast*, making him a sitting duck.

Hans peeled off his mask, unclipped the buckles on the buoyancy harness and slipped out of it. Then, clutching the equipment and his flashlight, he finned hard for the surface and burst through with as much commotion as he could muster.

The speedboat came around for a second run, throttle fully open, its bow rising and propeller biting down ready to tear him to shreds. Hans left it until the last possible moment and, with another sharp exhale, sunk beneath the surface, playing the beam of his flashlight overhead. He waited until he spotted the white arrow shape of the boat's hull slicing through the water and then thrust the jacket and cylinder upwards, rolling into a ball and clamping his hands over his head for protection. There was an audible clunk as the propeller connected with the dive cylinder, then silence as the engine stalled and the boat glided away.

Desperate to breathe, Hans broke the surface and took a deep gulp of air, watching as the boat limped off into the darkness, the erratic pitch of the engine confirming he had achieved his aim.

Hans unbuckled his weight belt and let it drop to the seafloor, then began finning out to sea using a compass back-bearing for direction. Twenty minutes later he located the *Outcast*, which had drifted far from the original drop-off point. He cussed, knowing this wasn't going to be good, hauling himself on board to find Silvestre lying on his back in a pool of blood, a bullet having gone clean though his head.

Wasting no time, Hans powered up the *Outcast* and headed further into open water as he considered his options. He concluded there was no ballistics evidence to glean from the scene, no family of Silvestre to notify of his death, and that reporting the murder would bog him down in a lengthy police investigation. Finding Jessica was his priority, which meant he had to cover up the crime scene, sinking the *Outcast* and effectively burying Silvestre at sea. It was what the treasure hunter would have insisted on anyway, since Hans stood a far better chance of bringing the killer to justice than Cape Verde's ragtag police force did.

Hans stopped the *Outcast* a mile out and dragged Silvestre into the pilothouse. He went below and lifted up a panel in the hold to reveal a drainage plug, which he unscrewed, before returning to the deck and bolting shut the pilothouse door. As water flooded aboard, he packed his clothes, wallet, passport and cell phone into a dry bag, then picked up his fins and jumped over the side to begin the long swim back to shore.

- 43 -

The next morning Mouthwash Man entered the corridor.

"Get into bed," Jessica hissed to Holly, and scrambled into hers.

Mouthwash Man walked into the cell carrying a foldout wooden chair. He set it up, took off his jacket and hung it over the backrest, then sat down.

Jessica pretended to emerge from slumber, yawning, sitting up and leaning against the wall. Unusually, he didn't give her breakfast or a pill.

"Maria, I have a question for you," he asked softly.

Staring at her feet poking out of the blanket, Jessica wasn't fooled by his tone. She gave a purposely timid nod.

"Do you want to live, or do you want to die?"

"Live," she mumbled.

"Then it is like this. We have found you a new place to live and a new mother and father," he lied. "Do you know where is England?"

"Uh-huh." She nodded. "I've been there before."

"Good!" The man leant forward in the chair. "Now, I am going to tell you about your new home and your new family and your new school. And you will remember what I say, you understand?"

"Yes."

The man reached into his pocket and pulled out a set of pruning shears. Then, grabbing her hand, he forced her to stretch out a finger, clamping it between the blades of the vicious tool. "Now, your new father, he is called David – David Dennis. If you give him any problem, he will cut off your fingers one at a time like this."

He clenched the grips just enough for the blades to pierce Jessica's skin, making her scream.

"Do you understand?"

"Uh-huh." The little girl nodded in terror.

"And if you do not remember what I tell you, then I will cut off your fingers, then your ears, then your nose. Do you understand, Maria Dennis?"

"Yes," she whispered.

David Dennis was the alias on the many forged passports of the fixer – a man connected to the dark syndicates making up Europe's extensive pedophile network. The fixer adopted a common English surname because it was easy for children he trafficked to spell and remember. It was the surname on Jessica's expensive fake passport, and they would travel under the guise she was his daughter. The fixer always invested in top-quality documentation, costing a considerable amount of money and taking time to prepare, a precaution that had saved him from a lengthy jail term on numerous occasions. He only dealt in English-speaking white children fitting with the cover story of a Brit or American holidaying in Europe with his child.

"Maria Dennis" wasn't destined for England, though. A high-speed launch would take her and the fixer north to the Canaries, liaising offshore with a crew from

Algeciras in southern Spain. From there the fixer intended to travel overland, exploiting Europe's nonexistent borders to deliver the kid to a pedophile gang in Belgium.

The fixer provided kidnappers with an identity the child needed to remember. If a child in his possession couldn't recall these details instantly, the fixer would see to it the kidnappers didn't receive payment. However, this was only a part of the reason Mouthwash went heavy on the brainwashing – he also enjoyed inflicting pain.

"What is your father's name?" he demanded.

"David Dennis," Jessica replied without hesitation, imagining the moment her papa would burst through the door and bust this guy's head.

"What's your name?"

"Maria Dennis."

"Okay. Dennis is spelled—"

Mouthwash Man's cell phone rang. He groped in the inside pocket of the jacket draped over the chair and retrieved it. "*Ola . . . Sí, sí. . . . Luego, luego.*"

He replaced the phone and resumed the lesson. "Okay, Maria, Dennis is spelled *d, e, n, n, i, s.* Spell it for me."

"*D, e, n, n, i, s.*"

"Say 'My name is Maria Dennis, and my father is called David.'"

Jessica obliged.

"You live in Tottenham in North London and you go to a school called . . ."

And so the indoctrination continued, four times a day every day, Jessica suffering torture and food deprivation when she got the details wrong.

- 44 -

"**Y**ou need some sleep," said Penny, peeling back the duvet.

"Agreed," said Hans, exhausted from his swim.

"Lights off?"

"Yeah." Hans' phone rang. "Odysseus, what you got for me?"

"The names from Hertz's booking system. Dumb administrator still hasn't found the backdoor I programed into their database when I infiltrated them four years ago. Hell, I coulda dumped fifty thousand credit card numbers and sold 'em on the black market for a fortune."

"And risked more jail time," Hans reminded the young reprobate. "So shoot."

"The rental agency has two E-Class Mercedes, both rented out at the time in question. One to a David Segal, a forty-seven-year-old Portuguese national. I done some digging, and he's senior safety inspector for the Sana hotel chain. Flew business class from Lisbon two days earlier."

Despite his fatigued state, Hans managed a smile. There wasn't much Jonah couldn't dig up when he set his mind to it.

"The other was to an Emmanuelle Viton, a thirty-six-year-old French businesswoman, who, going by her Facebook, is on vacation with her mom."

"Did you background-check Segal and Viton?"

"Yes, Orion." Jonah let out an audible Aspergic tut. "I'm not stupid, you know."

"Anything?"

"No, they're both on the level. Besides, they're foreign nationals with no significant connection to the islands."

Hans wondered if one of them may have lent the car to someone else but knew he was clutching at straws. It meant the vehicle that tailed him couldn't have been a rental – least not from Hertz, as the yellow license plate tag may have suggested.

"I also got a bunch of stuff on Logan," his fellow operative continued. "Guy's a regular Al Capone. I've hacked his personal and business bank accounts and uncovered an investment portfolio totaling one point seven million US structured by an offshore bank in Panama. Every three months between twenty and thirty thousand euros get deposited in the fund's holding account, as well as random smaller sums. The entries have the identifiers Criancas and Tapas on the bank statement. I'm guessing Criancas, 'Children,' is profit from trafficking, and Tapas, the smaller amounts, is money skimmed off Chico's to avoid the tax man. I've put all his online banking details, including usernames and passwords, in the file I'm emailing you."

"You breached his computer?"

"Yeah, I called Chico's pretending I was organizing a vacation for a football team. Said we wanted to hire the whole venue for a night and would pay whatever so long as they decorated it in our team colors. Emailed him a zip file containing photos of the football kit—"

"Which I'm guessing cloaked some kinda computer wizardry." Hans chuckled.

"Yes." Jonah replied deadpan, the compliment lost on his literal mind. "An SUI – stealth upload installer. Basically, a few lines of script bundled inside an innocent media file and delivered as an email attachment. When the recipient clicks the link to open the file, they're unwittingly installing a malware application that modifies the PC's operating system – to stay hidden and wipe all traces of its activity from the log files. At the same time it backs up the user's personal data to a remote server over an encrypted connection before uninstalling and erasing all traces of itself a week or so later."

"That doesn't explain how you hacked into his bank accounts."

"And phone records and Facebook and email," Jonah stated matter-of-factly, pausing to take a drag of his spliff. "The program also records and uploads a log of browsed websites and a chronological transcript of every character typed on the keyboard. You cross-reference the two to pinpoint the security protocols."

"So if the log says Logan visited his online banking webpage at, say, 4:00 p.m. yesterday, I check the corresponding keyboard entries to see what username and password he typed."

"Yes."

"What if he were to copy and paste his details in from, say, a Word document?"

"You've got a backup of his personal data, remember. You just have to trawl through his folders to find the

Word document."

"Of course." Hans kicked himself. "And how can I access this data?"

"It's stored on my server. You can preview the documents and files online via a secure interface I've set up and download the stuff you need. The web address and your security details are in the info pack."

Penny awoke the next morning to find Hans hunched over his notebook computer, set up on an antique writing desk with a spectacular sea view from the bedroom.

"Honey, did you sleep?"

"I got a few hours," Hans lied. "I've been finding out a lot about Logan, and none of it's good."

"Let me make some coffee, then I'm all ears."

Penny put on one of Karen's brand-new bathrobes and went into the kitchen, returning minutes later with two double espressos.

"Go for it."

"Jonah's done a first-class job. He's set up a secure online site where I can access the info he's hacked from Logan – a bit like Dropbox, only it doesn't show up in search engines. I haven't had time to sieve through all of it, but this is what I've got so far." Hans stretched and downed his coffee. "Every three months or so Logan makes a debit card payment for the equivalent of four thousand US dollars to Enaport, the company that manages the island's harbors."

"Charges for mooring fees?" Penny suggested, squeezing beside him on a green-leather-upholstered piano stool.

"That's what I thought, but looking at Logan's Facebook page it appears he lives in a luxury cliff-side villa with its own dock. So I figure the money must be outlay to fuel his speedboat, and he's paying Enaport because they own the diesel pump at the harbor."

"If it's not for a berth, then it has to be for fuel," Penny agreed.

"But here's the thing – four thousand dollars would completely fill the tanks on a speedboat that size, and every skipper knows for performance and economy you never carry more diesel than necessary. In fact, he often buys far smaller quantities of gas. It's just this big three-monthly purchase that doesn't change."

"So it's obviously for one hell of a long trip. We're talking fifteen hundred miles or more."

"Exactly! Enough to deliver a kidnapped child to the African mainland or further."

"Hmm." Penny frowned, nodding in agreement.

"Let me show you something else." Hans opened a PDF file in which Jonah had saved screenshots of Logan's offshore bank statements dating back monthly for three years to when the account was opened. "You see this deposit?"

"Twenty-seven thousand US." Penny eyed the sum.

"Converted from euros and transferred to the Panama account through a partner bank here in Praia. They've listed the exchange rate and the local bank's eleven-digit identifier. BANA stands for Banco Nationale."

"Didn't Jonah say a similar amount has been paid in every three months?"

"Yeah, I've highlighted them all. But get this: the transfer always takes place within three to four days of

Logan's big fuel payment."

"Whoa. That can't be coincidence."

"My guess is that Logan delivers these kids to the next handler in the chain – somewhere in a seven-hundred-mile radius – and earns his blood money for doing it."

"Do you think he traffics more than one child at a time? I mean, twenty thousand euros seems a lot of money, especially if they're being sold in Africa."

"I don't think that's the case," Hans said quietly. "The Canary Islands lie seven hundred miles away. It's the ideal location to transit kids onwards to the adoption market in Europe."

"And that's big money."

"Sure, and there's something I haven't shown you."

Hans opened a web browser and signed in to Logan's Facebook account.

Penny fought back tears. She could see how much this nightmare had taken out of the man she had met less than a year ago. He still hadn't regained his regular bodyweight, his skin had lost its healthy tanned sheen, and his hair was noticeably graying. Yet still he persisted, unemotional and focused, on the job of getting his daughter back, putting her welfare above his own. She felt the urge to tell Hans how much she loved him but instead placed her hand on his thigh and studied the computer screen.

"It's a photo I found." Hans' features strained as he scrolled down the page. "He hasn't uploaded many, but this one's the smoking gun." He turned the notebook toward her.

"No!" Penny's mouth fell open.

It was a shot of Logan and a blond woman surrounded

by grinning local children in front of a ramshackle building. A faded sign nailed to the shack's weathered wooden planking had one word written on it: *Orphanage.*

- 46 -

"**R**ight, we need a plan of attack." Hans slapped down the laptop's screen. "Here's how I see it. I have to get into Logan's speedboat and download the data from his onboard computer."

"To find out where he goes on these long trips?"

"Yeah. I figure if he's making them on a regular basis, then the coordinates must be programmed into the GPS. It'll be a big part of the puzzle, and if he skips town with Jessica, at least we'll know his waypoints and can organize an intercept."

"Would that be possible?"

"There's always a US or British warship on exercise in the area, plus coastguards looking for a piece of action, and Muttley never has a problem pulling a few strings."

Penny let out a small gasp, leaving her mouth ajar as if about to speak.

"What is it?" Hans pressed.

"You just reminded me of something Muttley said when he was here with Phipps organizing the search when *Future* went missing." Penny stared into nothing for a moment. "He said someone was putting pressure on the Pentagon to block his request for US military intervention. Said they'd issued a Code . . . *Purple*?"

"Really?" Hans grimaced.

"Something about the Pentagon can refuse to provide support, and Code Purple means in the interest of national security they don't have to give a reason why."

"*Baxter*," Hans spat under his breath. "Do you remember I told you what happened to my team in West Africa?"

Back in 2000 Hans' SEAL team joined a squadron from the British Royal Marines' Special Boat Service, the SBS, for a mission to take out a rebel force, the West Side Boys, in Sierra Leone. Headed by a charismatic psychopath, Fodim Kassay, the rebels modeled themselves on Tupac Shakur, the gangster rapper, and were always high on drugs. They'd taken a group of American and European medical workers hostage in an old hospital on the coast and were using the building as their headquarters. The SEALs and Marines were on standby on an aircraft carrier out in the Atlantic when their orders came through. They were to drop into the sea from choppers a mile offshore and swim in under the cover of darkness, then put in a dawn attack and conduct a rescue mission.

Only it didn't go to plan. Blood diamonds fueled the conflict, a dirty trade that went all the way to Washington. Protecting their own interests, someone in DC made sure the Pentagon delayed the patrol's clearance to disembark the aircraft carrier. What should have been an easy swim for the men turned into a battle for survival. The tide was on the move, a swell kicked up and waves as big as apartment blocks smashed down on them. The one mile the special ops team had to cover became the equivalent of four. Thirty-two men went into the water, six got out. Hans lost thirteen of his closest buddies that day, their bodies mutilated by the rebels when they washed up on shore. The six remaining troops continued the mission, linking up with a detachment of Special Air Service troopers at first light to take out the West Side Boys and rescue the hostages, one of them being Kerry, an American nurse, who later became Hans' wife.

"I remember you telling me about the mission," said Penny. "Are you saying Baxter was the one putting pressure on the Pentagon?"

"Let's just say the Concern has had its sights on him awhile. Guy's a real-life Patrick Bateman, Ivy League *psycho*. Spent time in the CIA in the nineties orchestrating all kinda atrocities to overthrow governments down in Central America. Torture was always his MO – that and cocaine smuggling. Guy's floated around the Republican cause for years. He's been a strategist and policy advisor on foreign affairs to both Bush administrations. It's given him the cover and contacts to leech money from all kinda ill doings around the globe. He's a total sociopath, knows how to cover his back, and him and his neocon cronies are puppets for some serious men behind closed doors. Hence why the Concern has held off."

"And . . ." Penny hesitated. "You said he had something to do with Kerry's and JJ's murders."

"When this is over, I'll tell you all I know. But for now I need to focus on getting Jessica back."

"Will he be brought to justice?"

"He'll get justice all right . . . at the first chance I get."

Hans was lost in thought for a while, before bringing the conversation back to the present.

"We need to get Logan's cell phone number. Jonah couldn't find any phone bills, only the ones for Logan's bars, and there's nothing out of the ordinary there. He must be using pay-as-you-go. We have to find out who he's been calling."

"I think I can help," said Penny, an idea forming in her mind.

- 47 -

Over the next couple of weeks Jessica did her best to keep Holly's mood up, but her fellow captee was always tired and distant and spent a good part of the day asleep. Jessica reckoned she must have been swallowing the pills, probably too scared or not understanding the importance of spitting them out. She hoped nothing bad would happen to Holly and, not wanting to alarm her, didn't mention the new identity and trip to Europe business. Besides, her papa – her *real* papa – would be here soon to kick up hell and put things right.

"Jessica," Holly whispered through the grate one afternoon.

"Yes, I'm here." Jessie crouched down on the floor.

"I feel sick."

"It's because you've been eating the pills. I told you not to."

"I'm sorry."

"Ah, it's okay, you're just a kid. Hey, you wanna play a game?"

"Uh-huh."

"It's called I Went to the Store."

"What's a store?"

"It's like a place where you buy things."

"That's called a shop."

"Oh well, we'll call it . . . I Went to the Shop-Store,

okay?"

"Uh-huh."

"Okay, I have to say, I went to the store – the *shop-store* – and I bought some . . . cat food. And you have to say, I went to the shop-store and I bought some cat food and something else."

"I went to the shop-store and I bought some cat food and something else."

"No! You have to buy cat food and you have to buy something for yourself!"

"But we haven't got a cat. We've got a dog and he's in the kennels while we're on holiday."

"O-kay." Jessica drew a deep breath. "Then you say, I went to the shop-store and I bought some dog food and something else."

Holly's gentle snores came through the grate.

48

As the cab drove along Praia's seafront, Penny looked out of the window to see the lush green fig trees sprouting from the beach's gray volcanic sand fading into the growing darkness, leaving only a thin line of frothy white surf visible.

"*Aqui*," said the driver, pulling up outside Chico's Bar.

Penny was impressed. Somehow she'd expected Logan's place to be a spit-and-sawdust affair, like an old-school London pub, but Chico's was far from it. Stretching along the bar's frontage was an elevated deck the length of a tennis court, with a bamboo transom overhead creeping with vines and interlaced with tiny yellow fairy lights, giving the impression of fireflies. On the deck were smart dark-wood dining tables with pristine white cloths and napkins, sparkling cutlery and crystal-cut wineglasses set out neatly on them. Dotted around were hanging-basket chairs and swing seats, allowing drinkers to relax while taking in the sea view.

Hans had tried to talk Penny out of this, arguing that the Concern could fly an operative in, but she'd held firm, saying that would take time. Hans worried Logan might recognize Penny from the night the fishing boat exploded, but she pointed out it was dark and whoever blew the *Rosa Negra* out of the water had done so remotely and likely from a distance. Nonetheless, Hans insisted on waiting around the corner in the jeep with the M9 locked and loaded and that Penny took a walkie-talkie in the event Logan compromised her.

Penny had the story straight in her head. She was a tourist named Jenny staying in the Pestana Trópico hotel whose middle-aged female traveling companion was having a quiet night in. Jenny, an English scuba instructor living in Cannes in the South of France, fancied a few drinks out on the town, and the Pestana Trópico's concierge had recommended Chico's.

She approached the restaurant's smoked-glass doors and pulled on a long gold handle to find the place equally as impressive inside, a glitzy affair with its restaurant and bar area doused in subtle lighting and decorated with modern sea-themed art in vivid pastels. Uplifting samba played in the background, the progressive drumbeats, shrills and whistles complementing the perfect harmony of a black female choir.

Stepping through the door, Penny spotted Logan's bald head in her peripheral vision but headed straight to the mock-ivory bar and sat on one of its faux-zebra-skin, chrome-legged stools. The musclehead sat drinking half-liter glasses of lager with a loud group of Englishmen, who, unlike Logan, in his smart black trousers and a white dress shirt, wore shorts, flip-flops and sleeveless vests, showing off the mismatched tattoos on their lobster-red skin. Penny could see they were tourists and that Logan was throwing himself into the role of playboy host. She ordered a rum and coke from the young mestizo bartender and pretended to peruse the tourist leaflets stacked in a display holder, glancing at Logan every few seconds until they finally locked eyes. She produced a shy smile and went back to picking out and scanning the brochures.

Hans and Penny assumed the blond woman in the Facebook photos was Logan's partner, but other than her name, Krystal Cavenele, neither they nor Jonah could come up with any more intel. Banking on fidelity not being the flash merchant's strongest point, Penny planned to lure him into conversation and, if all went well, come away with his cell phone number. Playing the part of a carefree tourist, she wore a denim miniskirt, emerald singlet and leather flip-flops and, unusually, a trace of makeup. A whalebone pendant in the shape of a fluke hung on a leather thong around her neck, a piece she had crafted herself.

"I can highly recommend the 4x4 jeep tour, me darling," came a voice, making Penny jump.

"Oh," she recovered, turning to see the man himself. "You live here I take it."

"Been on the island a few years now," Logan replied, immediately hooked by Penny's smiling eyes and self-assuredness. "This is my bar. I'm Eddy. Can I get you another drink?"

Penny accepted the offer and made small talk, choosing the appropriate moment to ask, "So, do you run this place alone or . . . ?"

"If you mean do I have a girlfriend, yes." Logan chuckled. "But we're going through what you might call a patch."

"I'm sorry to hear that," said Penny, sounding genuinely concerned. "Trouble in paradise?"

"Ah, you could say that. She's desperate for a child.

We've tried for years, but it hasn't happened. Kinda pushed us apart."

At the mention of a child, Penny felt an immense urge to claw Logan's eyes out but forced herself to remain in character. "And this 4x4 island tour – you've been on it?"

"Ha!" Logan grinned. "I own a jeep, *and* I know the island like the back of my hand, so I make my own tours."

"Hmm." Penny pretended to read the information on the brochure, buying time while she considered what to say. "It looks fun. I'd love to see more of the island – especially with a guide who knows the sights. Where do I sign up for this tour?"

"Penny," said Logan, seizing the moment, "I've got tomorrow free. If you like, I can give you the tour myself."

"Eddy, that's so kind of you to offer," Penny replied, thinking one step ahead. "But I need to run it by my friend."

Oh." Logan looked down at his feet. "Of course. The offer's open to both—"

"No!" Penny giggled, sliding a hand down his arm and letting it linger a moment at the wrist. "She won't want to come. She's not what you'd call the adventurous type. I mean I need to check she's okay to spend the day on her own. Do you have a mobile number I can get you on?"

"Sure." Logan reached into his shirt pocket and pulled out a business card. "If you can't get hold of me for any reason, leave a message here at the bar."

"Brilliant!" Penny seized the opportunity for a polite hug and a kiss on the cheek. "I'll call you first thing."

49

Penny hailed a cab outside Chico's and asked the driver to take her to the meeting place she'd agreed with Hans, a bohemian joint, Tima Tima, a couple of miles along the seafront. She checked over her shoulder several times, as Hans had instructed, to make sure Logan wasn't following her.

"Good effort, Penny." Hans joined her in the backstreet café bar. "How was it?"

"Interesting. He certainly thinks himself Mr. Smooth. It was hard to imagine the double life he leads. I wanted to dig my nails into his face and demand where Jessica is."

"I bet."

Hans scanned Logan's business card and then caught the waiter's attention and ordered two Strelas.

"I feel – *urrrh!*" said Penny, a feeling of repulsion coursing through her as she began telling Hans about the meeting with the trafficker.

Not long into their conversation, Hans' cell phone rang.

"It's Enrique. Something's come up. Can we meet?"

"Sure," Hans replied, sensing this was to do with Silvestre. "We're in Tima Tima. Do you know it?"

"I'll be there in five."

In no time at all Hans and Penny heard a throaty roar as Enrique's Porsche pulled up outside. He entered the café bar wearing his smart cream jacket and black Armani jeans. Sporting his permanent grin, he hugged Penny and shook hands with Hans.

"Small matter of a certain treasure seeker who's disappeared in his boat." Enrique gave a theatrical frown. "You did say you planned a dive last night."

"Unfortunately, Eddy Logan was there to meet us," said Hans. "Took out Silvestre and tried to put an end to me."

"You are sure it was him?"

"It was the same model of speedboat, put it that way."

Enrique looked down at the table, nodding thoughtfully, then clicked his fingers at the waiter and ordered a glass of white wine and more beers.

"Your 'activities' – if we can call them that – have come to the attention of Praia's mayor, Senhor Videl Gonzales. He runs a tight ship here on Santiago, likes to know what's going down in his front yard."

"Activities?" Hans raised an eyebrow.

"People are dying and going missing, and it's obvious to the police you're the common denominator."

"Why haven't they hauled me in?"

"Because it would cause a diplomatic incident, and besides, the mayor pulls the strings around here, and he wants to meet you first. He's asked me to invite you and Penny to dinner with him at his home tomorrow night. He's a good man, and he'll do what he can to help you find Jessica."

Enrique took a small white envelope from his top pocket and slid it across the table.

"La Laguna." Hans read aloud the mayor's address, printed in neat gold lettering on the invite.

"It's a converted fortress up in the hills a little further around the island from where you're staying."

"I better put on a tie," Hans joked.

"Ah, don't worry," said Enrique. "He'll take you as you come."

Enrique insisted on paying for the next round of drinks.

"How's the investigation going?" he asked.

Hans thought carefully before answering, not wishing to divulge too much information for fear of having to explain his sources.

"We're building up a picture on Logan. Everything indicates he's trafficking local orphans by speedboat, likely to the Canary Islands to supply the European adoption market."

"That figures." Enrique bit his lip and stared into his wineglass. "What's your next move?"

"Tomorrow night I was planning to hop aboard his boat and pull the GPS history from the onboard computer to see if his excursions *are* to the Canaries. But I guess if we're meeting the mayor, it'll have to wait."

"You know the location of the boat?"

"It's moored on a private dock at his home. I'm figuring if Chico's shuts at two, then I'll leave it until three to give him time to get off to sleep. Penny stopped by Chico's tonight and managed to sweet-talk Logan into giving her his pay-as-you-go cell phone number. If he's signed up to one of the big network providers, then I've got a contact through my detective agency who can run a search on his phone records."

"May I see?" Enrique asked. "If you manage to expose this creep, then the agency will want his number for our own trafficking investigation."

Hans pulled the business card from his shirt pocket and handed it to the CIA man, who wrote the number down in his small leather-bound notebook with a pullout gold pen.

"So, Penny, have you ever thought about becoming a special agent?" Enrique winked.

"Ha! I'm not sure hanging around in bars chatting up sleazeballs is my thing," she replied, and they all chuckled.

"What are you gonna do?" Enrique looked to Hans.

"It depends what we're able to turn up. There's no point involving the police if the evidence is circumstantial and inadmissible in court. The most they can do is invite him in for questioning, which will tip off the trafficking syndicate. I'm thinking a spot of surveillance might be in order, see if his movements give us any indication where Jessica's being held."

"And if it doesn't?"

"Then it might be time to come clean with what we know to Interpol. See if anything cross-references with the search for Holly Davenport. If we're still drawing a blank, then the only option is I pay Logan a visit and beat her whereabouts out of him."

"Hans, as you know I can't get the agency involved in this – not unless you're willing to file a report – but if I can help on a personal level, just ask. The thought of this scumbag laying a hand on a child makes my blood boil."

"Thank you, Enrique." Hans raised his beer bottle. "I'll certainly do that."

- 50 -

The woman shuffled toward the check-in desk at Banjul International Airport. The air was stifling in the Gambian capital. She mopped her brow with a Kleenex and cursed the flies landing on her golden-brown skin.

It had been a two-day boat journey from Kankaba, a small city sprawling along the banks of the Upper River, where the All Saints Home for Abandoned Children sat. The woman's skin itched from the mosquito bites she'd received while sleeping on deck. She prayed she hadn't contracted malaria again. It would be the fifth time in as many years, and she'd spent enough time lying in sweat-soaked bedsheets with a fever raging so high death seemed the better option.

In front of her in the check-in queue was a loud, fat, sweating Mandinka wearing white robes and a skullcap, and, dressed in a gold sari and turban, his equally as vocal and ample wife. The woman waited patiently as the Mandinka couple attempted to haggle over the luggage allowance with the pretty Fula behind the desk. Repeatedly she told them that the bulky collection of food and other goods piled high in cardboard fruit boxes on their trolley was eighty kilos over the airline's limit. Each time the man tried to bluff his way out of the additional fee by handing her his *kora*, a stringed instrument made from a calabash and cow's hide, and suggesting she take it as payment.

Finally the role play ended, and the Mandinka pulled a fat roll of banknotes from a faux-crocodile-skin shoulder bag and slapped down half of what he owed. The petite Fula feigned a polite smile, opting for discretion over valor and the chance to move the annoying couple on.

The woman placed her passport and ticket on the counter and was soon walking through the departure lounge toward her gate. On the flight she mused as passengers broke out pack lunches of fish, chicken, rice and beans *before* takeoff, raising an eyebrow at the footprints some confused individual had planted on the toilet seat. The woman spent the flight reflecting on the circumstances that had conspired to put her in this position.

Born in Mali to Christian missionaries, a Mozambican father, an American mother, she had studied law at the University of Bamako in the capital and had gone on to serve as a junior government official. She fled the country during the buildup to the brutal Northern Mali Conflict, when Tuareg rebels declared war on the government and issued a hit list with her name on it. She had crossed Senegal to seek political asylum in Gambia, settling in Kankaba, where with her university education she was ideally suited to take over the running of the children's home, a neglected operation surviving on sporadic handouts and UN food parcels.

Since arriving at the home, she had accessed several funding streams, allowing for a complete overhaul of the building, its dormitories, classroom and kitchen. She'd gotten computers and Internet installed and set up a website displaying staff profiles, pictures of the orphanage and a Sponsor a Child link. In her sole piece of luggage, a sackcloth shoulder bag, the woman carried a cheap laptop storing files on each child, including photographs, personal characteristics and skills, and the circumstances surrounding their orphanment.

Many of the children at the All Saints Home for Abandoned Children were anonymous, having no traceable histories, and although a humanitarian at heart, she was a businesswoman first. Surely everyone had the right to create a little nest egg for themselves, particularly when it involved trading children no one would miss who were destined for sweatshops or worse anyway.

When the woman passed through immigration at Cape Verde's Nelson Mandela Airport and the official asked, "Business or pleasure?," "Pleasure," she replied – although in view of the children's profiles stored on her laptop, the declaration wasn't entirely honest.

51

Hans drove the jeep ten miles northeast along the coast, following satnav directions leading them inland and up a winding country road. As they came over a brow, the mayor's magnificent fort crowned a hilltop to their front.

"Wow!" Penny reached for Hans' new camera. "Let me get a shot."

"Looks like our man's not short of a few bucks."

Hans pulled to a stop a hundred yards from La Laguna. Penny jumped out and snapped a few pictures but immediately felt guilty, reminding herself this was not about tourism.

"I wonder if our meet will be mutually beneficial," said Hans, continuing on to cross a vast grit-strewn courtyard lined with antique cannons and passing through a huge stone archway, complete with a raised portcullis, into an inner quadrangle enclosed by the building's solid walls.

"How do you mean?" Penny slipped the camera back in its case.

"What with people dying left, right and center on the islands, I can understand why the mayor's taken an interest, but I'm wondering what he can do for us."

"Good point," said Penny. "Enrique seems to think

this guy's something of a gentleman with a good grasp on local affairs, so fingers crossed."

They stepped out of the jeep and began gazing around at the magnificent refurbished stonework – only two yapping dogs rushing out from behind a huge oak door interrupted them, closely followed by the mayor.

"Hello!" Penny bent down and petted the excited Jack Russells as they jumped up and pawed her.

"Senhor Larsson, Senhorita Masters," a booming voice echoed off the walls. "It is good to finally meet you."

"Lord Mayor, thank you for inviting us," Hans shouted back.

A dapper-looking gent with slicked-back, white balding hair, the mayor wore duck-green slacks, a navy-blue blazer, burgundy cravat and highly polished wingtips. After ordering the dogs inside, he pumped Hans' arm up and down with a cast-iron grip but was gentler with Penny.

"It is my pleasure," said Gonzales, a glint in his little flitting eyes. "I have followed your story with interest and thought it was time I offered my services."

Hans and Penny smiled. However, in view of recent events and the trail of devastation in their wake, they knew Jessica wasn't the only item on the agenda.

"La Laguna is quite some place, Senhor Gonzales," said Penny, turning to take in a glimpse of dazzling ocean through the archway.

"Thank you, but please, my first name is Videl." The mayor gave her a warm smile. "The castle was originally called Forte de São Paulo, built to defend the Portuguese from the English after the colony was plundered by Sir

Francis Drake in 1582."

Penny looked at Hans and winked, for Jessica knew all about Sir Francis Drake, Queen Elizabeth I's favorite sailor, from the history lessons her father gave her during their stay in England.

"Only it was sacked by the French in 1712" – the mayor shrugged – "and has undergone extensive renovation ever since."

"Why can't we all just get along, Videl?" Hans joked.

"Exactly!" said the mayor, chuckling. "Come, let's go inside."

He led them through the oak door, set into the seaward wing next to the entrance tunnel, and into a vast corridor with large maroon-and-white-checked floor tiles and oaken paneling on the walls. Hans and Penny would have loved to have stopped to inspect the suits of armor, gilt-framed portraits and other antiquities decorating the refreshingly cool hall, but Gonzales, pausing only briefly for their approval, continued up a burgundy-carpeted stairway to the next floor.

"My office away from the office," Gonzales announced, opening a door on the landing to reveal a suite with a stunning sea view and the pomp and regalia associated with municipal government. "For the days I work from home."

"Incredible," said Penny, rushing across the deep-pile carpet to the window, for the ocean view meant far more to her than antique furniture, rare book collections and photographs of the mayor meeting VIPs.

"You've got your very own city hall," Hans remarked, taking in the stately desk and gold floor stands supporting poles bearing Cape Verde's, Praia's and the mayor's flags.

"One must be comfortable." Gonzales sat down in his throne-like chair, reveling in his own importance. "And how about we get a photograph, the three of us?"

"Sure," said Hans, catering to the mayor's ego. "Only I haven't got a tripod, so can I set it up on this?" He indicated to a display pedestal holding the warhead of a rocket-propelled grenade. Olive drab in color and biconical in shape, Hans figured it was left over from Cape Verde's struggle for independence, backed by the Soviets.

"Yes, yes," Gonzales replied, dusting down his lapels and remaining seated for the shot.

As Hans set the camera up, a photograph of four soldiers, obviously comrades-in-arms, on the wall behind Gonzales caught his eye, so surreptitiously he zoomed in and focused on it, then joined Penny to stand either side of the mayor.

"Smile," said Hans as the self-timer began to beep rapidly. "Perfect!"

"Excellent! You must send me a copy." Gonzales stood up and put his arms around them. "Now, how about we eat?"

The mayor ushered them through the door next to his office and into an impressive dining room, its polished-walnut table long enough to host twenty guests. A thickset Spaniard, who must have been in his sixties, stood waiting to greet them with a tray of bubbly. Bald on top, with his remaining hair pomaded back from the temples, he sported a goatee beard and dressed in a simple black suit and tie. An ugly scar rose above the collar of his shirt. Hans could tell immediately it was a shrapnel wound and that, from the way he held himself, the man had seen some serious combat.

"Fernando, *gracias*," said Gonzales, passing a glass to Hans and Penny before taking one for himself.

"Senhor Alcalde," the butler grunted. He half smiled and disappeared, leaving the three of them to seat themselves at one end of the enormous table.

"*Salud!*" Penny raised her glass.

"*Ah, hablas español.*" Gonzales acknowledged that she spoke Spanish.

"*Más o menos,*" she replied modestly.

"*La dos ustedes?*" The mayor waggled his finger at both of them.

"Hans speaks a little," Penny said, switching to English for his sake. "But tell me, Videl. How does a Spaniard get to be mayor of Praia?"

"I was born in Madrid to a Spanish father and a Cape Verdean mother, so I have Spanish, Portuguese and Cape Verdean citizenship. Like Hans, I served time in the military, and I came here just as the country held its first open elections. I campaigned for the Democratic Alliance, and when Prime Minister Carlos Fonseca was voted in, he gave me a junior role in his cabinet. I eventually ran for mayor, and several terms later I am still here."

"And do you live in the castle alone?" Hans asked.

"Along with Senhor Chavez – that's Fernando, my butler – yes," said the mayor, uncorking a bottle of red wine and filling their glasses. "My wife, Catalina" – he looked over to a portrait painting on the wall of a naturally beautiful, dark-haired woman – "she died in childbirth many years ago."

"That's harsh," said Hans.

"When you understand this life is cruel, it makes it easier to live, no?" Gonzales paused to look at the picture once more, the pain evident in his birdlike eyes. "I guess it is why I wish to help you find your daughter."

"What makes you think she is still alive?" Hans asked.

Before the mayor could answer, Fernando entered the room pushing a trolley laden with starters. As he set down goat cheese salad, shrimp soup, fried moray eel and thick-crust brown bread, Penny caught the distinct smell of *aguardente* on his breath, a type of moonshine popular in Portugal and Latin America.

"It is not what I think, Hans, it is what you think." The mayor broke off a chunk of bread and dipped it in his soup. "I know you came to the islands to recover Jessica's body. You didn't find it, but you are still here. I would say that is something of a clue, no?"

Hans half nodded and shrugged, giving nothing away as he helped himself to salad.

"I also know you have received special mission status from the US embassy and that the treasure hunter you hired has rather curiously disappeared."

"You know a lot." Hans smiled politely, not wishing to appear defensive.

"Enough to know you believe your little girl has fallen into the wrong hands," said the mayor, locking eyes with Hans as the mood turned serious.

"Are you referring to the traffickers?" Hans asked, although the question needed no answer.

"*Os traficantes.*" Gonzales turned his head and made a spitting motion. "It is the islands' ugly secret, and the evil vermin responsible need to be brought to justice."

"I heard on the radio your offer of a reward for information about the English girl's disappearance."

"The money is the easy part, Hans. Even as mayor I can do little else, except to put pressure on the police to do their job. But I must warn you this business is centuries old. As Europe and the West modernized and your law enforcement developed ways to fight crime and corruption, Cape Verde remained in the dark ages. It is only recently, when we follow the international example to receive investment and support, that we have started to get our act together."

"And your point?" said Hans.

"That the foundations of this business were laid many years ago by men who care nothing for accepted rules, who have moved quicker than the times and who will let *no one* get in their way." The mayor's fist clenched, and it looked as if he would start banging it on the table. "I am trying to warn you, Hans. If you persist, you and Miss Penny will not get off this island alive."

"Are you suggesting I forget about my daughter and go home?" Hans fought to keep his temper.

The mayor reached forward, gripped both their hands and lowered his voice. "Hans, I am saying that you and Miss Penny have been through a lot already. You cannot afford to lose each other. You must go back to the States and let the authorities do their job."

Hans refrained from asking if these were the same authorities who let a fugitive from English justice move to the island, then start a business with the proceeds of his crimes and buy weapons and a boat for trafficking kidnapped children – but what the mayor said next made him glad he kept silent.

"*Amigos.*" Gonzales clenched his grip and looked them in the eye one at a time. "I *beg* you to go home, but if you *must* stay and continue the search for your daughter, then I suggest you focus on one man."

Penny's eyes flicked to Hans.

"And you must tell no one you heard this from me – *comprende*?"

They nodded.

"We have an Englishman here running a bar in Praia. It is called Chico's. Do you know it?"

"We've driven past it," said Hans.

"Then I say no more."

"But how do you know this?" Penny asked.

"I cannot know for certain," Gonzales replied. "But let's just say, to serve four terms in office it helps to have connections in the right places."

He didn't need to explain further, for the first thing Hans spotted in the mayor's office wasn't so much a landscape painting of a goat basking in the sun's rays on a hilltop but the esoteric symbolism behind it.

52

"**T**he mayor seems a good man to have on side," said Penny as they drove down the winding mountain road away from La Laguna.

"He's certainly making an effort to combat the traffickers," Hans replied. "The radio station said the reward money he offered for information about Holly's kidnapping came out of his own pocket, and he's certainly connected."

"Yeah, I saw you go quiet. What was that about?"

"The painting in his office – a goat standing on a pyramid of rocks in the sunlight." Hans threw her a knowing look.

"Masonic symbols – or are you thinking Illuminati?" Penny referred to the 'enlightened ones,' a global cabal of Satanists, originally an offshoot from Masonry, who manipulate mankind through financial and media control and by orchestrating a perpetual state of war.

"The goat might represent the devil Baphomet." Hans shrugged. "Or our mayor might just be a high-ranking Freemason."

"Don't tell me he gave you the handshake?" Penny grinned.

"Ha! A mason will tell you that's a myth." Hans braked for the T-junction at the bottom of the hill and pulled onto the coast road. "You certainly impressed him with your Spanish."

"We do our best." Penny squeezed his knee. "It was funny, though. I noticed he switched between Castilian and South American."

"How do you mean?"

"Castilian is the modern parlance of Spain, but in Central and South America they speak the language of the conquistadors – basically, an older dialect. He said *ustedes*, meaning 'you' plural, not *vosotros*."

"Probably due to the influence here. We're closer to the South American continent than we are to Spain."

"Yeah, I hadn't thought of that. The butler was a bit of a bruiser, hey?"

"You can say that again. Did you see the shrapnel wound?"

"Is that what it was?"

"Yeah, he's certainly been in the thick of it somewhere." Hans checked his mirrors and pulled over to the side of the road. "I need to speak to Mike Davenport."

He called the Englishman's number.

"Mike, Hans Larsson."

"Hello, Hans."

It didn't sound good.

"Any news?"

"No, nothing – only the usual police inefficiency."

Hans looked at Penny and shook his head. "Are you still in Praia?"

"Yes, staying at the Fortuna."

"Is there any chance we can meet, say, tomorrow for lunch? It would be good to catch up, and there's something I wanted to ask you."

 "Sure, do you have anywhere in mind?"

 "How about Tima Tima. It's a—"

 "Yeah, I know it. It's near the hotel."

53

The Malian woman made her way through immigration at Cape Verde's Nelson Mandela Airport and, with no luggage to collect, straight into the arrivals area. It thronged with disembarked passengers and expectant family and friends, most loud in dress and voice. Chauffeurs held up cardboard signs with names of their pick-ups scrawled on them in marker pen, and eagle-eyed cabdrivers and hotel touts pounced on hesitant-looking travelers to try and make a buck.

This airport was far more modern than the one she had flown from in Gambia. The mix of white tourists and coffee-colored and black Africans meant that with her light-brown skin she stood out a lot less than on the mainland. However, born and raised on the African continent, she had gotten used to the stares.

Before exiting the airport to grab a cab from the rank, the woman haggled with a moneychanger to get a good rate for the euros she'd brought from Banjul. Then, after picking up a map of the city of Praia from the tourist information desk, she bought a pay-as-you-go SIM card in a cell phone store and topped it up with credit.

Intending to stay within her budget, the Malian asked the driver to drop her at a boarding house she'd researched on the Internet. A prestigious establishment frequented by Portuguese officials, merchants and ships' officers in its heyday, the two-story colonial building had long since fallen into disrepair. It sat in a long terraced row on a street dividing the booming tourist area from the shantytown housing the third of the city's population that lived below the breadline.

The woman gave the building a once-over. Its terra-cotta roof tiles were broken, faded and mottled with age. Dark-gray mortar patched crumbling yellow walls in desperate need of paint. The balcony's handrail was broken in places and missed several balusters. She climbed two limestone steps, worn into polished-smooth troughs over the years by thousands of feet, to enter the lobby. After crossing the stone-tiled floor, careful not to trip in the gaps where tiles were missing, she woke with a polite cough the middle-aged local man sprawled over the reception desk.

"*Kantu noiti*?" he asked lazily in Creole, propping his head on an elbow.

"*Uma semana, por favor,*" she replied in Portuguese, figuring a week's stay should be sufficient for her mission.

He picked a key off a row of numbered hooks and slapped it on the desk, then laid his head back down.

"*Pagar agora*?" She reached for her purse.

"*Mais tarde,*" the guy waved a dismissive hand in the direction of the stairs.

The room was a simple affair and sufficient for her needs – a wooden bed with clean, if not dated, linen, a wardrobe, and a table and chair next to the louver doors onto the balcony.

After unpacking what little clothing she had, the

woman hid the SIM card purchased at the airport in the lining of her shoe. She undressed and wrapped herself in one of the hotel's threadbare towels, picked up her toiletry bag and room key and headed for the communal bathroom at the end of the landing.

Standing under the spray, washing off two days of travel grime, the woman felt the occasional niggling doubt, sending a tingle of anxiety through her shoulders, arms and torso. The Trade was a serious business – as its name suggested. Life was cheap, yet dealing in those lives created vast fortunes for amoral individuals who played by their own set of rules. These players weren't going to throw open the door and welcome her into their midst because she had cute little orphans for sale. She had to find an in and then be prepared to prove her intentions and trustworthiness by passing whatever initiation they had in store. If she didn't play it right, her fate didn't bear thinking about. Then there were law enforcement personnel to avoid – and not only local police but agents from a number of countries' intelligence organizations operating covertly in Cape Verde, the hub of international trafficking.

The woman put this out of her mind and concentrated on the next move. She needed a contact through whom to ease her way into the Trade. It had to be someone on the fringe, someone not too smart, a bit player she could blackmail.

- 54 -

When Hans and Penny entered the Tima Tima the following day, Mike sat sipping coffee and staring intently at his laptop screen. They both understood what he was going through. The café bar itself was quite some place, its bohemian ambience and neorustic decor setting it apart from the local food parlors, *churrascarias* and touristy eateries. The proprietor had acquired a series of enlarged prints of Jack Kerouac's original manuscript for *On the Road*, including authentic rum stains, handwritten by the Beat Generation author without paragraphs on a single roll of paper, which ran in segments along one of the café's redbrick walls.

"Hans, Penny!" Mike looked delighted to have company with whom he had something in common – as opposed to police, journalists and hotel staff. He stood up and welcomed them with a hearty handshake. "Let me get you some drinks. The espresso's good." He raised a thimble-size cup. "Or if you want milky, I'd go for a *galão*."

"*Galão* sounds great for me, Mike," said Penny, "but I reckon Hans will have a beer."

"Brilliant. Then I'll join you, Hans. I'm glad you suggested this place. I've been coming here every day to get out of the hotel."

Mike caught the waitress's attention and asked for the drinks and two more menus.

"So, how's tricks?" he asked, attempting a smile, but his haggard face spoke of only exhaustion, his bloodshot eyes of utter helplessness.

"No, you go first," said Hans. "And lunch is on us."

Mike took a deep breath and closed his laptop screen. "It's like whoever took Holly was invisible. Several people have come forward saying they were on that part of the beach the same day, some even camped right near us."

"But no one saw a thing?" Hans ventured.

"Nothing, Hans."

"I've come across this in my detective work. Those folks who did actually see Holly being led away wouldn't have registered it, because their brains weren't interpreting it as a crime, and the other beachgoers could have been preoccupied with a million and one other things at that exact moment."

"Yes, yes." Mike shifted forward in his seat.

"It's like a thief who goes into an electrical store and walks out with a huge TV. Because he's not acting all suspicious and no one's screaming 'Thief,' he gets away with it. It's called crime in plain sight."

"How come you've explained to me in ten seconds what no policeman here has been able to?" Mike looked both gobsmacked and cheated.

Hans spread his palms and gave an *I think you know the answer to that* look, adding, "It's my job, Mike."

The waitress returned with the drinks and menus and gave them time to order.

"I hope this doesn't sound inappropriate," said Mike, "but have you noticed how much you look forward to eating out when you're in a crisis?"

"Drinking beer too," said Hans. "It's a combination of replacing energy lost through stress and taking your mind off things."

"And having an excuse to eat whatever you want and stick it on a credit card," Penny joked, and the three of them laughed.

"Well, I'm going for the *jagacida* – bean and sausage stew," said Mike. "I've had it every time here, and it's really good."

"If it fills a hole, then I will too," said Hans, never picky when ordering food.

Penny had the same, and as they dipped chunks of freshly baked bread into the delicious *jagacida*, Mike filled them in on events.

"The media back home is having a field day – which has been hard for Carrie to deal with on her own. But it's getting difficult for me here too, what with the local backlash."

"Really?" Penny stopped her fork midway to her mouth.

"The islanders thrive on tourism. The more this thing drags out and the more journalists arrive here to stand on public beaches giving frantic news updates, the harder it's gonna be on their economy."

"Let's hope there's an end to this sometime soon," said Penny.

"I think if the British police had been given access to the case, it may well have been solved by now." Mike shook his head and blew through pursed lips. "But the cops here are next to useless."

"Have they given any indication who might be involved?" asked Hans, locking eyes with Penny for a moment.

"No. Why do you ask?" Mike put down his knife and fork, having spotted the nonverbal communication.

Hans looked at Penny again before continuing, not wanting to give too much away but feeling it disingenuous to keep the desperate man in the dark.

"Mike, we have reason to believe Jessica has also been taken."

The Englishman's mouth fell open. "B-b-but I thought you said she had drowned . . . When your yacht sank, I mean."

"We were tipped off she was pulled from the water and passed on to the traffickers," said Hans.

"So . . ." Mike wrung his hands, struggling to get his head around the dramatic turn of events. "We're in the same situation."

"It might even be the same kidnappers," Hans replied. "Which is why I need to ask you if the police have ever mentioned a guy named Eddy Logan to you."

Mike thought for a moment, but only out of politeness. "No, Hans. They looked into a couple of local guys, and nothing came of it. But I'd remember if a Westerner's name came up."

"When you first arrived, you said you flew into Praia and spent a couple of days here," Hans said.

"Yeah, we did."

"Did you visit a bar and restaurant called Chico's?"

No, I've not heard of it. Why are you asking this stuff?"

"Because Logan is a name that's been mentioned, and Chico's is the bar he runs." Hans screwed up his paper napkin and chucked it in the empty bowel.

"Have you been to the police?"

"Believe me, Mike, if we had anything to go on, we would. But at this stage the cops would only blunder in and send the traffickers scurrying underground. I'm making inquiries, and I've got powerful people behind me and the resources I need to do a thorough investigation. But I can't stress enough how important it is for the girls' safety that you don't tell *anyone* we've had this conversation."

"No, of course not, Hans," said Mike, looking ever more bewildered. "You have my word."

- 55 -

In Goldman Sachs' Boston office, Innes Edridge checked he was up to speed with the morning's itinerary, the final action being a phone call with Liechtenstein's finance minister advising him of the effect issuing shale gas exploration permits would have on the national oil company's share prices. Then he sat back in his office chair for ten minutes of mindfulness meditation before eating – or drinking – his lunch of vegetable juice, a combination of cucumber, spinach, celery, carrot, tomato, garlic, chili pepper and ginger, blended with a dash of Worcestershire sauce. The latter, along with the carrot and tomato, was not particularly alkalizing on the body, but it added a fruity flavor, and the result was certainly far healthier than his colleagues' choices – ham and cheese subs, pasta mixes, and the previous evening's leftovers.

He steadied his breathing and focused on the barely perceptible pause at the end of each inhale and exhale, gradually emptying his mind of anxiety and clutter. Occasionally, a random intrusive thought interrupted the exercise, like a fly buzzing into a peaceful room. Innes acknowledged the thought and let it slip gently into the ether, but as he achieved a tranquil state free from the stress of modern life, his cell phone rang.

"Orion, dear boy," the Scotsman answered in his well-to-do brogue.

"Muttley, any news on the prints?"

"I've been tracking the package, but somehow it's got lost after leaving the sorting office in Dallas."

"Anything you can do?"

"I'll call the company again in the morning."

"Thank you."

"Did you get the toys I mailed you?" Innes referred to the satellite-tracking emitter Hans had requested to plant on Logan's boat and an electronic gun pick to bump the locks.

"They arrived at the embassy this morning."

"Excellent!"

"And the cell phone records?" Hans pressed.

"Yes, our symp at Velafon's come up trumps. I emailed them to you earlier, along with a rundown on the numbers from Odysseus."

"Good news, thank you. I've also sent you the detonator cap fragment from the fishing boat."

"Yes. I forwarded the photos you emailed to our ballistics man. He came back to me right away saying it's most likely US military."

"Oh." Hans' mind began running through plausible scenarios.

"But don't get excited," said Muttley. "They're openly available on the market and one of many used by mining operations the world over."

"I see."

"Look, how about I send in a surveillance team?"

"I was gonna ask for Triton and Achelous if they're available," said Hans, using the code names for Phipps and Clayton, both former SEAL buddies and African American Concern operatives. "Let me think on it."

"Say the word and I'll book the Learjet."

"Roger that."

56

Logan's luxury villa nestled in a rocky inlet with its own dock a couple of miles south of Karen's apartment. Hans studied the terrain using Google Earth, and after toying with the idea of driving there, parking the jeep up and covering the last few hundred yards cross-country, he opted to take Karen's boat around the coast and swim in under the cover of darkness. Penny insisted on accompanying him, and once again Hans tried to talk her out it.

"You'll need someone to keep a lookout while you sneak on board."

"I . . ." Hans was about to suggest Enrique, but it wouldn't be fair to ask someone in his position to get involved in what was essentially a criminal act. Besides, the less he knew about the information the Concern had sourced on Logan, the better. "Okay, but if I get compromised, like the lights come on in the house, I want you to get the hell out of there. This guy's responsible for the death of four people."

"You want me to *leave* you?" Penny looked at him askew.

"Honey" – Hans gripped her arm – "this is serious. We'll take the walkie-talkies, and at the first sign of trouble you buzz me and head back here. Our little boat is no match for his. I'll swim home."

"And what if he tries to run you down again?"

"He won't even see me, but he'd easily see Karen's bright-orange boat."

After conducting a radio check, Hans put a walkie-talkie in the dry bag he'd taken from the *Outcast*, along with a head torch, scuba mask, 32 gigabyte memory stick, the satellite tracking device, his M9, switchblade and other tools for the job. Then they carried the outboard down the steep rocky steps and readied the little craft.

Penny hugged the coastline with the throttle at half revs, the gradient of the cliffs blocking out the waning moon. Hans had memorized the outline of the island they needed to skirt and, estimating their speed at four knots, timed the journey on a cheap black plastic watch he'd bought to replace his shiny Rolex. Pointing the compass at a lighthouse marking a treacherous reef south of Praia, Hans waited until the needle aligned with the bearing he had taken from the map. He raised his hand, and Penny cut the engine – as the security light on Logan's villa came into view higher up the cliff. A few meters out, still in the shadow of the cliff, they dropped a paint can filled with cement over the side to serve as an anchor.

Hans put on the black metalworker's balaclava he'd bought, which, unlike a scuba hood, covered most of his face. Having buckled the dry bag around his waist and tightened the straps on his Teva all-terrain sandals, he gave Penny the okay sign and slipped into the warm water, using a scissor kick and sidestroke to get him to shore.

A slight wind and the sound of waves lapping on the rocks muffled those of Hans' movement. He swam into the long inlet fronting the property and headed for the state-of-the-art speedboat, which Logan had moored to a smart wooden dock jutting into the sea. A row of car tires lashed with thick blue nylon cord to the dock's hefty wooden posts protected the craft from damage as it bobbed gently in the swell. Using the decked walkway to keep out of sight from above, the American swam underneath and clambered up through the gap onto the boat using the tires for hand- and footholds.

Hans crouched on the aft deck for a minute or so, calming his breathing and listening for any sign of human movement. He opened his mouth wide to act as an amplification chamber for any sounds, a trick learned in the military.

Satisfied he remained undetected, Hans wasted no time, opening the dry bag and clipping the walkie-talkie to the collar of his black acrylic rash vest and hooking on the earpiece. Then he took out the electronic lock-picking gun.

Muttley had informed the Concern's leading locksmith of the speedboat's make and model, and the man had pinpointed the locks used on the boat in the extensive database available to the profession. Knowing the specifications of the door and ignition locks, the locksmith fashioned two attachment rakes for the gun. The rakes housed vibrating teeth that worked on the principle of Newton's cradle, transferring energy to the spring-loaded pins in the lock and suspending them in the open position, thus allowing the lock picker to turn the barrel.

In seconds Hans was in. Leaving the rake attachment in place, he dashed through the plush saloon and emptied the contents of the dry bag onto the white leather couch nearest the cockpit. He unfurled a rectangular length of black curtain fabric, onto which he'd sewn six suction cups from windshield-mounted cell phone holders bought in a motoring accessories store. He licked the cups and stuck the fabric over the inside of the windshield to block the red-filtered light from his head torch, the filter lessening the illumination and preserving Hans' night vision.

Using the lock-picking gun, Hans turned the cockpit's ignition to flash up its airplane-like console and navigation system, then pressed the on-screen buttons to scroll through the menu as Jonah had instructed. Arriving at the button labeled "Backup," Hans inserted his memory stick into the console's USB slot and began downloading the computer's stored history. The download bar indicated this would take some time, so Hans went to work unscrewing a plastic panel below the ignition to expose the wiring loom. He located a brown wire that went live once the ignition was turned and a blue earth wire, clamping on the tracking device's quick-fastener connections with a pair of pliers and replacing the panel.

Checking the download bar, Hans saw there was an estimated four minutes left, so he spent the time searching the boat for anything that might link Logan to the trafficking operation. Underneath the sofa's leather cushions he found life jackets, barbecue equipment and snorkeling gear, and in the galley's cabinets the expected seagoing victuals – coffee, tea, canned and dried food, a few bottles of wine and beer. Opening the wardrobes and drawers in the master bedroom also turned up nothing. Hans was about to give up when he lifted the mattress on the king-sized bed to reveal a storage compartment. Stowed inside it were reels of duct tape, bulk packets of baby formula and children's clothes – brand new, and for ages ranging from babies to young teens.

"Hans!" Penny's voice came over the radio. "Lights have come on in the villa, and there's a dog barking."

"Okay, I'm out of here," he replied. "Go back to Karen's, and I'll meet you there."

Hans returned to the saloon, packed up the gear and switched off the head torch. He considered the M9 for a moment, but a discreet getaway would be preferable to a shoot-out, so he shoved it in the dry bag and then checked on the download. Still thirty seconds left – *Damn!*

The dog's barking grew louder. Hans peeled back the makeshift curtain to see someone with a flashlight running down the path from the villa. The GPS console flickered with the message "Download complete," but Hans knew the dog would soon be upon him. He yanked out the memory stick, turned the ignition off and removed the lock-picking gun. Then he ripped down the curtain and wrapped it around his right forearm for protection.

A shotgun blast rang out in the darkness.

Hans ducked instinctively but figured it was only a warning shot, the beam of a powerful flashlight playing on the windshield and illuminating the cabin. He scrambled outside, relocking the door as another shotgun blast saw a patch of water erupt only feet away.

Strapping the dry bag around his waist, Hans heard a long bloodcurdling bark and looked up to see a Doberman, teeth bared, leap from the dock.

In one fluid movement Hans thrust his bandaged forearm into the dog's salivating jaws, rammed a fist into the angry beast's abdomen and dived overboard. The second his feet got purchase under the surface, Hans powered downwards with all his might, dragging the animal by one of its legs, intent on giving it the fright of its life.

The terrified Doberman released its bite on Hans' arm and flailed for the surface. Hans hit the sandy bottom four meters down and let go of the powerful animal. Then, staying true to his SEAL training, he fought to remain calm, preserving the air in his lungs and swimming out of the inlet. He could see nothing except blackness but knew from experience that twenty strong strokes would get him the thirty-five meters into open sea. Turning left, he put in another twenty strokes to seek the protection of the headland.

When at last Hans sensed he was out of Logan's line of sight, he broke the surface, took a deep breath and then duck-dived and swam another stretch of the rocky coastline underwater. Finally, he felt safe enough to swim in the open and continued onwards using sidestroke to keep his splashes to a minimum.

Hans rounded an outcrop and considered his options – whether to clamber ashore and go cross-country in case Logan gave chase in his boat, or finish the two-mile swim back to the villa. As Hans opted to keep swimming, he heard "Psst!" echo in a gulley in the cliff. Craning in the darkness, he made out Penny rowing Karen's boat toward him.

"I thought I told you to—"

"Shut up and get in," Penny whispered.

Hans gripped the hull and wrenched his body up and down twice, the third time kicking like hell and rolling aboard the small craft. Knowing the distance sound travels on water, they remained silent as Penny pulled smoothly on the oars. She had rowed for the best part of half a mile when Hans raised his hand.

Penny lifted the oars off the water, and they listened intently.

"Okay, we're good." Hans nodded at the outboard.

Penny flicked the kill switch to "On," closed the choke on the carburetor and gave the pull-cord a solid tug. As the engine fired, she opened the choke, twisted the throttle grip and they whirred away.

Meanwhile, Logan watched his Doberman swim to the rocks and clamber out of the sea. The trembling dog shook water from its fur and, tail between its legs, ran to meet him.

"What was that about, Mani?" Logan asked, pulling out his cell phone and autodialing the last number to ring him. He had no idea who the person was that had called him to warn him his boat was being broken into – probably one of his drunken mates having a late-night laugh.

Somewhere on the island a pay phone rang and rang.

57

"**W**hat?"

Penny stared at Hans in disbelief – although in reality their suspicions were confirmed.

". . . and baby formula, duct tape and diapers," Hans continued. "Basically, everything needed to traffic kids by speedboat to a new life."

Penny took a long slug of beer. "And do you think someone saw us approaching his boat this evening and warned him off?"

"More likely my breaking in triggered an alarm in his villa. Luckily, I downloaded everything I needed, including the charts."

Hans held up the memory stick.

"Thank heavens."

"Thank Jonah. His instructions were spot on." Hans powered up his notebook and double-clicked an icon depicting an *M* emblazoned on a globe. "This is the Marin GPS software I installed, the company used by the speedboat manufacturer."

He inserted the memory stick. When the folder-view window popped up, Hans copied the one containing the boat's navigation history and pasted it into the GPS application in accordance with Jonah's instructions. He clicked "My Data" and then "My Locations," which brought up a series of dated folders going back years. As he checked the dates against Logan's offshore bank account, it soon became apparent the journeys were all two to three days before the large deposits. They also tied in with the fuel purchases from the pump at the harbor.

"Here goes nothing," said Hans, right-clicking a folder and selecting "View" to bring one of the recorded voyages up on the notebook's screen.

The brightly colored chart covered the southeastern part of the North Atlantic, taking in the West African coast, a jagged purple line highlighting the speedboat's route. Scrolling the mouse arrow along the route flashed up an information box displaying progressive coordinates.

"There it is."

Hans sat back on Karen's couch, arms folded and staring at the screen.

"The Canaries," Penny murmured, tracing the line north to where it stopped short of the island group. "But what's with the dogleg?"

Initially, the line ran west from Praia for fifty miles into the mid-Atlantic, clearing the archipelago before abruptly shooting north.

"At a guess I'd say he heads out into the commercial fishing grounds, using the trawlers for cover from the coastguard's radar," Hans replied. "Once in the channel he breaks away from the fleet and makes north for the Canaries."

"But if Logan's trying to avoid known smuggling routes, why does he head directly back to Praia from the Canaries?"

"Because he's already handed the kids over to the next traffickers in the chain and has nothing to hide – with the exception of his payoff. But there's no law against having a few thousand euros on board."

"I see."

"Penny, can you grab a couple more beers and the rum? It's time to have a look at this guy's cell phone calls."

Jonah had taken the records provided by the Concern's symp at Velafon and put the last twelve monthly call summaries into a PDF file, adding annotations elucidating on destinations of interest. Some of the calls were to known criminals on the island or in the UK, but Jonah's notes explained the individuals were not linked to trafficking and that the calls were so infrequent they were likely social and didn't point to a possible kingpin.

"Anything?" Penny set the beers down on the coffee table and went back into the kitchen area to fetch the rum.

"No," said Hans, perusing the most recent telephone statement before scrolling back two months. "Ah!"

"What is it?" Penny sat down on the couch and unscrewed the bottle cap.

"Have a look." Hans turned the notebook toward her, taking the rum and filling their glasses.

"Orphanage on São Nicolau," she said, reading Jonah's note, São Nicolau being another of the islands in the archipelago.

"And the one below," Hans prompted.

"A pay-as-you-go number in the Canaries."

"Check the date," said Hans, passing her a list he'd

complied from the GPS records of the speedboat voyages to the Canary Islands, along with the respective fuel payments and offshore bank deposits.

"It's the day before Logan's last big trip."

"And look." Hans took the notebook and flicked through the PDF, pointing out the corresponding calls to the Canaries, as well as numerous ones to the orphanage.

"So what's next?"

"I need to call a team in. Bug Logan's house and put surveillance on him for a few days. If that doesn't turn up anything, it's time to get heavy."

58

"**A**rhhh!"

Jessica pushed out her thirtieth push-up, finishing her morning fitness regime. Then she climbed back onto the bed and lay there thinking of her family.

JJ was dead.

Mommy was dead.

Miss Potter, her class teacher – whom she and Hans referred to as the Old Witch – had been unusually nice to her that day, taking her out of class and putting her in the care of Matt and Kelly Mason, family friends, who'd made a surprise visit to the school to pick her up, along with their own daughter, Pearl.

However, Matt and Kelly didn't take Jessie home. Had they done so, they'd have met with a scene from a Hollywood movie – emergency vehicles and flashing lights everywhere, the house cordoned off with police tape, the bomb squad in attendance, helicopters overhead and a SWAT team on alert as detectives questioned local residents and other potential witnesses to the atrocity.

Back at the Mason's place, Jessie had been playing with Pearl in the yard when her father arrived with the news that changed their lives forever. She still didn't know the full extent of what had happened, only that a bad man had hurt Mommy and JJ and made them dead.

Whoever carried out the hits were professionals, leaving no traces of their identities for the investigators, which was clue enough for Hans to know who had ordered them. It was something he would have to live with forever. He'd done his best to explain the loss to Jessie in terms she could understand, giving the angels-in-heaven scenario a miss. When they'd sprinkled Mom's and JJ's ashes on East End Beach, Hans had told his little girl how they would always be with them in the waves, the flowers, the birds and the trees.

Tired from her workout, Jessica drifted off to sleep but awoke to the sound of raised voices. Mouthwash and another man stood outside the cell having a disagreement. The other man was unhappy Mouthwash had brought the English girl to them when the American was poking his nose into their affairs and the island crawled with journalists and police.

"*Lo siento,*" Mouthwash Man apologized.

"*Mátala y deshacerse del cuerpo!*"

"*Bueno, voy a salir con ella en el barco,*" Mouthwash Man agreed, saying he would take the English girl out on the boat and dispose of her.

From the tone of the conversation, Jessica knew the outlook was not good, but from Spanish lessons with her mom and their domestic help back home, she understood what "*El americano está aquí*" meant: her father was coming to get her!

59

Hans called Muttley in the morning to request backup, disappointed to hear Phipps and Clayton were tied up and wouldn't arrive for another two days. Now Logan was clearly in the frame, Hans needed to start the surveillance operation and begin watching his villa for any comings and goings giving a clue as to Jessica's whereabouts. He planned to sneak into a reconnaissance position somewhere on the hillside and find a suitably large shrub to act as a hide, offering camouflage while he observed the house through the sniper spotting scope loaned from the US embassy's armory.

Penny drove him into town to buy equipment and supplies. In a supermarket Hans chucked three loaves of bread into the cart, a pack of thick-sliced ham, some local cheese and a jar of pickled gherkins, adding a roll of saran wrap and a few bars of chocolate for good measure. From a hardware store he bought two plastic gas cans and a pair of pruning shears, and in a sports outlet a backpack, camping roll and two-inch-long red anglers' glow sticks.

Knowing there were no military surplus stores on the island, they met Enrique in a coffee shop to pick up a camouflage net procured from the US Marines in the barracks.

"Be careful out there, Hans," said Enrique. "You know this guy has some serious firepower, and he's not afraid to use it."

"Thanks for the warning, friend." Hans smiled. "But so do I."

Back at Karen's place, they were surprised to find gifts on the doorstep – two bottles of vintage red wine, a bouquet of flowers, chocolates and a card.

"Hmm." Penny smiled. "This fairy can come again!"

"Most definitely." Hans peeled open the card. "Ah, they're from the mayor. He says, 'Once again I urge you to leave this matter to the authorities, but if you must continue, please let me know if I can be of assistance. Wonderful to make your acquaintance. Your friend, Videl.'"

While Penny cleaned and oiled the Beretta as Hans had taught her, he sliced the bread and made twenty ham, cheese and gherkin sandwiches. He filled one of the gas cans with drinking water – the other would be for when it came out the other end, the saran wrap for when he needed a dump. He strapped on the holstered M9 and shoved all the gear, including the camera, into the backpack.

As evening fell, Penny dropped Hans off a mile up the coast from Logan's villa and then continued into town to keep an eye on Chico's from a discreet distance. Hans ducked off the road and shouldered the backpack. After crouching awhile to let his eyes adjust to the dark, he began clambering over the rocky terrain and brushing through the shrubs to reach a suitable vantage point.

In the blackness Hans wasn't overly worried someone might spot him, and the gentle but steady breeze covered the sound of his tracks. Nonetheless, he got down on all fours three hundred feet from his predicted lookout and crawled on his belly the rest of the way.

The security light on Logan's property came into view in the gulley below, and Hans continued another fifty yards before stopping to find cover. Fortunately, several clumps of spurge, known locally as *tortolho*, sprouted from the otherwise barren ground. Hans knew it would have to do and began preparing the hide.

Using the secateurs, Hans carefully snipped away foliage to form a tunnel in the bush. Once inside he widened the space enough for him and his rucksack. The bush was sparse, so the camo net came in handy. Hans strung it around the hide using spring clips to hold it in place. He took the roll mat, sniper spotting scope, camera and gas cans out of the rucksack, then unholstered the M9 and placed it inside. Having unrolled the compressed-foam mattress, he maneuvered himself onto it – not an easy task in the confines of the hide – and then set up the scope on its tripod. Finally, he tied back some of the leaves in the front wall to form a viewing hole.

Now all Hans had to do was what Navy SEALs did best – to watch and wait – figuring there was enough food and water to last until Phipps and Clayton arrived in a couple of days to take shifts. He hadn't gone as far as applying camouflage cream to his face, since this wasn't a military scenario, where a determined enemy would have sentries posted watching for any sign of movement, an out-of-place shape in the brush or light reflecting off skin and equipment. Nor had he bought military fatigues, which would arouse suspicion should he bump into an islander, but instead wore jeans, sneakers and a long-sleeved shirt. Hans chuckled. He couldn't imagine anyone had ever lain in the dirt conducting covert operations in Armani, Ralph Lauren and New Balance.

Despite applying the strongest mosquito repellent available, neat DEET, to his exposed skin, Hans felt insects biting through the thin fabric of his shirt. Having experienced far worse, he didn't flinch. Years of self-discipline had taught him that if you resist the urge to scratch, then the itch disappears in two days and, besides, bugs weren't his problem tonight. He rested his elbows on one of Karen's couch cushions – she wouldn't mind – and scanned the property in a figure-of-eight pattern with his naked eye, checking through the scope every couple of minutes in case he missed any subtle movement.

There were lights on in some of the villa's rooms, but drapes prevented Hans seeing what was taking place inside. Cupping a mini-glow-stick in the palm of his hand, he began drawing a three-dimensional map of the property and surrounding ground.

The villa itself sat fifty yards up the hillside and enjoyed a stunning sea view. It had an L-shape design, with a barbeque and sunbathing patio and swimming pool fronting the seaward wing. The other wing was furthest away from Hans' position, and nestling in the crook of the L-shaped design was a block-paved courtyard skirted with a triple garage and two outbuildings. Neatly manicured garden lay all around, and there was a fair-sized vegetable plot, its soil darkened by the water from a sprinkler system.

Hans suspected the property housed hidden rooms,

likely in a basement, and felt a pang of anxiety that his terrified daughter could be so close. He would conduct further reconnaissance later to check if the property was alarmed – highly probable in view of its secluded location and the fact the speedboat appeared to be. If he ascertained the type of alarm, he could ask Jonah to provide technical direction on how to disable it. The recon patrol would have to wait until tomorrow night, though, as he needed twenty-four hours to assess the movement at the villa and daylight to see whether there were any surveillance cameras.

Hans took out the radio and clipped on the earpiece. "Skipper, you there?"

"I'm here," Penny replied, her voice reassuring to Hans in his vulnerable position.

"Anything?"

"I buzzed past Chico's in the jeep. Logan's playing host to the usual suspects. I'm parked a block down watching the door."

"Okay, let me know when he leaves."

"Will do," said Penny. "Are you all right?"

"Having a blast, honey. Booked into the Ritz Praia."

"Ha! Don't eat your sandwiches all at once."

"Roger that. Later."

As Hans placed his eye back on the scope, the house lights extinguished. In the glow of the security lamp, he made out a local woman lock up the front door and hop on a moped. Figuring it was the domestic help, he wrote in his notebook, "2104 hrs – DH leaving property."

Nothing of significance took place during the next two hours. Hans was in two minds whether to get some sleep, knowing Penny would notify him when Logan left the bar to return home. If Phipps and Clayton had been there for backup, it wouldn't be an issue, the three of them taking turns to watch the villa. As it was, he worried a forty-eight-hour stretch awake with no possibility of moving about would tax his weakened body to the point where sleep overcame him. He couldn't afford to miss any intel or compromise tomorrow night's recon.

Hans lay there until midnight, listening to the breeze rustling the leaves of the hide, the whining of mosquitoes and waves crashing on the rocks far below. He felt something pad across the back of his hand and in the darkness could make out a scorpion, likely of the *Hottentotta* genus, one of the island's poisonous inhabitants. He smiled and watched as the creature clambered over his fingers and went on its way.

Hans bleeped Penny's walkie-talkie, a precaution before breaking radio silence.

"I'm here," she replied.

"Anything, skipper?"

"No, no change."

"Okay, in that case I'm gonna take a nap. Bleep me if there's movement."

"Roger that. Out."

Without changing position, Hans lay his chin on his crossed forearms and drifted off. Every few minutes a mosquito dipped its proboscis into his skin, the sharp sting keeping Hans from deep sleep. He dreamt a bizarre and fractured dream in which Logan caught him snooping around the house and, rather than blowing him away with the twelve-gauge, invited him for a barbeque and then laughed at Hans' paranoid accusations.

The radio beeped, shaking Hans from slumber. For a split second he remained in the dream world, his mood lightened by Logan's innocence, until Real World kicked in and a pang of anger coursed through him.

Hans keyed the mic. "Skipper?"

"Target's leaving the bar now with four other men," Penny replied. "Looks like holidaying Brits. They're climbing into a black convertible BMW."

"Thanks, hon. Go back to the villa and get some sleep."

"Okay, I'll leave the radio by the bed if you need me."

In preparation for Logan's arrival, Hans unscrewed the cap on the empty gas can and, shifting onto his side, relieved himself into it. He took a well-needed drink of water from the other can and gobbled down some of the sandwiches. In a tactical operation such as this it wasn't possible to cook with a stove, but under the circumstances his picnic easily passed as five-star cuisine. After stretching out his limbs one at a time, then his back, shoulders and neck, Hans settled into position as the lights of the BMW appeared up on the coast road. Logan turned into the long, hilly driveway and drove at speed toward the villa. He screeched to a halt in the courtyard, setting his Doberman off barking.

One of the men crammed into the sports car's backseat attempted to hop out of the car *Dukes of Hazzard* style. His mates roared with laughter as the drunkard crashed unceremoniously onto the block paving, where he rolled around, lacking the coordination to get up. The other men grabbed his arms and escorted him into the house.

The next thing Hans knew, the patio was ablaze in spotlights, and one of the high-spirited Englishmen was carrying a cooler loaded with beer and spirits on ice as Logan led them to the poolside.

"Last man shut the door on the dog," he ordered.

"Got it, Ed," his guest replied, a lobster-red bonehead bordering on obese and wearing a white tank top with the slogan "Don't Be Sexist to Bitches" emblazoned on it in comical pink lettering.

The men's raucous voices carried clearly across the gulley up the hillside to Hans' position. He wondered if they'd feel so entertained if Logan came clean with them about his *real* business.

"Who fancies a little Coca-Cola?" Logan bellowed as his new friends cracked beers and necked shots.

Hans got that it wasn't a reference to a soft drink.

"Rude not to, Eddy!" said the fat bonehead.

The others agreed – except the wasted guy, who'd fallen asleep on a sun lounger.

Logan went inside and returned carrying a mirror with a bag of white powder and a box cutter blade resting on it, placing it in front of the men on the plastic garden table.

"This better not be like the shite we have at home!" said the fat reveler.

"Ha!" Logan mocked. "This ain't Blighty, mate, and this stuff's the real McCoy, from the South American jungle!"

He proceeded to pour a good amount of powder onto the mirror and began chopping it up and furrowing it into neat inch-long lines with the blade.

"That gear don't look right," said another of his

guests, a weaselly-looking guy with thinning brown hair tied in a ponytail wearing an England football shirt, camo cargo shorts and black Adidas sports shoes. "Looks all sticky and that."

"That's because it's hundred percent pure," Logan gloated. "Not like that powdery crap back home."

"Here's a note," said the other holidaymaker still awake, holding out a clumsily rolled-up banknote.

"You Neanderthal," Logan scoffed. "This ain't fuckin' Bromley."

He rerolled the note but folded back one of its corners an inch so the paper tube neatly interlocked. "There – *that* won't come undone. Now shove your nose in it."

Up on the hillside, Hans snapped close-ups of the guests for the record. As the men snorted marching powder and washed tequila slammers down with gulps of beer, he listened intently for any swing in the conversation – particularly Logan's bragging – that might lead to finding Jessica.

In reality Hans knew Logan wasn't going to jeopardize his lengthy and profitable operation by divulging anything to these bozos. He knew from time spent in England that the country's working class, including its thugs and criminals, hated crimes against children more than anything else – even murder. One misplaced word from Logan would see him drowned in his own pool – after which these tattooed lager louts would snort all his cocaine and drink all his liquor in celebration.

The rest of the morning went as expected, with the booze and drugs inducing boast-and-bravado-filled speeches, discriminatory jokes and cringeworthy revelations – in addition to dive bombs in the pool and a belly flop competition, won not surprisingly by Mr. Misogynist, God's fat-bellied gift to women.

Come 6:00 a.m. it was clear Logan wanted his bed. Unlike his guests, the millionaire playboy indulged in this behavior most nights, and the novelty of a hedonist's paradise wore thin.

"Right, fellas, taxi's here!" he announced.

The three men roused their buddy and, following man hugs and false promises to keep in touch, lurched toward the cab waiting out front. Logan left the pool area in a mess of bottles, cans and overflowing ashtrays and went inside the villa. Seconds later all the lights went off.

Hans reviewed his notes, feeling a cloud of depression envelop him. Not once during the morning's festivity had Logan sneaked away to check on Jessica and Holly – only his dog – confirming the likelihood they were imprisoned at another location. He set the alarm on his cell phone for 8:00 a.m. and attempted to grab a little sleep, knowing the sun's relentless rays would bear down on the hide soon, making rest impossible.

- 60 -

Hans awoke to the *put-put* sound of the domestic helper returning on her moped. He hadn't expected to see her with it being Sunday, but as she began clearing up the poolside mess, the reason for the overtime became obvious.

Hans pressed his eye against the spotting scope and chuckled, for the young and pretty mestiza, unaware of anyone watching, racked up two fat lines of Logan's coke and snorted them through the left-behind banknote. Then, having pocketed the cash, she piled the contraband and paraphernalia onto the mirror and carried the lot inside. On her return she downed a couple of tequilas and, to Hans' surprise, peeled off her tank top, shorts and panties and dived in the pool. Hans glanced down at his notebook, figuring that, when he briefed Penny later, he'd leave this part of the proceedings off the record.

The girl swam ten lengths of the twenty-meter pool using an impressive front crawl, slipping seamlessly from the water to dry herself off with one of Logan's towels. After putting her clothes back on, she tidied the few remaining items, locked the property and sped away on her scooter.

Knowing Logan would be sleeping off his booze-and-coke hangover Hans didn't expect to see much action for the rest of the morning. He worried the Englishman might take Sunday off from Chico's, thwarting his plan to reconnoiter the property as night fell. Putting it out of his mind, he scanned the grounds, searching for surveillance cameras. He couldn't see any through the scope – although they might be out of his line of sight.

Hans drank some water and ate a couple more sandwiches, and not long after, his digestive clock told him it was time to take a dump. This was always a challenge in covert operations. Rolling back against the hide's scrub wall, he took out the saran wrap, tore off a generous length and spread it along the camping roll. Having unbuckled his belt and jeans, Hans rested on his elbows and relieved himself, then cleaned up with wet wipes and sealed the lot up in the plastic film. He wrapped a few more layers around to be safe and placed it in the backpack.

The sun rose in a cloudless sky, and the heat in the hide intensified – as did the pain from the hundreds of mosquito bites on Hans' back where they'd penetrated his shirt. Having accidently upset a scorpion during the night, Hans' left ankle had inflamed to twice its normal size and throbbed with intense pain. He reached into the backpack for the first aid kit and popped an ibuprofen and a couple of antihistamine tablets, washing them down with lukewarm water. The rank aftertaste of the pills, combined with soaring temperature, sleep deprivation and general discomfort, made Hans nauseous, but he put it out of his mind, for as far as the former Navy SEAL was concerned, he was alive, he'd been through a lot worse, and he would go through it all again if it meant getting Jessica back. He radioed Penny to let her know all was okay and that he would give her a further update when Logan surfaced.

Lying there, Hans found it impossible not to think about Jessie. Since his recovery in Boston, he'd done so every waking moment. He remembered when she came into the world with hardly a whimper and made him and Kerry such proud parents. She could swim the width of their pool back in Portland at two years old and scuba dived in the sea off Maine aged five. Carl, his younger brother bought Jessica a Rubik's Cube for her sixth birthday, which came with step-by-step instructions. When Hans went to tuck Jessica into bed that night and read her a Willard Price adventure story, he found the little girl fast asleep with the completed cube sitting on the nightstand. She was such a smart kid the school moved her up a year, and Kerry spent time in the evenings tutoring her.

When Kerry and JJ were murdered, Jessica displayed a maturity way beyond her years, dealing with her grief better than most adults would. Then there was the night Hans downed a bottle of Jack Daniel's and sat staring down the barrel of his Beretta – she had been his reason to go on living then. Now, checking the date on his cheap plastic watch, November 1, tears began to well. It was her birthday in three days.

With the time approaching 11:00 a.m., Hans let out a monster yawn. He had to get some sleep or he'd be no good to anyone, Jessica or otherwise. Setting the alarm on his cell phone for 1:00 p.m., he laid his chin on his hands and dozed off.

The sound of a shotgun blast rocked the hillside.

Hans woke in an instant, his mind flashing back to numerous enemy contacts during his days as a SEAL. Staying calm, he pulled the pistol from its holster and put his eye to the scope – *Phew!*

Logan stood on the terrace pointing his twelve-gauge out to sea.

"Pull!"

His automatic launcher hurled another clay pigeon into the air, and Hans heard the familiar zing as the disc whizzed skyward like a miniature flying saucer. Logan raised his barrel in a fluid motion and squeezed the trigger, shattering the imitation bird into a thousand pieces over the ocean.

"Pull! . . . Pull!"

Hans was impressed as he watched Logan dispatch two more clays in quick succession. The man could certainly handle a gun, prompting Hans to rethink his camouflage. He thought about pulling the balaclava from the backpack, although its solid black color wasn't ideal. A trained sniper would only have to glance at the hillside to spot the discrepancy immediately. Logan wasn't about to start scanning the surrounding area with optics, though, and in the cover of the hide, Hans wasn't overly worried. Besides, he was far enough out of range of the twelve-gauge for its ammunition to be effective.

Ironically, the impromptu target practice provided Hans with entertainment, taking his mind off the pain and discomfort. In between slugs of beer, Logan sent forty or more clays sailing out over the sea and hit almost all of them. Hans smiled when the Brit swapped to his pistol, which from its two-tone gold-and-black finish looked to be a German-made Sig Sauer 9 mm. As expected, he missed every one of the next ten targets, then stopped for the day and carried his equipment inside.

What happened next saw Hans raise an eyebrow. Still wearing a white tank top and Union Jack flag shorts, he emerged from the main door of the villa with his Doberman, having swapped his flip-flops for gumboots. He crossed the courtyard to one of the brick toolsheds and took out a garden fork and a rake. For the next two hours he worked flat out, digging over one of his vegetable plots, pulling weeds, smashing the clods of earth into smaller lumps and raking stones to one side, only stopping to throw a ball for his hound.

Content with his spot of gardening, Logan rinsed the tools under a hose and stowed them back in the shed. Then he went into his villa, emerging minutes later wearing brown-framed glasses and carrying a book and a long drink, complete with cocktail umbrella. He lay on a sun lounger by the pool and began to read. Hans zeroed in the scope to see the book's title: *Break Through the Barriers Inside*, by the world-famous American personal development guru Eric Jansen.

His involvement in the Trade aside, Logan lived a fulfilling life, and, bizarrely, Hans felt he had a lot in common with the man. Both of them worked hard in business, both liked boats and had a connection with the sea, both enjoyed handling weapons, self-improvement and drinking a beer or two. Yet Hans didn't need to remind himself there was a distinct possibility that circumstances might force him to put a bullet through Logan's skull before the day was out.

Darkness fell, and it looked increasingly likely Logan would spend the evening at home. Hans polished off the sandwiches as he watched the multicolored glow of a widescreen TV flicker across the courtyard. From the sound of intermittent cheering and running commentary, Hans guessed Logan was watching English Premier League soccer, the thought of a comfortable couch, cold beer and a ball game making him long for the day all this was over and he, Penny and Jessie could return to Maine.

To cheer himself up, he called Penny on the walkie-talkie. "Skipper, you there?"

"I'm here."

"Looks like Logan's staying home tonight, so the reconnaissance mission's off," Hans whispered, holding up the cushion to prevent his voice traveling in the night air.

"Can you wait until he's asleep?"

"I'd only wake his dog."

"Ah, I hadn't thought of that. Listen, how about I pick you up, and we can continue this when Phipps and Clayton get here?"

"To be honest that's not a bad idea, but I can't risk leaving this place. If anything happened while I was—"

Wailing sirens interrupted their conversation.

Hans looked up to see a convoy of vehicles with flashing emergency lights speeding along the coast road.

"Orion, what is it?" Penny hissed.

"It's a police raid. Stay off the radio until I make contact."

"But—"

Hans twisted the volume knob to "Off."

Blue-and-red light bathed the hillside, the sirens growing louder as police cars and SWAT team vans poured down the villa's driveway.

How not to conduct a covert operation. Hans scowled, strapping on the M9 and shoving everything but the sniper scope in the backpack. He had his eye to the scope when the first car pulled up in the courtyard and none other than Chief Inspector Barbosa Amado jumped out, pistol in hand.

If you put my little girl in danger . . . Hans cursed, recognizing a bungled operation when he saw one.

As the police tactical unit rushed the front door with a battering ram, Hans caught a movement at the seaward side of the house. He turned the scope to see the Englishman dashing across the floodlit veranda, manhandling a large suitcase, which he lowered over the parapet and vaulted after. From the exertion on Logan's face, Hans could tell it contained something heavy.

Jessica!

Leaving the backpack and scope, Hans was out of the hide and bounding down the hillside, realizing Logan was making a dash for his boat in an attempt to sink the evidence of his involvement in the Trade to the bottom of the Atlantic. Pain rocketed up Hans' leg from the scorpion bite, but he hardly felt a thing as he powered toward the dock, hurdling rocks and scrub and sliding down the steep drops on his backside.

Logan had the speedboat's engine fired up in no time, thrusting the throttle forward to roar away from the jetty. Hans sprinted down the walkway but knew his efforts were in vain. Even if he jumped he would miss landing in the boat by a matter of inches. He was about to give up the chase when he saw something dragging through the water. In Logan's haste to cast off he'd let the stern line drop in the sea.

The American needed no prompting, launching himself at full pelt from the end of the walkway and flying through the air to come down in a belly flop on top of the trailing line. He grabbed the thick hemp rope with both hands and plunged underwater for what seemed an eternity before the pull of the boat towed him to the surface.

With the thunder of the diesel engine and the cabin door shut, Hans hoped Logan wouldn't notice he had company, but if he did and came out on the offensive Hans would do everything in his power to put a bullet through his skull and give Jessica a chance to live.

He quickly realized this wasn't going to be an option, for as the boat picked up speed it was all he could do to hold on, let alone think about drawing his gun. The churning seawater surged over him, placing enormous strain on his arms and preventing him drawing a breath.

Desperate for air, Hans knew he had to let go but was determined to fire a few shots into the cabin before the speedboat disappeared into the night. Praying he wouldn't get tangled in the rope, Hans counted, "One . . . two . . ."

Logan realized something impeded the boat's progress, so he throttled back, and the speedboat slowed. Fueled on adrenaline, Hans seized his opportunity, hauling himself along the line to within a yard of the hull.

Fearing the stern line had wrapped around the propeller, Logan grabbed a sheath knife and left the cabin to investigate. When he saw Hans gripping the stern ladder, his jaw dropped, and he rushed for the suitcase.

Hans leapt on board as Logan heaved the case over the side. Logan turned and, unsheathing the knife, rushed at Hans. The American blocked the thrust with his forearm and shattered Logan's nose with a crunching head butt.

Air bubbled from the suitcase as it slowly sunk into the depths. Hans dived into the sea and powered downwards. He managed to locate the case's handle and kicked for the surface, no easy task lugging the deadweight.

"Jessie, Jessie!" he screamed, gasping for air as the boat's momentum carried the craft forward.

He tried the catches on the case but Logan had locked them – *Damn!*

Hans struck out with his legs and one arm. It was a good minute before he managed to grab the mooring line and pull himself to the ladder.

"Urr . . . uur . . ." Logan started to come around.

"Stay down!" Hans ordered, using his remaining strength to drag the case over the fiberglass coaming.

"Jessie! It's Daddy!"

He grabbed Logan's knife and broke open the catches.

Clutching his nose, Logan looked both shocked and bemused.

Hans threw open the case. "Wha—?"

It was filled with cracked and chipped clay pots and figurines.

He collapsed back on the deck, his mouth trying to form words that wouldn't come.

"So, you're Interpol I take it."

Logan's nasal tone sounded ridiculous. Blood dripped down onto his sweat-and-brine-soaked T-shirt and spread out in an ugly red blossom.

Hans came to his senses, leaping up and pulling out the M9. "Where's my daughter?" He leveled the pistol at Logan's head.

"Mate" – Logan held up his hands – "I've got no idea what you're on about."

"Alvarez! He passed her on to you after he pulled her from the water."

"Who?" Logan looked utterly confused. "I don't know anyone called Alv—"

"And this?" Hans jerked his head at the suitcase.

"I'd rather not say." Logan broke eye contact.

Hans tensed and pressed the barrel of the M9 into the Englishman's forehead.

"Okay, okay, okay!" Logan made a to-ing and fro-ing movement with his palms as if he were telling a car driver to stop, his demeanor more guilty schoolchild than international child trafficker. "They're ancient artifacts. Colombian – mostly terra-cotta from the Piartal Period."

Hans let the muzzle drop and sank back on his haunches. It was his turn to look confused.

"AD 750 to 1250," Logan continued. "In fact, archaeological evidence proves ceramics were produced on Colombia's Caribbean coast earlier than anywhere in the Americas outside of the lower Amazon Bas—"

"Stop!" Hans had heard enough of the history lesson. "Is *this* the reason behind your boat trips to the Canaries?"

Logan gave a mournful nod. "Some guy from Tenerife came into my bar one night. We got chatting over a beer, and he said he was an art dealer. When I told him I owned a boat, he asked if I was interested in making some serious cash. All I had to do was meet a fishing trawler from South America offshore, collect a package and take it up north and collect the money."

"Hence the dogleg," Hans muttered, remembering the GPS coordinates.

"Huh?"

"Nothing." Hans waved the pistol. "Go on."

"I got greedy. A lot of the items were similar, so I figured no one would notice if I helped myself to the odd piece. Only I couldn't work out a way to sell them on."

"So you shoved them in a suitcase."

"Yes, mate."

Hans gripped the Brit's bloodied shirt. "Up!"

He marched him through the doorway into the cabin, down the ladder and along the passageway into the stateroom, then ripped the mattress from the double berth and lifted the lid on the storage compartment beneath.

"Explain the children's clothes."

"Th-th-they're for an orphanage . . . over on São Nicolau," said Logan, still visibly trembling. "Before my partner, Krystal, up and left, we'd been trying for a baby. In the end we decided to adopt. We've visited the orphanage several times to meet the kids. The clothes cost nothing in the market and—"

"Yeah, I get it . . . and the baby formula too. But what about this?" Hans picked up the duct tape and gave Logan a knowing look.

"Actually, the formula and the tape are for something else."

"Care to explain?"

Hans felt his whole being deflate as anger and suspicion flowed out of him, along with the last traces of hope. Logan might look like a thug, but he certainly wasn't an international child trafficker. In fact, he sat somewhere between nerdy and pathetic.

"Yeah, I can explain, but listen, er . . . ?"

"It's Hans."

"Hans, are you going to arrest me?"

"I'm nothing to do with the police."

"Then what the hell was all that about?" Logan flicked his eyes in the direction of the villa.

Mike Davenport, thought Hans, but didn't say anything. "I have no idea."

"You mentioned your daughter?"

"She's been abducted."

"And you think *I* did it?" Logan looked horrified.

"I have – or at least I *had* – good reason to believe that."

"Then I'm gonna do everything I can to help you and prove my innocence, honest. But let's get this boat out of here first before the coastguard comes."

"Okay," said Hans. "I know just the place."

- 62 -

Logan dropped anchor in the inlet by Karen's villa. "I don't know about you, Hans, but I could do with a drink," he said, nodding to the saloon.

Hans took his drenched and defunct cell phone from the pocket of his jeans and sat down on one of the plush white leather couches.

"Give that to me," said the Englishman.

"Sorry?"

"Your mobile. I'll put it in Eddy's onboard repair shop."

"You can fix it?"

"Ha! If you knew how many people have been pushed in the drink off this baby, then you'd know why we have a system," said Logan, chuckling as he opened the back of the phone and removed the battery. After rifling through a drawer in the galley, he pulled out a clothes peg tied to a length of cord with a wire hook at the other end. "Wait a minute."

Hans watched, intrigued, as Logan disappeared down the ladder to the deck below. He returned a minute later with a grin on his face

"I've hung it below the hand drier in the head," he explained and then pressed down on the jazzy coffee table. Its smoked-glass top rose up like something from a sci-fi movie to reveal a fully stocked liquor cabinet and glasses. "Ice?"

"Be rude not to." Hans forced a beleaguered smile.

Logan went to the galley area and peeled off his T-shirt, exposing his dragon tattoo. He wet a corner of the shirt under the faucet and wiped the blood from his face. Then he opened the refrigerator and hit a button, dispensing an avalanche of ice cubes into a built-in plastic bucket.

"Pretty neat," Hans mused aloud.

"Yeah, but a pity it doesn't make this." Logan pulled a half-eaten sleeve of chocolate chip cookies from its box and tipped a fat packet of cocaine out onto the drinks table.

"Oh."

"The South Americans" – Logan shook ice from the bucket into their glasses – "often slip a kilo or two in with the artifacts. "The guys I deliver it to think I don't notice or they don't care."

"And you charge a little tax?"

"I take a bit out for my personal use, mix some milk powder – formula – in with the rest so they can't tell and—"

"Tape up the packets with the duct tape."

Hans dropped his head into his hands as the last piece of the puzzle fell into place.

"Here." Logan slid a tumbler brimming with whiskey across the tabletop. "You look like a man who needs a drink."

Hans let out a long sigh and downed it in one.

"So, who are you anyway?" Logan's eyes flicked to the bag of coke, like the proverbial kiddy in a candy store. "A vigilante or something?"

"Private detective," Hans replied, and told Logan the bones of the story, feeling a pang of guilt his head butt put paid to the man's powdery pleasure.

"So were you on my boat the other night?" Logan reached for the scotch. "I wasn't sure if the phone call was one of my mates having a laugh."

"How do you mean?" Hans' antenna pricked up.

"Some guy called from a Cape Verde number saying my boat was being broken into and I should get down to the dock right away. I didn't see anything, but my dog was behaving pretty weird."

"Was the guy a Westerner or local?"

"He spoke English, put it that way. But I was pretty drunk, and his voice was muffled."

"Is the number still on your cell phone?"

"Yeah, but I Googled it already – a pay phone in Praia."

Hans thought back to the murders of the Fulani, Alvarez and Silvestre. The traffickers always seemed to be one step ahead. He admitted to Logan that he'd broken into the boat and explained his reasons, then accepted another drink and turned the subject back to Jessica.

"They call it the Trade here." Logan shrugged. "Everyone knows about it, but . . . you know, it's underground."

"Do kids ever go missing from the orphanage you visit?"

"Hell, Hans, I hadn't even thought about it."

"Do you think your contacts might know anything?"

"I can ask around."

"And to clear up a couple of loose ends, where were you the evening the fishing boat blew up in the harbor?"

"Saturday I was at the restaurant. In fact, Sergio Horne walked in. He's an actor, pretty famous in these parts. I texted a photo to Krystal. Here, check it out."

Hans looked at the picture on Logan's cell phone and read the date and time of the text.

"And my sources mentioned something about you being arrested for having a kid on the boat."

"Ha! Police harassment more like. Look, Hans, I did a stretch in jail in the UK for laundering profits for a cigarette smuggling ring through a betting shop I ran. I got completely ripped off and didn't make a penny. But when I was released from prison early, they expected me to pay a whole load of money back under the Proceeds of Crime Act. I didn't have any bloody proceeds, so I skipped the country and moved to Cape Verde. The authorities here have been on my back since I arrived." He paused to dab his finger in the coke and rub it around his gums.

"And the boy?"

"Hmm." Logan licked his lips. "A local street urchin, Hans. I told you, me and Krystal love kids. It's not like the UK or the States here. You don't have to undergo a criminal record check or sign your life away to the health and safety muppets to take a youngster for a spin in your boat. You just have to make sure the little beggars don't rob you blind while you're doin' it!"

From his own experiences, Hans knew it to be true. The sense of community and extended family in African culture meant children were far more trustful of adults. He didn't bother interrogating Logan further. He'd heard enough. But one question remained.

"Eddy?"

"Shoot."

"Can you think why anyone would want to set you up for my daughter's disappearance?"

"How do you mean?"

"Is my cell working yet? I wanna show you something."

While Logan put the Samsung back together, Hans told him about his meeting and the subsequent demise of Djenabou, the Fulani.

"Look at this." Hans flicked through the phone's picture gallery.

Logan, ⍦

"That's harsh," said Logan, squinting at Djenabou's ugly bloody scrawl. "But to me that's not a dragon's claw."

"What is it then?" said Hans, taking the phone back to look for himself.

"It's a downwards-pointing arrow."

"And why would she write that next to your name?"

Logan shrugged. "I have no idea."

Cobra Azul, "Blue Snake," ripped a slip of paper from his youngest sister's schoolbook and formed a V-shaped tray, into which he sprinkled a good amount of ground-up marijuana. He took a rock of crack from a vial worn on a thong around his neck and placed it on a CD case lying on the simple wooden table. After bashing the rock into powder with the base of his cigarette lighter, he added it to the potent tray of herb, twisted it into a reefer and sparked it up.

Cobra always smoked his crack this way, since the pipe method produced too intense a high, one that only lasted a few seconds, leaving you craving for more. He'd witnessed many of his fellow pimps and dealers go down that route, desperately chasing another hit to produce the elusive initial euphoria, spending all their earnings and then hustling and cheating to buy more.

Adelina, the middle of his five sisters, curled up on the shack's dilapidated couch watching cartoons on a beat-up television set. Every so often her eyes flicked to her brother, for in the shantytown of Rocinha most kids smoked the rock, and this eleven-year-old was no different.

"*Nau!*" Cobra yelled in Creole. "You wanna get high, you buy it yourself!"

"Phuh!" she pulled a face and went back to watching *ThunderCats* dubbed in Portuguese.

Cobra's real name was Artur, after his late father, stabbed to death in an argument over a card game when the boy was four. His mother, a crack addict, smoked herself into the sanitarium, recovered and returned home only for the cycle to repeat. She would get cleaning jobs and sex work to provide for the kids, staying sober for a while until the addictive psyche took hold, conning the poor woman into scoring "just once," seeing her mental health, promises and earnings go up in bittersweet smoke.

The young mestizo stood up and looked in the mirror. He fingered the mini-dreads in his bob-length hair into place before putting a black baseball cap on backwards. Then he reseated his faux-gold chain and medallion and admired his trademark blue eyes. He was Cobra Azul, and it was time to go to work.

- 64 -

Two blocks over, fourteen-year-old Angel sat in the front room of her grandfather's shack as the drunken pig slept in a chair. Listening to emphysemic snores emanating from a pathetic skinny chest, she wished the half-empty bottle of cane spirit he clutched like a baby would slip and pour all over his filthy pants. Angel hated the sick old pervert for subjecting her to so many heinous acts over the years but knew if she didn't take the bottle from him she would pay dearly: the cigarette burns on her arms testified to that.

The teenager went to the bathroom and filled a bucket with cold water from a sole faucet, then stripped off and rinsed herself down with a wetted washcloth. Cobra would sniff her armpits before work that evening, and if they smelled of body odor she could expect another beating and an even smaller share of the cash.

Angel shut the door of her bedroom and pressed "Play" on an antiquated cassette player, her mood lifting to the *na-na-na* of Kylie Minogue. After putting on a skintight pink minidress and a pair of hand-me-down yellow heels – two sizes too big – she began gyrating in the mirror the way the girls in the lap-dancing clubs taught her.

The mirror was a triangular shard not much bigger

than a dinner plate. Angel had to keep adjusting its angle on the tea chest serving as her dressing table and repeat the dance routine to analyze her moves top and bottom. She fantasized about the day she would be old enough and suitably accomplished to work the poles herself.

A bottle of cedar oil perfume she had bought from a Moroccan in the Várzea quarter sat alongside an Afro comb and a pair of earrings on the purple, sequined headscarf draped over the tea chest for decoration. Angel shook a drop of the oily, woody-scented essence onto her fingertip and rubbed it behind each ear, intending to make the tiny amount of perfume in the small but deceptively bulbous bottle last. It was the only fragrance she had ever owned, and buying it used up all her savings. The earrings were a cheap mock-gold hooped affair. Angel inserted one into her left piercing without a problem, but the right lobe was infected and swollen, and having located the hole, she forced the dirty wire through, resulting in a trickle of pus and blood running down her neck.

Angel didn't own a cell phone or a watch but could tell from the growing darkness that it was time to leave the slum and meet Cobra on Rua Ribeiro in the red-light district near to the harbor.

- 65 -

Penny opened the door of the villa to find her dripping-wet boyfriend on the doormat.

"Hans! I was worried!" She threw her arms around him. "What happened, and why are you so wet?"

"Would you believe me if I told you I've just swum ashore from Eddy Logan's boat?"

"What?" came the expected reply.

"Let me get out of these clothes, and I'll tell you all about it. And if there's a beer going spare, I wouldn't say no."

Hans went into the bathroom and, after taking his wallet and cell phone out of the resealable bag Logan gave him, threw his clothes in the tub. He put on a bathrobe and joined Penny in the living room.

It wasn't until they'd drunk a fourth beer and polished off half a bottle of rum that Hans finished retelling events.

Penny cupped her chin, shaking her head as she stared down at Karen's marble-tiled floor. "So, we're right back at square one."

"Afraid so, honey." Hans could see the exhausted Penny was on the verge of tears. "Let's sleep on it and come up with a plan in the morning."

Neither of them could stomach breakfast, so after a

shower and coffee Hans drove them back to the previous night's drop-off point to go and retrieve the gear from the hide. By now Hans' saran wrap package stunk to high heaven, so he placed the backpack in the rear of the jeep and wound down the windows.

"Don't ask," he told Penny, seeing her face screw up.

Hans was about to turn the ignition key when his cell rang, a Praia number he didn't recognize.

"Hans Larsson."

"Senhor Larsson, Chief Inspector Barbosa Amado. Can we meet?"

"Is this so you can arrest me?" Hans asked, with so many implicating factors buzzing through his mind – the Fulani, Alvarez, Silvestre, Mike Davenport – that he made a concerted effort to clear his head and focus on Amado's words, listening for any nuances giving a clue as to what was afoot.

"No, Hans. You have done nothing I would want to arrest you for," Amado replied. "But something has come up, and I feel it is time to share what we know. Or if you prefer, you can just listen to what I have to say."

"Do you want me to come to the station?"

"No, no! Erm, where are you now?"

"About five miles from town on the coast road east."

"Okay, then there is a turning right, about one kilometer. Fifty meters up is a bar called O Cacto, er, The Cactus. I can be there in twenty minutes."

"*And?*"

"Interpol? No, only me I promise."

- 66 -

Toweling dry after her shower, the Malian considered the clothes in her functionalist wardrobe. Not wishing to appear too smart for the evening's mission, she opted for lightweight beige pants, a dark-blue tank top, flat shoes and a cheap denim jacket. As a precaution she slipped a switchblade into her pocket and, having checked the tourist map, left the ramshackle hotel to head in the direction of Rua Ribeiro.

The woman passed by open-air bars playing upbeat folk music and taverns and tapas restaurants frequented by locals, but there was no nightclub district to speak of, most of the tourists enjoying entertainment laid on in their hotels. Although on her own in a rough part of town, the woman felt safe, and no one paid her unwanted attention. Arriving at one end of Rua Ribeiro, she decided to take a brisk walk along it to familiarize herself with the street scene. Before doing so, she entered a small convenience store, bought a soda and a loaf of bread and placed them in a plastic bag so it looked like she lived in the area. Keeping her head high and adopting a purposeful pace, she headed up the street, giving the appearance of minding her own business but taking in every movement with her peripheral vision, along with the sheer poverty of her surroundings.

The working girls weren't difficult to spot. Three, all of different ethnicity, leant against a brick wall leading off down a side street, waiting to step forward when a punter pulled up. Others – some of them white, likely Russian or Eastern European – stood on their own in doorways, hands and feet fidgety from the prework smoke of the crack pipe. There were no pimps in view, although the woman felt certain they were around, and the girls looked to be of legal age. This did not fit with her plan, so she continued down the street, and when there were no more sex workers in sight, she took a left turn at the next junction and a left again to bring her back to where she'd started.

The woman took a seat outside a café and ordered a beer. She was in no rush, and it was important to get this right. In the meantime she familiarized herself with life on Rua Ribeiro, keeping a wary eye out for anyone who might prove trouble.

An hour passed and a good many sex workers too, either arriving for work, rushing to the nearest drug dealer with their latest payment, or hurrying a car-less tourist off the street into an unlit alleyway in case the police appeared.

Finally, the woman spotted a contender. Walking several yards behind his "property" – a girl no more than fourteen wearing a skimpy pink dress and stumbling along in oversized yellow heels – the pimp had a cocky air about him and wore a black backwards-facing baseball cap on top of short dreadlocks. He had his shirt open to the waist, exposing a fake-gold medallion, and only looked to be a teenager himself. But what stood out the most was the young man's eyes. Like the woman's, they were turquoise blue and unmissable against his brown skin.

The woman watched as they continued up Rua Ribeiro and made a left down a side street. She threw a five-hundred-escudo note down on the table, picked up her shopping bag and went after them. Turning the corner, she saw the pimp and the girl arguing on the sidewalk. *Perfect*, she thought, taking out her cell phone and hitting the video mode. Then, walking down the street pretending to have a conversation, she turned the phone at a slight angle to capture the couple's dispute.

Having a Mozambican father, the woman spoke Portuguese and although not entirely fluent in Cape Verdean Creole, a variant of the mother tongue, she understood the gist of what they were shouting. Drawing level with the pair, she stopped, making no attempt to hide her actions.

Cobra continued his dressing down of Angel, having not forgiven her for mistakenly charging a tourist the locals' rate for oral sex the previous night. He backhanded her across the face, and as she fell to the ground he noticed the woman filming.

"Wha—?"

"Do you know the punishment for forcing underage girls into prostitution?" she asked in Portuguese, putting the phone back in her pocket. "Especially right now, when the police are having a major crackdown and looking for arrests."

"Fuck you," he scowled, and threw a lightning punch.

The woman blocked it with her forearm, barreling his arm downwards and gripping his thumb, levering the vulnerable digit away from his body.

Pain rocketed up the pimp's wrist, sending him crashing to the ground. "*Ah-ah-ah*, okay, okay!" he screamed.

Angel watched in astonishment, then, contemplating the beating Cobra would give her for not coming to his aid, she took a step forward.

"Don't even think about it, *amiga!*" the woman warned, stopping a high kick short of Angel's nose.

The girl looked to Cobra for direction. He shook his head rapidly, his eyes saying the consequences would be painful for both of them.

"Okay, I'm going to let go, but if you try anything funny you have my word I will break your arm."

"Sure, sure," Cobra replied, the thought of no more pain far outweighing the humiliation he'd received.

The woman released her hold.

"Arrh!" He shook his arm out. "So who are you – a cop or something?"

"I'm in the same business as you."

"Yeah?" He eyed her in disbelief.

"Yeah," the woman replied, pulling a photo of one of the orphans from the pocket of her denim jacket. "See this girl?"

"Uh-huh." Cobra massaged his wrist.

"There are many more in my care, and I'm looking to trade."

"Why you telling *me* this?"

"Because I need to see the Man."

"Which man?" Cobra tried to get smart.

"That's up to you. But if it's not someone I can do business with, then the video in this phone" – she tapped her pocket – "will be on the vice squad's desk first thing tomorrow morning, and I will write a full statement about what I saw tonight and then testify in court."

Cobra and Angel made eye contact, unable to hide their nerves, the girl about to burst into tears any moment.

"What jail term are we talking for pimping a minor – five to seven years?" the woman said and tutted. "That's if you don't get shanked by a fellow prisoner for preying on a child."

"Okay, okay, I'll speak to my boss," Cobra pacified her. "He knows a guy. How can I get hold of you?"

"Room Eighteen, Pensão Lisboa. Ask for Brenda Umchima."

- 67 -

O Cacto was the most authentic establishment Hans and Penny had visited on Cape Verde, with none of the glitz or faux-culture associated with the touristy places. Not much more than a wooden shack, it was reminiscent of a truck stop out West, though with bare floorboards and rust-blemished road signs adorning the walls – genuine signs and not the Route 66 type bought off the Internet – it was a deal humbler.

Hans and Penny took up seats at a table by the window. After ten minutes it became obvious the man wearing a white cotton tank top and eyeing them with suspicion from behind the bar wasn't going to take their order, so Penny went up and asked for a beer and a bottle of mineral water. The barman made a show of taking his time, refusing to look Penny in the eye, and then slapping the change down on the graffiti-engraved bar.

"Who says racism's only for white folks." She handed Hans his beer.

"Probably not so much racism but a distinct dislike of spoilt tourists," Hans replied, having witnessed this kind of behavior before.

If it weren't for recent events, both would have got a kick out of being off the beaten track. As it was, they were happy when Amado arrived, bursting out of a Hawaiian shirt and driving what must have been his own dusty white jalopy.

"Hans, Miss Penny." He shook hands and sat down, still looking as flustered as the time they met him at the airport. "Boy!" He clicked his fingers at the barman, who dropped the ashtray he was wiping and ran over to their table.

Hans felt a touch of panic, worrying this notable difference in service was to do with Amado being a police officer and that the meeting wasn't as hush-hush as he'd hoped. But he soon relaxed, remembering it was Africa's class system in play, Amado having a significantly lighter skin tone than his compatriot.

"Three more beers," Amado spat in English over his shoulder, purposely not giving the barman his full attention. Then, "Hans, I gather you spoke with Mr. Davenport about a man named Logan."

"And?" Hans remained noncommittal.

"I'm sorry, Hans. I did not mean to interrogate you. Just to say that a search of Logan's place turned up nothing of any significance. We took a load of paperwork and a computer away to see if our detectives can come up with—"

"You'll be wasting your time." Hans' tone spoke for him.

"Yes, yes, exactly." Amado mopped his brow with a handkerchief, then took a slug of beer. "I am throwing myself at your mercy, Hans."

From the bags under Amado's eyes, they could see he was exhausted.

"Barbosa, my mercy has pretty much drawn a blank,"

said Hans. "You're the insider here. You must have come up with *something*."

"We have a lot of people on this case. Interpol are guiding us through the process, and we have the British police lending support."

"But?" Hans spoke into the neck of his bottle before taking a swig.

"Friends, I was born and brought up on these islands. I've been a police officer for twenty-six years. I have a good idea of the people who are responsible for abducting your daughter, but there are other powers at work."

"Other powers?" said Hans.

Amado squirmed, gripping his thighs and scanning the empty bar. "Yes, *other*." He put his hand down by the side of the table and made the sign of the horns.

Hans nodded and gave Penny an *I'll explain later* look.

"You must understand, Hans, these are evil people in high places who are not about to let a tired old cop expose them. They play by their own rules, and my life means nothing to them." He wrung his hands, attempting to look apologetic.

"Amado, if you don't tell me who this is, then *I* will kill you." Hans' face darkened as he leaned over the table. "And that's whether I get my daughter back or not."

"If after a lifetime in law enforcement I cannot do my rightful job, then there is no point to live. So please, I will approach my superiors one last time – later today – and if I don't get the right response I will tell you everything. This is my promise. But I have a question for you."

"Shoot." Hans reached down for Penny's hand, and

she squeezed it in return.

"In your inquiries, have you come across this woman?"

He passed them a profile picture taken off a website. Penny looked at it for no more than a second before shrugging and shaking her head. Hans had no idea either.

"Her name is Brenda Umchima, the manager of an orphanage in Gambia. She's on Cape Verde attempting to make contact with *os traficantes*, er—"

"The traffickers," Penny muttered.

"How do you know all this?" asked Hans.

"Our vice squad pulled in a girl last night, a fourteen-year-old prostitute from the slums. Her pimp ran off and left the poor kid terrified. She – how you say? – squawked, no?"

Hans nodded.

"Said she had information if we released her from the cells and gave us this woman." He nodded to the photograph. "She's looking for a contact in the trafficking and staying at the Pensão Lisboa."

"Have you checked her out?" Hans asked.

"There's nothing on record for Umchima, either local or international, so I searched the Internet and found her details on a website for a children's home in Kankaba."

"Did you pull in the pimp?"

"Calls himself Cobra Azul – Blue Snake. My detective traced him to a house in the slums, but his kid sisters hadn't seen him. We have an informant living two doors down who's going to let us know if he returns."

"Is your informant reliable?" said Hans.

"When it comes to crack addicts, they're more reliable than anyone when a bribe's at stake."

"Can I take that picture?"

"Sure." Amado pushed it across the table.

- 68 -

Brenda Umchima awoke late in the humble hotel room. She groped under the pillow for her switchblade, dropped it into her toiletry bag and headed for the shower. If everything went to plan, the traffickers would be onto her already, although she didn't feel in danger at present. Skilled in the art of subterfuge, these people wouldn't neutralize a player without first ascertaining their identity to establish the level of threat that existed.

Umchima posed no danger to the traffickers. She was exactly the sort of twisted individual they sought to do business with, someone with a conflict of identity resulting from a lifetime of oppression through being different, someone feeling bitter, insecure and unworthy. Brenda Umchima had been victimized all her life for her skin and eye color and mixed parentage, her Mozambican father branded an outsider in Mali who got lucky by marrying a rich, white *toubab* wife.

Umchima threw open the louver doors to the balcony and stepped outside into glorious sunshine. She stretched her arms above her head and yawned in a show of obliviousness and contentment, yet immediately spotted the man in a shiny black BMW attempting to park innocuously – though failing miserably in this impoverished borough – a few yards up the street.

The Malian went back into the room, grinning in satisfaction. She had her in, and being the manager of a shabby orphanage in the back end of beyond was about to pay dividends. Purposely leaving the balcony doors open, she placed the laptop containing information about her role in the orphanage on the rough wooden table and left the Pensão Lisboa for a celebratory brunch.

Walking in the direction of the new town, Umchima took out a compact and dabbed her cheeks with foundation. She hardly ever wore makeup – with frizzy brown hair bleached into highlights by the African sun, and stunning blue eyes accentuated by golden skin and natural eyebrows, she possessed a beauty a lot of women yearn for – but the compact's mirror allowed her a snatch view of the BMW's occupant. It was a bald tough guy with a goatee beard who looked as though he'd been around the block a few times.

Fifty yards from the hotel, she noticed a white man and woman sat chatting in a jeep parked on the other side of the road. It had a yellow Hertz rental logo on the license plate, piquing her interest, since this wasn't a tourist area. She made a mental note of the registration number and hailed a cab, wishing to put time and distance between her and the hotel, for it wasn't hard to predict the trafficker's next move.

"Here," Umchima told the cabdriver as they pulled onto Praia's seafront, having picked the first establishment advertising breakfast.

She ordered a *cachupa* stew of bananas, vegetables, pork sausage and bacon, and to calm her nerves, a bottle of local beer.

The meal arrived, but with a million thoughts

occupying her mind, Umchima had no appetite. She reflected on her past, the orphanage and the Trade, running through an escape plan in case things turned sour. She reached into the pocket of her denim jacket and took out her cell phone but paused, as if realizing something, then went up to the bar and asked the barman the whereabouts of the restroom. When the Malian returned, she sat back down and made a call.

After an hour and two more beers, Umchima stopped pushing lumps of banana and sausage around the plate and paid the check. At the Pensão Lisboa, she walked past the sleeping concierge, who remained blissfully unaware of events going on around him, and went up to her room. Upon opening the door, she smiled. The laptop was missing from the rough wooden table.

- 69 -

While Penny typed "Pensão Lisboa, Praia" into the satnav, Hans drove toward the city. He didn't hold out much hope that tracking down Brenda Umchima would turn up any new leads – with respect to the Trade, she was obviously looking for a connection herself – but with nothing else on his detective itinerary, he thought he might as well check her out.

The area the satnav directed them to cast further doubt. Any person staying in a run-down location such as this had to be a chancer attempting to make a fanciful buck.

"Rua Michelle, next left." Penny pointed at the satnav screen, its synthesized voice telling them to turn into the street and that the destination was on the right.

"Would have been quite the place in its day," Hans mused, taking in the rotting palm trees along Rua Michelle's central reservation, their drooping fronds blackened by car fumes and volcanic dust.

"Agreed," said Penny, eyeing the gray, cracked whitewash on the palms' once-dazzling trunks and the forlorn state of the colonial buildings.

"That's the place there." Hans pointed out the old hotel, stopping the jeep fifty yards before it.

"What's the plan?" Penny pulled down the sun visor.

"I was hoping you had one." Hans sighed, staring at the hotel's entrance, awaiting inspiration.

"Oh honey." She buried her head in his neck.

Hans looked at the photograph Amado had taken off the orphanage's website. "I guess we wait and see if this woman turns up. Perhaps something will come to me."

They didn't have to wait long. Hans tapped Penny on the leg as he spotted a beautiful bronze-skinned woman with frizzy, sun-bleached brown hair leave the building. She began walking at a brisk pace in their direction but on the other side of the street.

"Okay, pretend we're chatting, but hide your face behind me," said Hans, turning his back to the window as the woman passed.

"She's flagging down a cab." Penny realized she was whispering, watching the action out of the corner of her eye.

"Is this one stopping?" Hans asked calmly as a taxi drove by.

"Yes, she's getting inside."

"Then I guess we should follow."

Hans fired up the engine and made a U-turn through a gap in the red-and-white-striped curbstones protecting the palm beds. Keeping a discreet distance, he tailed the cab to the seafront, where its driver stopped at the first restaurant and let the woman out.

Hans pulled up behind a parked truck a hundred yards away. He waited until the woman entered the establishment and took a seat at a table out front and then fetched the sniper spotting scope from the rucksack in the trunk and ditched the package of crap in the nearest garbage bin.

"Well, she's not stupid," Hans remarked as he observed through the scope. "She's sitting in a chair facing the sidewalk."

"Do you think she's expecting someone?" asked Penny.

"No, she's keeping an eye on anyone walking past or entering the place. She's taken the table nearest the bar so no one can sit behind her."

"She could be paranoid," Penny remarked with a giggle.

"You know what they say about paranoia?" said Hans.

"Go on."

"If you think you're paranoid, you probably have every reason to be."

Hans watched as the woman reached into the pocket of her denim jacket and took out a cell phone. She paused, as if remembering something, then went up to the bar, spoke briefly to the barman and disappeared into the back. When she returned, she sat back down and made a call.

Clever, Hans mused, but didn't say anything.

There was nothing to gain by observing the woman any longer, and Hans didn't want to risk her seeing the jeep a second time, so he U-turned and drove back to the villa, needing peace and quiet and time to think. He also needed a beer, plus both of them were hungry, having skipped breakfast.

- 70 -

For the umpteenth time in three days, Brenda Umchima walked out onto the balcony to check the street below.

Bingo!

The BMW had returned, looking completely out of place on the forlorn boulevard, confirming the thickset bald guy in the driver's seat was a trafficker and that Umchima had her in.

She left the hotel and crossed the street. The trafficker held the door open, and she climbed into the backseat. Once she was inside, he turned and shoved a pistol in her face.

"He wants to meet you, but if you fuck with us, then this bullet has your name on it. *Entiendes*?"

"*Sí*," the woman told the Spaniard – of course she understood. But as they drove east along the coast road, she still contemplated how to kill him if things turned nasty – a stranglehold or simply sticking the switchblade into his neck or through an eye socket.

A couple of miles from the city the man pulled over and, with a wave of the pistol, ordered Umchima out. He patted her down at the roadside, finding the cell phone, switchblade, her passport and a small wallet. He smiled at the stiletto – a precaution he could relate to – then placed it in his pocket and thumbed through the contents of the wallet. There were business cards with her contact details at the orphanage stamped on them in simple black lettering, a Visa debit card, a Gambian driving license and some of the money she'd converted at the airport. He handed everything back to Umchima but the switchblade, then took a black hood from the driver's-door compartment and pulled it roughly over her head.

"In," he ordered, forcing her to lie down on the backseat.

Umchima expected this and wasn't overly concerned. She began counting to sixty in her head, making a note of the minutes that passed with her fingers and concentrating on the changes in the road surface and gradient and the car's turns. After an uphill climb, meaning they were heading inland, she heard the crunch of rubber on gravel and sensed from the lack of breeze and an echo that they had entered a large enclosed forecourt.

"Out."

The trafficker manhandled her from the car and into a building, slamming a heavy door behind them. It was cool inside. Umchima felt solid stone tiles under her feet and smelled the odor of antique furnishings. She guessed it was a precolonial build and the owner an established figure not short of money – hardly surprising with the revenue the Trade generated.

The man grabbed her arm and shoved her along a long hall, down a flight of steep steps into a room she sensed was small and windowless. Having steered her into a chair, he pulled off the blindfold. Another man –

sprightly, with slicked-back white hair and a short-clipped gray beard – sat in the feeble glow of a bare lightbulb. He stared at her across a simple metal-framed office desk. With the exception of two chairs, there was no other furniture in the room, only an expensive-looking computer, which seemed out of place in the damp and moldy surroundings.

Curiosity evident in his birdlike eyes, her host remained silent a while before speaking in near-perfect but accented English.

"So, you have met Fernando. He is – how can we say? – my butler, chauffeur, aide-de-camp. Naturally, he is also somewhat protective of our little operation and of me, no? He was once Sargento Chavez, when he and I were soldiers. We have been through rather a lot together. Er, English is okay?"

"English, Portuguese, French, Bambara, Mandinka . . ."

"If we are to do business together, I feel it is best to use English. Besides, my Mandinka is a little rusty, no?" He smiled. "But tell me, how come the manager of an orphanage in Gambia speaks so many languages?"

"How do you know I'm the manager of an orphanage in Gambia?"

The man reached into a drawer and held up her laptop. "I have taken the liberty of reading your files and Internet history. It all checks out – but for security you shouldn't leave yourself logged into your email."

He handed the laptop to Umchima and then turned his computer's screen around to show the orphanage's webpage.

"Then you will know from my staff profile I was born in Mali to an American mother and Mozambican father

– and of course it helps to speak French in a French-speaking country."

"Yes, yes, but we couldn't find any official records relating to your parents, only an entry for you on the Ministry of Justice's website. It hasn't been updated since 2011 – I'm assuming because of the collapse of democracy following the rebel takeover."

"Correct. My parents were Christian missionaries, murdered in the initial uprising when the Islamists forced sharia law on the North. As a government official I was on the Tuareg's kill list, so I escaped through Senegal to seek asylum in Gambia."

"Terrible, terrible," the man muttered. "But tell me, if your mother was American, why you did not flee to the USA on your American passport?"

"I've never owned an American passport," Umchima spoke with venom. "I am African, and I will live and die in Africa. When the fighting is over, I will retake my rightful place in government and work to rebuild *my* country."

"It's okay," said the man, his smile warming as the conversation unfolded. "I know you don't have a US passport – I have contacts in high places. But tell me, why do you want to trade in *los niños*?"

"Children – why not? What other life can they have? When they leave the orphanage, someone will try to exploit them for financial gain – either that or they'll end up living on the street with a drug problem, prostituting themselves to survive. I know that you have the connections to send them to a new life in Europe."

"This is true, but you must understand their new life can be even harder there. Do you know what I am saying?"

"*Senhor*!" Umchima glared into his strange flitting eyes. "I watched my parents dragged into the street and mutilated, screaming as they burned to death wrapped in gas-soaked car tires. I know hardship, and I know life is not fair. But if one or two children sacrifice themselves so we can prosper, how can that not be worth it?"

"*Exactamente*!" The man beamed, but then his demeanor changed abruptly. "Just one last thing."

The brute Fernando stepped forward with the woman's cell phone.

"Call up your orphanage and say hi." A reptilian blink appeared to flicker across the man's cagey green eyes. "And use the loudspeaker so we all can listen."

"Okay," she replied, thumbing the phone's keypad and then placing it on the desktop.

It rang . . . and rang and rang.

The man's face twisted into a sneer. "So, there is no—"

"*Kairabe*, Kankaba Dindinoly Dimbaayaa," the voice of the secretary came over the speaker, greeting the caller with the name of the orphanage.

"Isatou! How many times have I told you to answer the phone in English?" Umchima reprimanded the woman for speaking Mandinka and not the national language.

"Miss Brenda!" the secretary replied, giggling in delight. "How is the life in Banjul?"

"The capital is busy, Isatou, and smelly," Umchima replied, having lied to the staff about the destination and purpose of her trip.

"And did you manage to raise more funding for us?" the secretary shouted above the noise of the children running around yelling in the background.

"I am working on it, Isatou." Umchima gripped a fold in her pant leg with her free hand. "I have a meeting with the Red Cross this afternoon. And how are the children?"

"Musa ran away."

"Don't worry. Musa is a street child. He will always run away."

"Nyima has the fever, and a man arrived saying he was Llana's uncle and removed her. Shall I call the police?"

"The police will only want a bribe and then do nothing to find her. Has Nyima seen the doctor?"

"Yes. Sister Ungjina took her this morning. She is with me now. I will pass the telephone."

"Hello, Brenda," the nun greeted her, and then screamed at the children to keep the noise down.

"Sister Unjina, how is Nyima?"

"Ah, the doctor says she will live! How is the big city?"

"The city is fine, Sister, but I must go now and meet another charity. Will you be okay until I get back?"

"*Yeeess* . . . of course we will be okay! Take care in Banjul. It is a very dangerous place. And may God walk with you."

"And with you too, Sister – oh!"

"What is it?"

"Please tell Isatou she must answer the telephone in English."

While Penny fired up the gas-assisted barbecue, Hans stripped to his boxers and dove off the patio wall into the Atlantic's inviting aquamarine water. A passionate reader of all things adventure since childhood, he'd long followed the practice of the South Pacific Islanders, who believe in going for a swim when faced with hardship or crisis. His powerful front crawl saw him half a mile offshore in eight minutes, where he floated on his back, emptying his mind and feeling the movement of the sea and the sun's warmth on his skin.

When Hans experienced complete relaxation, he turned his thoughts back to the investigation. Sherlock Holmes once said when you have eliminated the impossible, whatever remains, however improbable, must be the truth, so rather than cluttering his mind going over old ground, such as Logan's boat and bank accounts, he focused on the discrepancies in the case – the missing links between all the events. If only he could work out the connection, it would expose those lurking in the shadows, revealing the kingpin and leading to his daughter's return.

Everything pointed to someone who knew the Fulani, someone she would invite willingly into her home, someone who knew Alvarez and had the means to blow his boat to kingdom come. Someone who knew Logan – at least well enough to have his cell phone number – to warn him Hans was breaking into his boat. Someone who had spoken to Silvestre and learned of the plan to dive on the wreck of the Rosa Negra . . .

The problem was these people were all so unconnected that any theory Hans came up with was instantly doubtful, any suspect immediately expunged by the sheer implausibility of it all.

Larsson, stop!

Hans had let his mind go into overdrive. Instead, he went back to the beginning, starting with the car tailing him on Mindelo the night the Fulani was murdered. The yellow tag on the license plate had to be a Hertz logo. It couldn't have been a car leased out without the rental agency logging it on the database, because they only had two E-Class Mercedes, and Jonah accounted for both hirers at the time.

Impossible . . . impossible. Floating on his back with the midday sun directly overhead, he crossed off hypotheses in his head. *Impossible . . . impossible . . . impossible . . . Yes!*

The answer stared him in the face – the midday sun!

Improbable, but not impossible!

He rolled onto his front and began hauling himself through the water to reach the shore.

Penny waited on the rocks with a towel.

"What is it?" she asked, having seen this look on Hans' face before.

"I need to call Jonah," he panted, rushing up the steps to the villa.

"Won't he be asleep?" she called after him.

"That's the problem!" he yelled back. "He's nocturnal!"

Hans picked his pants off the patio wall and took out his cell phone. He hit Jonah's number, praying the night owl would still be awake. Midday on Cape Verde meant it was 5:00 a.m. in Los Angeles.

"Orion, dude!" Jonah's Aspergic monotone made him sound the least likely candidate for a surf bum, his condition allowing Hans to cut to the chase without fear of offense.

"Odysseus, the info you gave me from the rental agency's database."

"Hertz – both the E-Class Mercedes were rented out on the night in question. One to a French lady and—"

"Yeah, yeah, I know. But what night was it?"

"Orion, it was around midnight here when you called – er, you asked for last night's records, so the twenty-fifth I think."

"Odysseus, did you pull info for the twenty-sixth?"

"No, dude, only what you asked me for."

"Listen, I need you to get me the names of whoever hired the Mercs on the twenty-sixth."

"Okay, but if their administrator's found the backdoor I programmed into their software, it might take a bit of time to hack into the database."

"Just get back to me as soon as you can, huh? Code Zero. It's really important."

"Your wish is my job, Orion," Jonah replied, knowing Code Zero meant urgent, like *yesterday.*

As Hans ended the call, he could have kicked himself for such an amateurish error – *Damn!*

"What's wrong, hon?" Penny placed a hand on his

arm.

"I messed up. Do you remember when I called Jonah from the airport the morning after the Mercedes followed me, asking him to hack the records from Hertz?"

"How could I forget – the day after the Fulani woman was murdered and a fishing boat exploded in my face!"

"I asked him for the records for *last night*. I was forgetting LA is six hours behind – seven with daylight saving."

"So he would have thought you meant the previous evening."

"Exactly! His Asperger's means he takes everything literally and wouldn't have questioned it."

"Hans, you really are quite some detective."

"Yeah, I'm a regular Sherlock Holmes."

- 72 -

Satisfied with the background checks and reassured by the phone call to the orphanage in Gambia, the man invited Umchima to spend the day with him. He led her out of the dingy underground office and up a flight of stairs into one of his castle's many hallways.

"Wow! Are you the King of Cape Verde?" she joked, gazing at the ye-olde artwork and historical paraphernalia adorning the impressive stone corridor.

"I am the mayor of Praia," he announced with an air of self-importance. "Would you like to walk around the grounds, Senhorita Umchima?"

"I would love to, er . . . ?"

"Videl . . . Videl Gonzales, but call me Videl please."

"Thank you, Videl, and call me Brenda."

She tilted her head flirtatiously and for a brief moment looked deep into his eyes.

A pair of yapping Jack Russells joined them on the tour, during which Gonzales showed her the former servant's quarters, still recognizable but now renovated and lived in by Fernando. They passed through what would once have been the soldiers' barracks and entered the great hall, which was too large to suit any modern domestic purpose and empty of furnishings, bar an aging maroon carpet. Gonzales then showed Umchima the antique cannons lining the courtyard out front.

They sat on a bench, looking out over the rock and scrub on the hillside to the cobalt-blue sea beyond, discussing the logistical and financial aspects of their newfound partnership. Gonzales, despite a penchant for prostitutes and young boys, felt a stirring at the thought of the "other" partnership occupying his mind, his lust heightened by the power he held over this beautiful woman.

The plan they came up with was simple. Every couple of months a handler would collect a child from the orphanage to transit down the River Gambia by passenger boat. Because of the system of extended family in Africa, it would be unlikely to raise suspicion. Besides, few people carried any form of checkable ID, and corruption ran rife amongst police and officials. The handler would have more than enough cash to grease greedy palms should the need arise.

In Banjul, Gonzales' connections would traffic the kids by speedboat via the Canaries to Europe, or bring them to Praia while a sham adoption and the relevant documentation were organized.

"What if a speedboat gets intercepted by the coastguard?" Umchima wrung her hands.

"The kids are shackled to a concrete block, and at the first sign of trouble they follow the block to the bottom of the ocean."

"Good." Umchima gave a slow and satisfied nod. "And what if a trade falls through for any reason?"

"There is still good money to be made selling children here on the islands – begging syndicates and factory labor – and some of our curb crawlers and sex tourists like them young." Gonzales' lips curled into a slight but heinous smile.

"So I have seen." Umchima returned it.

"Anyway, enough business talk for one day. Are you hungry?"

The mayor stood up and offered his hand.

"I've had nothing since breakfast." Umchima grasped it without hesitation.

"Then we must go and see what Fernando has prepared for us. He is a little dumb, but his food is the finest."

The mayor led Umchima to the dining room, where Fernando had laid two settings at one end of the long polished table and stood waiting to pour drinks.

"Cordornìu." The mayor held up the cork to display a black four-pointed star, the symbol of a true Spanish cava. "So much crisper than champagne, don't you think?"

"I will have to take your word for it, Videl." Umchima flushed a little, too embarrassed to make eye contact. "I can't say I've ever drunk cava, and I doubt the bubbly served at government functions in Mali is of the quality you are used too."

"Well, we must rectify that, mustn't we?" Gonzales ran a finger up Umchima's cheek, his smile still indistinguishable from a sneer.

She took his finger gently in her hands and kissed it, adding a playful wink, since this was a man who could get her results, and she wasn't about to upset him.

Fernando entered carrying a tray of traditional Cape Verdean starters. "*Pastel com o Diablo dentro,*" he announced, setting down plates of pastries filled with devil-hot chilies, tomato paste, onion and garlic.

"Please enjoy," Gonzales urged. "But tell me, how did you end up managing an orphanage in the Gambia?"

"My parents lived in a small town in the north of Mali near Timbuktu. After they were murdered, I fled west. There were thousands on the road, all heading for a refugee camp in Mauritania, but word came back the camp was overflowing and many were dying of malnourishment and disease, so I headed for Senegal. It was a long, tough journey. I joined a family, and we had to avoid the main roads for fear of rebel checkpoints. We walked for many days, stopping in the villages and begging for water and food. Finally, I crossed into Gambia. I knew former Malian officials who now lived in the capital, but when I got as far as Kankaba, the nuns at the orphanage took me in and insisted I stay until I got my strength back. It was a good life – living by the river, getting over the loss of my parents, helping out with the kids, free from the stress of government."

The mayor opened a bottle of Tinta Roriz 1978 as he listened.

"The nuns were kind but they knew nothing of funding, promotion or social media. When I helped out, they begged me to stay and suggested I become manager, so I applied for a residential permit."

"And you haven't gone back?" Gonzales began filling Umchima's glass.

"How can I go back? The Mali military overthrew the government, and at the same time the rebels joined forces with the Islamists to take control of the North. In the meantime al-Qaeda and other extremist networks have established themselves in the country. What was initially a straightforward issue of land rights has turned into a civil and religious war."

"You have every right to feel bitter."

"I've lost my parents, my roots and everything I worked hard for."

"Then" – Gonzales raised his glass – "we must drink to you getting it back."

Umchima lifted her wine and, with a dreamy smile, gazed around at the palatial setting. "We must, Videl. I think I could get used to this life."

Fernando removed the plates from their starters and returned with a large silver tureen. He peeled off the lid and began ladling a delicious-looking yellow stew on their plates.

"Hmm, what is it?" Umchima looked at the butler and smiled.

"*Rondon, senhorita,*" Fernando grunted, and disappeared.

"*Rondon*?" Umchima turned to the mayor.

"A Nicaraguan recipe, one of my and Fernando's favorites." He ladled a huge helping onto her plate. "Breadfruit, sweet potato, banana, yucca, coconut, onion and lobster."

"And the sauce?"

"Chicken stock flavored with garlic, green herbs and lime juice."

"It looks amazing."

"I will drink to that." Gonzales raised his glass.

By the time they finished dessert – sweet papaya cooked with cloves, cinnamon and lemon – Umchima felt on the drunken side of tipsy. This didn't stop Gonzales opening a bottle of port and pouring glass after glass while flattering her in true Hispanic style.

"Videl, a girl might think you were trying to get her drunk." Umchima gave a cheeky flutter of her eyebrows.

"It is a long time since I had such a fine woman's company to get drunk in. I hope you are not planning to eat and leave." He placed a hand on top of hers on the white satin tablecloth.

"Is that an invitation to stay the night?" She put on a churlish look.

"I feel it would be more comfortable for you than a run-down guesthouse."

"Then how could I say no?" She giggled and leant forward for the kiss.

Hans and Penny spent the rest of day at the villa, soaking up the sun, barbecuing mackerel kebabs and going over the missing pieces in the jigsaw in search of a smoking gun. Late afternoon, Hans received a call from Innes Edridge, his handler in Boston.

"Orion, dear boy, just to let you know the glasses you sent for fingerprinting finally turned up and I've sent them to ForTech, overnight delivery, with an instruction we need the results Code Zero."

Based in a state-of-the-art building in Phoenix, ForTech was a forensics laboratory under contract with the Arizona Department of Public Safety. However, unbeknown to the many law enforcement divisions under the DPS's umbrella, the Concern owned ForTech, and many of its staff were operatives.

"Muttley, this is great news."

"Don't raise your hopes, Orion. Even if they can raise a decent print, there's no guarantee anything comes back from AFIS."

He referred to the Automated Fingerprint Identification System, an electronic gateway allowing law enforcement agencies in member countries to submit search requests to an international fingerprint database managed by Interpol. Naturally, ForTech had end-user access.

"Muttley," said Hans, "following the Logan debacle, one thing I won't be doing is raising my hopes."

"Good chap. I've also spoken with our ballistics man about the detonator cap."

"And?"

"Confirmed what he told us before – US military grade, but available to commercial operations worldwide. He says the salt mines in Cape Verde order thousands of the bloody things."

"Gotcha." Hans hid his disappointment. "On a positive note I had an error in comms with Odysseus over the rental of the hire car. He's gonna get back to me with a fresh set of data. It's possible another name turns up."

"Bear in mind they could have used a fake driving license and credit card," his handler warned.

"I don't think so. That would have taken time to organize, and whoever this person was they were onto me right away."

"I hear you."

"Any news on Triton and Achelous?" Hans mentally crossed his fingers.

"They should be with you in forty-eight hours. If you need someone sooner, say the word, and I can be on the Lear tonight."

"That's very kind of you, sir."

"She's my goddaughter, Hans. Carter comes first, but family comes a close second."

"Thank you, sir."

Hans ended the call.

As Hans relayed the conversation, Penny didn't need

to see the strain on his face to know how much rested on the fingerprint results and Jonah's second hacking of the Hertz database. They couldn't act until they heard anything, so "Let's go fishing," she suggested.

"Er." Hans worried there was something to do.

"Come on! Let's chuck some beers in the boat, grab Karen's fishing poles and see if we can catch a monster with the leftover mackerel."

Hans knew Penny deserved a break from the constant stress too. "Catcher of the biggest fish gets breakfast in bed?" he suggested.

"If you don't mind cooking." Penny winked, running a finger up his chest and pretend-poking him in the eye.

Hans grabbed the beers and rum and rowed out into the channel as Penny cut the mackerel into strips.

"Here's good," he said, shipping the oars.

Using hefty leads and stainless-steel hooks, they set up paternoster rigs and, making sure to keep a thumb on the spool to prevent the line from bird's-nesting, lowered them over the side.

"Good idea of yours, Penny." Hans gazed at the spectacular pink and orange sprays firing up the lilac sky.

"Yeah, we should have left a note saying 'Gone Fishing'!"

"Up until this last eighteen months it was always the answer to life's problems. Chuck a line in the water, crack open a beer, and if you caught a fish it was an additional bonus. Now . . ." Hans' shoulders slumped.

"Honey, there's a big difference between 'problems' and the life-changing events you've had to go through."

Penny hated seeing Hans beat himself up.

"Yeah, I know. When I was in the life raft with Jessie . . ." Hans stopped himself.

"It's okay. I know what you mean." Penny swapped hands on the fishing pole to lean across and squeeze his arm.

"When I was in the life raft *thinking* I was with Jessie, I promised myself if we ever got rescued I would give everything up – the house, the business, the Concern – and buy an RV and travel the country. You know, seeing the sights, sleeping under the stars, grilling the fish we caught on an open fire."

Hans reached for the beers and handed one to Penny.

"No, I'll stick with the Sprite."

"Oh, okay. You haven't had a beer all day?"

"Good to have a break every now and then."

"Yeah, it is – what was I saying? Oh yeah, it seems ironic that we *were* rescued, and yet the nightmare's even worse now."

"Worse, but you will find her. I know you will."

"Thanks, Penny." Hans forced a smile, then unscrewed the rum and gulped from the bottle.

"Do you ever think you could give it up – the Concern, I mean?"

"Ha, it's funny. We used to have the exact same discussion in the military. Like, how can you *leave*, man? There's *no* jobs out there, you gotta *great* career, and all this kinda stuff. In the Concern it's known as Buying the Chains."

"Explain." Penny sipped her Sprite.

"You know, like when the slaves on the plantations gave up the fight, stopped trying to escape and going against their masters' wishes, because buying into their own oppression actually became an easier option."

"If you can't beat 'em, join 'em, you mean?"

"Exactly. The difference being, in the military you're wearing the chains. You're owned by Uncle Sam and used and abused for the Illuminati's sick agenda. Getting out ain't a bad option." Hans pretended to spit into the water.

"And working for the Concern is the other way around?"

"In the Concern you feel like you're doing something worthwhile, like you're working for the benefit of mankind. No one's trying to make off you. You're not sitting in a crummy office typing irrelevant bullshit into a computer all day long to make some creep rich, while he gives you two weeks a year to spend with your family and a crummy watch at the end of forty-five years."

"I guess I've been lucky." Penny smiled, thinking of a life spent on the ocean.

"Damn right you have! Sailing this beautiful planet, meeting folks from all cultures, and the only damage you're doing is leaving a few bubbles in your wake."

"Have you always thought like this?" Penny's curiosity kicked in.

"Hell no! Remember I told you after I left the SEALs everything went downhill – started drinking, fighting, getting sacked from god-awful jobs by jumped-up managers, wondering what the hell this life was all about?"

"Uh-huh – before you met Kerry."

"I hit rock bottom. When there's no more way down, you either stay there and die or you learn your way back up. All that stuff they indoctrinated you with at school, like it's good to be a doctor or a lawyer or a goddamn whatever, and all that stuff your parents tried to instill in you – respect authority, play by the rules, mow the lawn on Sunday, go to a bullshit church and vote in some phony-baloney political system – you gotta *un*learn that stuff. You gotta do in your heart what you know is right, follow your own path, realize it's all a big game put in place by a twisted ruling elite that only cares about money and power, who've been playing it since the time of the pyramids and know just how to sucker you in."

"The Coca-Cola dream," Penny chuckled.

"Ha! Do you know the average American thinks drinking that stuff is actually good for them?"

"And did Kerry feel strongly about this stuff too?"

"Acht . . . I loved Kerry. She came along in my life when I had nothing else, and I wouldn't be here today if she hadn't. I never tried to change her. But she thought by putting a link on Facebook she could help achieve world peace."

"Tphuh!" Penny choked on her Sprite. "So, I'm guessing life in a sleepy suburb is not for you, Mr. Larsson."

"Penny, I'm trying to say that *yes*, maybe one day I'd be happy to give up the Concern, accept a life of obscurity and hightail it around the good ol' US of A in a camper with my daughter—"

"Er-hum!"

"Sorry, with the lovely *Penny* and my daughter, but I . . ." Hans fell silent, the thought of Jessica spawning a pang of anxiety bringing him abruptly back to reality.

Penny understood. Constantly being in limbo was hard for both of them, but for Hans it didn't end there.

Circumventing the system by conducting his own investigation, he'd taken sole responsibility for Jessica's safe return.

They fell silent awhile, sipping beer, jigging the lines up and down and watching the city's lights come on as the sky turned to graphite.

"It's just . . . look at us here now, Penny. If it weren't for the circumstances, would you wanna be anywhere else? A beer, a hook in the water, fresh air, the rise and fall of the sea and an incredible view. To think most kids today will never get to experience being in a boat, let alone casting a line or gutting a fish, but it's perfectly fine to spend all day with your nose stuck to a smartphone or an iPad making synthetic friendships and clicking buttons for corporations who tell you how to think, feel and do. You know I ended up buying Jessie a cell phone, a tablet *and* a PC. Not because I believe a seven-year-old needs to be text-messaging her friends when she's bored or surfing the net, but because I don't want her getting left behind in the technology stakes."

"You talk about being controlled by a sicko elite – don't you think technology and social media help bring people together, like it's easier to spread the word on, you know, chemicals in our food, illegal wars and stuff?"

"I think it's the opposite, Penny. Disinformation is just information being used against you."

"In what way?"

"Take three weeks ago, an Ausair jumbo jet on route from Sydney to Rome shot down over Jakarta. The media went crazy, right?"

"Uh-huh. At first they thought it was Muslim separatists using rockets supplied by al-Qaeda. Then the blame shifted to the Indonesian government for creating a false-flag operation."

"Exactly. Bringing the plane down so they had a legitimate excuse to go after the extremists, all of which set off a thousand and one theories on TV, radio and social media. But do you really wanna know who killed those innocent passengers?"

"Go on."

"MIT – Turkey's intelligence agency."

"MIT? But Turkey has nothing to gain by stirring up trouble in that part of the world."

"What if I were to tell you that the day the plane went down, the Turkish Army waged an all-out offensive on several Kurdish villages under the pretext of destroying PKK rocket-building factories? That four hundred innocent Kurds were killed, many of them children."

"I saw something about that, but—"

"You were caught up in the hullabaloo created by the plane being shot out of the sky."

"Oh, Hans, I thought I kept abreast of the madness, but the more you learn about the world, the sicker it gets."

"Can you understand now why I'm not ready to buy the chains?"

"I don't think you'll ever be ready – oh-oh-oh!" Penny's fishing pole bowed.

"Hell, does this mean I'm cooking breakfast?" Hans joked.

"Whatever it is, I don't think it will take much cooking." Penny grinned, playing the fish as it jittered about trying to shake the hook.

"I'm thinking great white shark." Hans downed his

beer and stretched a hand toward the line, ready to help.

"No, *bigger* than that!" Penny laughed.

"Do we need a gaff, or shall we let it tow us into shore?"

"I'm thinking we should cut the line to save us being chomped!"

"Well, it better be worth us sacrificing our breakfast mackerel!" said Hans, the thought of the jazzy fish's oily flesh perking his appetite.

"It's . . . it's . . . it's . . ."

The fish's white underbelly began flashing below the surface.

"It's . . ." Penny lifted the rod to bring the catch on board. "A mackerel."

"Ahhh-hah-ha-hah! It's not just a mackerel, Captain Penny. It's a smaller mackerel than the one we had!"

"It's a start!" She poked her tongue out.

They fished on awhile, Penny pleased her monster catch had lightened the mood on an otherwise miserable day, particularly as Hans' clenched jaw told her that today was especially difficult for him.

"It's her birthday tomorrow, Penny." Hans stared at his line disappearing into the shimmering black brine.

"Oh honey, I could see something was up. Why didn't you say?"

"Because I can't bear to think she's out there somewhere." Hans nodded at the myriad of yellow dots scattering the landscape. "Just the thought that she probably doesn't even know it's her birthday kills me."

"Hans, I hate to ask, but what if the fingerprints on the Fulani woman's glasses aren't on record and Jonah doesn't come back with anything for the hire car?"

"I've been thinking the same. Maybe it's time we contacted a couple of the newspapers here. Start with the biggest. See if we can meet with an editor to get their take on this Trade business."

"Perhaps we should have done that earlier."

"It's not as if we've had the time. Anyway, knock on wood" – Hans rapped his knuckles on the gunwale – "Muttley and Jonah will have some news for us tonight or tomorrow."

Penny stared at the distant lights without replying.

"Honey, you okay?"

Hans could see something was on her mind.

She turned to face him. "It's that I've got some news too, Hans."

"Go on."

"I'm pregnant."

74

As Hans cooked scrambled eggs in the morning, a million thoughts ricocheted around his mind. *Where the hell were we six weeks ago? It must have been in the hospital in Boston.* He smiled.

Penny's bombshell had a bearing on everything. Hans intended to spend his every breath, if that's what it took, keeping up the search for his daughter. If, heaven forbid, any harm came to her, he would hunt down the traffickers like the rats they were and eliminate them one by one. Should this happen, he'd decided to take his own life, for losing a wife, son and daughter, there was no reason to go on. But the fact he was going to be a father again put paid to that idea.

Stop it! Hans told himself. Jessica wasn't dead, and this passive speculation wasn't helpful. He *would* get her back. That was the plan, and he intended to see it through.

Carrying a tray of coffee, eggs, bagels, fried tomatoes and mushrooms through to the bedroom, Hans turned his thoughts to Penny. He knew her mind was still in turmoil following the abortion two years ago. He also knew she loved him as deeply as he did her. They hadn't exactly planned this pregnancy – but then it wasn't unplanned either. Both knew fate had brought them together for a reason and that they were in this for the long haul. Now, along with so many thoughts and feelings surrounding Jessica, Hans had Penny's and the baby's welfare to consider. *One day at a time, frogman,* he reminded himself. *One day at a time.*

By 10:00 a.m. neither Muttley nor Jonah had called. Hans didn't need to chase them – they would be in touch the second they got a result. To make use of the waiting time, Hans called the *Expresso das Ilhas,* the national newspaper, and arranged to meet Nelson Cabral, its editor.

75

Mouthwash Man unfolded the chair and draped his jacket over the backrest, preparing to give Jessica another dose of brainwashing in preparation for her trip to Europe with the fixer. His eyes were even more bloodshot than usual and the smell of liquor on his breath strong.

"Whhhaa . . . school you . . . you go to, Maria *Dennis?*" he slurred.

"Kelloway Primary School," she replied, knowing the answers off by heart now.

"Whhhaas your mother's name?"

"Sarah."

"Whhhere you live in . . . in . . . in London?"

"Number 25 Allcourt Road in Tottenham."

And so it went on.

Mouthwash was about to ask Jessica to spell her surname for the umpteenth time when the sound of high-pitched barking interrupted him. A small dog burst into the room, made a beeline for the bed, jumped on Jessica's lap and licked her face in between yaps.

"Hello, little doggy!" She hugged it tight.

From somewhere outside the other man shouted and whistled for the dog to return.

Mouthwash Man wasn't happy. Grabbing the scruff of its neck, he pulled the dog off Jessica and shook it violently. Then he left the room to return it to its owner, slamming the door behind him.

Jessica was off the bed in a flash and shoving her hand into the man's jacket, searching for his cell phone. It wasn't in the first inside pocket, and her hopes sank. Perhaps he didn't have it with him.

She tried the other pocket, and her hand closed around the phone. The little girl's heartbeat stepped up as she pulled out a Nokia similar to the one she had at home. Her father always insisted she memorized the emergency services number for each of the countries they visited on the yacht trip. England was 999, France 122, but she couldn't remember Cape Verde's. Jessica didn't even know if she was on Cape Verde. Perhaps when the pirates plucked her from the sea they had taken her to another country.

One thing she did remember was her father's cell phone number. He also taught her to prefix the area code with 001 when calling from abroad. Listening out for Mouthwash Man's return, she punched the keypad and put the phone to her ear.

Nothing – not a ring or even the engaged message.

Jessica checked the signal bars. There were none. She knew if this happened you could send a text message and the person would receive it when the signal improved. She typed "Help me" and her father's number and pressed "Send," then replaced the phone in Mouthwash Man's pocket and hopped back onto the bed.

Only, in her haste she'd forgotten to check the Nokia's predictive text.

76

On the drive to the office of *Expresso das Ilhas* to meet the newspaper's editor, Hans' cell phone beeped. Penny picked it out of the center console and read the message.

"Who is it?" asked Hans.

"I think it's Mike Devonport." Penny looked puzzled. "It says, 'Help md.'"

Hans took the phone and glanced at the screen. "That can't be Mike, unless he's using someone else's phone. His name would come up. Besides, it's not a UK cell phone number, it's local."

Without warning Hans hit the brakes and pulled off the road.

"What is it?" Penny asked.

"That's not 'Help md.' It's a typo. It's meant to say, 'Help *me*'!"

They looked at one another in utter shock – *Jessica!*

"Right, keep absolutely quiet," said Hans, closing the electric windows. He thumbed through the phone's icons, brought up the voice recorder and hit the red *R*. Then he pressed callback, set the phone to loudspeaker and turned the volume right up.

As the number started ringing, neither of them had ever felt so much anxiety flooding through their veins.

One ring . . . two rings . . . three . . . The line crackled a second or two.

"Papa?"

In that instant Hans went into professional mode, controlling his nerves as if adrenaline didn't exist.

"Jessica, Daddy's coming, but I need you to answer these questions. Can you do that?"

A barely audible –s could be heard.

Checking the signal bars on his Samsung, Hans cursed the other phone's reception.

"Honey, describe the man who is keeping you."

". . . older . . . you, Papa . . . speaks . . . ish . . . José . . ."

"Jessie, describe the room you are in."

". . . ark and col . . . lik . . . time we . . . asco . . . stle . . . Mommy . . ."

Hans prayed the voice recorder was getting all this and that he would be able to make sense of it later.

"Jessie, can you hear any noises—any cars or people or animals, anything you can tell me?"

". . . saw . . . ike Lucky in . . . mouth . . ."

"Listen, Jessie, the first chance you get, I want you to run away. Do you hear me? Run and find an adult and ask them to take you to the nearest police station."

She didn't reply.

"Jessie, can you hear me?"

The sound of a man's heavy breathing came over the loudspeaker.

Hans looked at Penny – and the line went dead.

The two of them sat in silence for a moment, both trying to take in what happened.

"Penny." Hans handed her a Bic and pad from the driver's-door compartment. "Write down what I tell you."

Hans replayed the recording –

". . . older . . . you, Papa . . . speaks . . . ish . . . José . . ."

– craning to make out the syllables, mouthing the words he understood and attempting to fill in the blanks.

He pressed pause. "Right, it's a Latino or Hispanic in his sixties."

Penny began scribbling. "How do you know that?" she asked, not questioning Hans' judgment but curious.

"Because José is the husband of our Mexican domestic back home."

"And the age?"

"She's saying he's older than me. If it were ten years or so, Jessie wouldn't be able to distinguish it. But in his sixties he'd likely be graying and possibly balding with wrinkles, and that would look significantly older."

"Why not seventies or eighties?"

"Do you think many people that age make money from trafficking kids?"

"Good point."

Hans pressed "Play."

". . . ark and col . . . lik . . . time we . . . asco . . . stle . . . Mommy . . ."

"Ach! Something about a dark and cold place. She must have been somewhere similar with her mom."

". . . saw . . . ike Lucky in . . . mouth . . ."

"Okay, the guy owns a terrier – Lucky was a Jack Russell belonging to a homeless guy we met in Plymouth."

Hans adjusted the voice recorder's graphic equalizer, turning up the bass and treble, and then replayed the middle part of the call.

". . . time we . . . asco . . . stle . . . Mommy . . ."

"Those two syllables, they have to be the name of a

place back home."

Penny kept silent. She could see Hans' mind was in overdrive going through the possible permutations.

"Oh *no!*" Hans let the phone drop in his lap.

"What is it?"

"No, no, no!" He slammed his hands against the steering wheel. "Why didn't I *see* it before?"

"Hans, you're scaring me." Penny was visibly shaking. "What is it?"

"Take a look at the photo again." He scrolled through the phone and brought up Djenabou's final message.

$$Logon, \downarrow$$

"What if I said that's six letters and an arrow – not five letters, a period and a claw?"

"I-I-I—"

"Penny, the place Jessie mentioned was Trasco Castle – it's a cheesy theme park in Portland built around the nearest thing we have to an actual castle."

"Are you saying . . . ?"

"Elderly *Spanish* guy. Lives in a *castle* and owns *Jack Russells?*"

Penny look at the Fulani's handwriting again.

"That doesn't say 'Logan,'" Hans prompted.

"No," she whispered. "It's 'Laguna,' and the arrow means she's in the dungeon."

- 77 -

As Fernando approached the cell door, having returned the Jack Russell to its owner, the mayor, a conversation saw him freeze in the gloomy corridor.

". . . and he talks like José."

Sobering immediately, he tiptoed forward.

"It's dark and cold, like the time we went to Trasco Castle with Mommy."

Hearing this confused Fernando. No one could have got into the cell in his absence. The little pissant appeared to be talking to herself.

"I saw a doggy like Lucky in Plymouth."

Then he realized – she was using his mobile phone!

Fernando threw open the door, ran across the cell, snatched the handset from Jessica and put it to his ear.

"Jessie, can you hear me?" asked a man – an *American*.

Fernando terminated the call and put the phone back in the pocket of his jacket hanging on the chair. He turned to Jessica, face red and looking about to burst.

Once again terror had her in its ugly grip.

Fernando began openly shaking, and spittle built in the corners of his lips. Jessica tried to back away, but once again chilling fear paralyzed her body.

The butler felt an overwhelming urge to grab the little bitch by the throat and strangle her until her face went blue, her eyes bulged and life drained from her body. Everything told him to smash her pretty little face into the wall and listen to the satisfying crack of her skull splitting apart, and to keep ramming his fist into her brain cavity, relishing the experience as hideous green matter splattered his face and torso.

As the butler stepped forward, Jessica wet herself again without even realizing. His face contorted beyond the extreme, the tendons in his neck, arms and legs as taut as bowstrings. Jessica's innate sense told her something terrible was about to take place, something primeval. Her legs gave way, and she collapsed with a jolt on the bare stone floor.

Then a strange thing occurred. Despite his intense rage, the Spaniard experienced an external locus of control telling him if he put a single mark on the kid, the fixer would see to it that the mayor, Gonzales, wasn't paid. The rings in Europe liked their children unblemished and unadulterated, for torturing and abusing the innocents was a large part of their sick, twisted game.

If Fernando's actions jeopardized his boss's massive paycheck, his life would not be worth living. For, an old man now and past fighting prime and the cunning of his youth, he relied on his boss's charity, knowing many younger, more able men would gratefully take his place with the profits on offer.

There was a time, over the water in the fog of war, when he could do what he liked to the innocents. His boss not only laughed and egged him on but also praised him for it. They would see who could frighten the children the most, who could abuse them the most, followed up by the most sadistic death. He'd liked that time: no rules . . . no anxieties . . . just reaping the rewards of the slaughter . . . the *glorious* slaughter . . . But all that had changed.

No, he couldn't harm the girl.

Fernando began to shake. A tear built in the corner of his eye and rolled rapidly down his cheek to drip onto the cobbled floor. Then another tear and another, and before long he was blubbing like a baby, shoulders shrugging up and down as he lost control.

He turned and left the room.

78

Hans drove flat out toward the villa, but as they came around a bend on the coast road, a tractor held up a line of ten cars. "Damn!" he muttered, instinctively checking his wing mirror.

"Hold on, Penny."

He floored the jeep's accelerator and took the oncoming lane, passing the sleepy island drivers one by one.

A heavy goods truck approached head-on.

"Hans, look out!" Penny curled up in the fetal position.

Hans didn't flinch, timing his maneuver perfectly and sliding through the narrowing gap to leave the traffic in his wake.

Back at Karen's, he connected his cell phone to the notebook and opened a secure Internet browser used by the Concern. He typed a code into the address bar and accessed a nondescript portal hidden from search engines. Putting in a username and eighteen-digit alphanumeric password brought up a dialogue box requesting insertion of a security token – a memory stick generating a synchronous dynamic password from a cryptographic algorithm. This brought him to a futuristic-looking interface with links to all areas of the

Concern's operation and a constantly updated newsfeed scrolling down one side.

"Wow!" said Penny, blowing her sun-bleached fringe away from her face. "It looks like something from that Tom Cruise film."

"*Minority Report*," said Hans. "It's actually designed for touchscreen operating systems. I just haven't upgraded my notebook, so I struggle through it with the mouse."

Through this front page, Hans could access a secure email platform, as well as several databases – each requiring differing levels of clearance – and a search engine to look up fellow operatives' profiles. Should Hans require a Russian-speaking electrician in Tanzania, he had only to toggle with the drop-down menus, click the relevant radio buttons and type the appropriate key words to find the closest match.

While Penny set to work cleaning and oiling the M9, emptying the rounds from the magazines, polishing and refilling them and replacing the batteries in the walkie-talkies, Hans navigated to the database storing the siphoned CIA records and began searching for information on Videl Gonzales.

79

Gonzales surprised Umchima. For a man past his prime, he sure kept up a performance in bed, subjecting her – how she'd describe it – to sex during the night more times than she cared to remember, along with his rancid breath, flaccid lily-white skin and maniacal eyes.

After each ravage, Gonzales lay back on the purple satin bedsheet and smoked a cheroot in silence, its coarse aroma mingling with that of the sex in the room to create a sickening miasma. Then he'd drift off to sleep without so much as a visit to the bathroom to wipe a washcloth over his increasingly stinking self.

Umchima put up with it. Business was at stake, and she was on a mission she had sworn to see through to the end.

The mayor was in his element, not having slept with an adult for some time, especially one as beautiful as this "crossbreed," as he thought of her, his preference being young boys and street sex workers – the more impoverished and sluttier, the better. Knowing he still had what it took to attract a good-looking woman, Gonzales experienced immense narcissism.

They slept until late in the morning, when the mayor called Fernando to request breakfast.

"May I use the shower?" Umchima asked.

"You may use the *bath*, Brenda," he reprimanded her. "This castle has never had a shower, and so long as I am living here it never will!"

Gonzales' eyes glinted with cognitive detachment, a sign the sociopath possessed zero ability for the self-reflection required to form meaningful relationships.

When Umchima entered the dining room after her bath, she found the mayor at the head of the long polished table, on which Fernando placed an ornate porcelain coffee jug and large, white, oval serving plates neatly stacked with smoked sardines, eggs scrambled with red pepper and chorizo, sauté potatoes, grilled tomatoes, mushrooms, think-crusted white bread and croissants.

Still unwashed, the mayor had wrapped a dressing gown around his skinny body, and combined with the aroma of smoked sardines, the pong was enough to make Umchima want to run from the castle and never return. She reminded herself how well she had done – not only to liaise with the Trade but also to contact *and* seduce a high-ranking trafficker, one who'd taken her into his confidence.

Now she needed a result, to sell a child, and all her efforts would be worth it. Umchima considered her next move. *What would a professional child trafficker do in this situation?*

Money! They must discuss money. A trafficker would want to know the rewards for putting their freedom on the line.

"Gonzales," she began, smiling disarmingly. "As much as I don't want to ruin the mood, after a perfect night" – she paused to cast a subtle seductive look – "I'm a businesswoman, and I need to know the economics of our proposed union."

"*Mi amor*, I didn't want to discuss such a crude matter during our most intimate evening, but of course you are right: no one ever got rich in business by letting other people make all the decisions."

"Especially taking into account the considerable risk," said Umchima, leaving the food in front of her untouched and only taking a sip of coffee – all part of her performance.

Gonzales was impressed, for the women he'd breakfasted with over the years – mostly desperate prostitutes – would usually gorge on such a feast, particularly after the all-night-long bondage session he subjected them to. Puncturing someone's back and buttocks with a thousand tiny holes using an electric drill, smearing their eyes and other sensitive membranes with piri piri sauce, whipping them until the welts became an indistinguishable mass of bloody purple and blue – or doing all three – generally tended to work up appetites . . . for the ones who made it through the night.

Putting business first was a true display of professionalism by this gorgeous creature, and it was reassuring to see she was equally as greedy, wanting to drop the preliminaries and start trading little brats.

"The first thing you must understand is that neither I nor you set the price – the market sets the price," Gonzales went on. "Naturally, I will strike the best deals I can with the traffickers in the North. You can expect to be paid ten thousand euros for children traded into the illegal adoption market in Europe, and five thousand for those going to the sex gangs. Of course, for the adopted brats it's a sliding scale depending on skin color."

"So how much for an orphan with my color skin?" Umchima held up her bronze wrist.

"Still negroid," said the mayor, not bothering to look as he chased a mushroom around his plate. "So about seven thousand."

"What if you can't strike a deal?" said Umchima. "Am I not putting myself through all this risk for potentially no reward?"

"Rarely will there be nothing, except when a child is terminated for security reasons, such as those thrown overboard from the speedboats when the coastguard interferes. Even the unwanted bastards fetch up to three thousand from local begging syndicates and the sex-tourist trade."

"And how often will you take children from me?"

"I think every six months or so, to keep the market from flooding. We have existing commitments to fulfill and limited space to hold them here at the castle—"

"You hold them *here*?"

"The valuable ones, yes. Does this surprise you?"

"I-I-I figured you'd keep a degree of separation. You know, as the middleman."

"Brenda, I am mayor of this city. I'm also a member of – how we can say? – a *special* club. No one is above me in these islands. *Entiendes*? Besides, the people know me for my kindness and charity – and do they not say the best way to hide such business is to conduct it in plain sight?"

Umchima felt an ice-cold pang of reality, having inadvertently opened yet another window through to the dark side. Gonzales was a serious player, on a par with illicit arms traders and drug lords. She knew now her time on this planet had considerably shortened. Gonzales didn't get to his position of wealth and influence by letting other people dictate his moves. He would use her while she was of worth to the Trade and then snuff her out like a discarded cigarette butt when the relationship was no longer profitable. In fact no, the wily old fox that Gonzales was, he would wipe the orphanage manager out before that, at a time she least expected it, to silence her and bury all evidence of their transactions.

It was tempting to formulate an exit strategy, but she needed to focus on the here and now and maintain her game face.

"Fifteen thousand euros for children traded into the adoption market and ten thousand for those going to the sex gangs. *That* is my minimum," she proffered, setting her coffee cup down on its saucer with a succinct chink. "You can take it – or you can leave it and we call this whole thing off. I'm not prepared to lower my price."

Gonzales was impressed. Umchima passed every test he set for her with consummate professionalism. Had this beautiful creature acquiesced and accepted his initial offer, she would shortly be on a boat traveling out to sea with her throat slashed from ear to ear – after he'd had fun with her corpse. But she'd held her ground, a true player refusing to kowtow under pressure and risk losing face. There would be one final part to her initiation, however, and with the little English girl requiring a bullet to the brain, he had an idea.

"Then I think we have a deal." Gonzales raised his coffee cup.

As Umchima lifted hers, the door flew open.

Fernando burst into the room, a frantic look on his moronic face. *"Commandante, tenemos un problema!"* he blurted, then explained in rapid-fire Spanish how Jessica got hold of his cell phone and called her father.

"Calma, calma."

Needing time to think, Gonzales motioned his former sergeant to sit down. This was serious. He'd known Hans Larsson would be trouble the moment he set eyes on him and had to predict his next move. It wouldn't be to go to the police – the American made it clear during their dinner party he thought little of their bungling efforts. Besides, even if Larsson did get the law involved, Gonzales was grand master of the Lodge, and most of the officers belonged to it. Those not in the fraternity were either in his pocket or smart enough not to cross him. No, the former Navy SEAL turned detective would take matters into his own hands and see his investigation through to the end – his downfall.

After thinking awhile, the mayor had a plan.

"Okay, call the Boy," he ordered the butler in Spanish. "Tell him we need to set up an ambush."

"Like Jinotega, Commandante." Fernando sniggered.

Gonzales nodded, remembering the trap his rebel troops laid on the outskirts of the Nicaraguan city, the success of which had been a turning point in the Contra's resistance.

"And what about the girls?" the butler grunted, praying he would put his huge hands to gratifying use.

"First we see what Senhor Larsson brings to our table. In the unlikely event he outsmarts us, we don't want two dead children on our hands. Even with my connections, that is a little too much to explain."

"I can take them out in the boat and—"

"No!" Gonzales scowled. "The American may arrive at any time, and I need you here with a gun. We will deal with him and then get his daughter off the island to avoid any problems until the fixer is ready to do the exchange."

"And the little English bitch?"

"When this is over, we will sink her in the channel as agreed."

"Commandante!" The butler clicked his heels together, going seamlessly into military mode.

"Brenda, you were surprised to hear we keep children here, no?"

"A little," Umchima replied, projecting an aura of calm yet digging her fingernails into her thigh under the table.

"Then I think it is time you met our VIP. I would like the two of you to take a trip together until things calm down, if this is okay with you."

"If we are to do business together, then it is the least I can do."

"Very good," said the mayor, his beady eyes glinting more than usual. "Fernando, after you have called the Boy, take Senhorita Umchima down to the dungeon and introduce her to our guest."

"Commandante!" The butler snapped to attention, about-turned and disappeared.

- 80 -

"**A**nything, hon?" Penny passed Hans a can of beer.

"Just kicking myself for not checking this guy out sooner."

He shook his head and flicked the notebook screen with the back of his fingers.

"Why, what you got?" Penny sat beside him on the couch and ran an eye over the CIA document.

"Videl Manuel Gonzales, born Videl Rodrigo Morales, made a name for himself fighting as a mercenary in the Nicaraguan Contra resistance, rising to the rank of colonel."

"Whoa! Didn't the Reagan administration sell arms to Iran and use the profits to fund these psychos?"

"Yeah, to overthrow the democratically elected Sandinista government, on the basis they objected to American imperialism in the region. The National Security Council set up an organization called the Enterprise, with its own airplanes, airfields and ships, staffed by covert operatives and using Swiss bank accounts to train, fund and supply arms to the rebels. CIA elements in Central America pretty much ran the show, and their method was simple: totally destroy the infrastructure of Nicaragua – hospitals, schools, businesses, communities – and destabilize the economy.

They killed anyone of note – doctors, nurses, politicians, government officials – even simple peasants suspected of sympathizing with the Sandinistas, who'd done great work for the people during their time in power. The Contras slaughtered thousands, and their MO was bayonetting pregnant women, executing captured enemy *and* their children, torture, rape, arson – all kinds of atrocities. The country disintegrated into such misery and chaos that even the Contras were sick of it and looking for a way out. Then the CIA slipped a puppet into power at the next election."

"So what part did Gonzales, or *Morales*, play in this?"

"In order to raise more funding for their terror campaign, the Contras began shipping cocaine to the US – organized, of course, by the CIA. Back then the drug was the privilege of the affluent – corporate types and Hollywood. They shipped so much of the product stateside that the market flooded – the CIA were literally stockpiling tons of the stuff – and the distributors and dealers had to find a way to increase consumption: basically, lowering the cost. So they came up with crack cocaine, a cheaper, purer and far more addictive form of the drug. The resulting epidemic ravaged impoverished communities and sent crime through the roof."

"And you're saying that Gonzales . . . ?"

"Was the kingpin in the drug operation – collaborated with the CIA, oversaw the supply chain and funneled the profits through Swiss accounts."

"Did he get brought to justice?"

"Ha! Justice isn't a word that features in this. The CIA later claimed they were under no legal requirement to report any knowledge of drug trafficking by foreign combatants and made sure to cover their tracks. The State Department argued the money they had paid to known drug traffickers was in support of humanitarian assistance to the Contras and that the conflict was justified, since the Sandinistas were supplying arms to rebels in El Salvador. The incoming Bush administration destroyed all documentation linking the players in the drug chain. Gonzales received the protection of Nicaragua's new US-backed president and couldn't go to trial in the States because he knew too much. Hell, he was a major card in a huge and tottering house. The deal he'd have cut with the congressional inquiry would've brought the US government crashing down. If I remember rightly, they laid all of the blame on some low-level drug dealer in LA."

"So Gonzales walked away scot-free?"

"Gonzales walked away with a clean slate and a small fortune. He turned up in Cape Verde in 1990 just as the country held its first open elections. Used his money and connections to bring Carlos Fonseca's Democratic Alliance party to power. Bar a three-year deposition in 2002, Fonseca's been there ever since."

"So Fonseca's likely in the US' pocket?"

Oh, he's a puppet all right. The US has been pouring aid money into Cape Verde since its independence in the seventies in return for certain favors. In 2006 Fonseca signed the US Charter for International Development – basically agreeing to whatever economic conditions and standards of governance Big Brother requested in return for ongoing financial assistance."

"And I'm guessing Gonzales still has ties to the CIA. Is there anything in the records linking him to child trafficking?"

"Get this. When rising up through the ranks in the Contra campaign, Commandante Tres-Ochenta – "Three-Eighty," as he became – had a penchant for taking the children of captured enemy combatants off into the jungle to 'show them his spiders,' and those kids never came back."

"No!"

"And in 2009 there was a huge police cover-up when a building contractor working at La Laguna reported seeing him in bed with a young boy who'd gone missing a week earlier and who was never seen again. Needless to say, the builder turned up dead on one of the island's beaches following a 'swimming accident.'"

"Oh, Hans." Penny buried her face in his neck.

"I know."

"What are you going to do?"

"I've got to move fast – this has wasted enough time already."

"Can you wait until Phipps and Clayton get here tomorrow?"

"Did you hear that guy breathing down the phone? That's not someone who's gonna give us enough time to organize a rescue."

"But you can't go on your own. I'm coming with you."

"No, you can be more use to me here. If I'm not back in three hours and I'm off comms, contact Karen and Muttley."

"You're not going alone?"

"No, I'm going to call Enrique and Eddy Logan. They both said they'd help out if it came to it."

Hans took out his cell and stabbed at the keypad.

"Enrique, Hans. We've found our man – it's the mayor."

After a distinct intake of breath, "This is not possible – he does much for charity, no?" Enrique replied.

"It is him, trust me. I've got proof – a recording on my cell phone of Jessica calling me from La Laguna."

"Have you told the police?"

"No, they'll only get in the way."

"What about Karen?"

"If I tell her now, then as US ambassador she's obligated to notify the authorities – but she won't. She'll cover for me, and that means unnecessary trouble for her down the line. I've told Penny if I'm not in contact within three hours, then to go ahead and tell Karen everything."

"What do you plan to do?"

"I have to go and get her out. Listen, Enrique, you said I could call on you for support. I know it means going out on a limb, and I'll go in there alone if I have to, but—"

"Hans, you got it, man. Where are you now?"

"I'm at the villa."

"Okay, I'll get there as soon as I can."

"Please do – and I'm gonna call Eddy Logan."

"Logan!"

"It's a long story, but he's promised me a favor."

- 81 -

Mouthwash Man entered the cell with a woman in tow.

"Maria, wake up!" he ordered.

Jessica raised herself, pretending to feel groggy from the pills. She fixed a wonky gaze on the woman, who looked a little like Penny. A similar age, they had the same height and build and shoulder-length sun-bleached brown hair. But this woman's tresses were frizzy, like Lianna the R & B star, her skin a little darker and eyes piercing blue, like the husky their neighbor old Jake owned back in Portland. A feeling of comfort came over Jessica. She hoped this woman would be as nice as Penny.

"Maria, this is Brenda."

The woman smiled. Jessica knew the game by now and nodded vaguely.

"Brenda is going to take you on a nice boat ride to a beach, but you must behave and do as she says, you understand?"

"Uh-huh," Jessica bluffed. "Do . . . they have ice cream . . . at the beach?"

"You can have all the ice cream you want." The woman chuckled. "If you are a good girl."

"I'll be good." Jessica made a pretense of flopping back down on the bed.

"I suggest you are." The woman thrust out a hand and

grabbed the little girl's hair, then pulled a knife from the pocket of her pants. She flicked open the blade, dragged Jessica's head into her lap and dug the knife into the side of her nose.

"Ouch!" Jessica tried to pull back, but the woman held her in an iron grip. Blood welled in the wound.

"If you mess with me, I will not hesitate to cut your pretty face so you're an ugly girl. Do you understand me?"

She nodded. The woman twisted Jessica's hair around her hand until the kid screamed and her eyes brimmed with tears.

"In fact, you horrible little bitch, I might kill you anyway. *Do you understand?*"

The woman's face contorted into an evil sneer, nostrils flared and eyes wide with hatred. She dug a nail into the top of Jessica's ear and spat in her face in frustration.

Behind her the man giggled quietly. The woman saw he had his fists clenched. She heard him wheezing with excitement and could see he was aroused.

"Okay, cut her hair," she ordered.

The man stepped forward with a pair of scissors. "Sit still!" he bellowed.

Jessica obeyed, and he began hacking off her long brown locks.

82

Logan said he'd leave Chico's immediately, stop by his place to pick up some hardware and meet Hans at Karen's villa. Twenty minutes later they heard the sound of his BMW skidding to a halt outside.

"Hans, how is it, mate?"

He popped the trunk and vaulted out of the convertible.

"Crunch time, Eddy," said Hans. "Thanks for coming."

"No problem. I owe you one for keeping quiet about my little import-export business."

Hans was about to introduce Logan to Penny when the Englishman's jaw dropped – "You!"

"Are we still on for that 4x4 jeep tour?" She grinned.

"We can explain later," said Hans, filling him in on recent events.

"There's some sick shits around." Logan grimaced. "Let's hope this mayor geezer comes out shooting so I can blow his head off with this baby." He reached in the trunk and pulled out his shotgun. "I brought the nine mil for backup." He lifted his Adidas jacket to reveal a shoulder-holstered pistol.

"Good man," said Hans, and then explained Enrique's part in the proceedings. "As soon as he gets here, we're all systems go." Hans checked his Rolex. "Damn! He's late."

They spent the waiting time checking the radios and going firm on an assault plan. Hans decided it was best to leave the car some distance from the fort and approach on foot, using the lie of the land for cover. As there were no feasible access points in the formidable walls, they would move through the entranceway in a pepper-potting motion, covering each other as they did. If the main door was locked, as Hans reckoned it would be, Logan would give it both barrels with the twelve-gauge, and then they would force their way inside and begin clearing the rooms.

"Do we know how many we're up against or exactly where Jessica is?" Logan asked, staring at a three-dimensional plan of the castle and the surrounding hillside Hans had drawn on paper.

"Hopefully it's just the mayor and his bruiser of a butler, but it's impossible to say. They know we're onto them because of the phone call from Jessie, but they'll figure we've gone to the police and that it will take time to get a raid organized. As for where she's being held, everything points to the dungeon, but who knows by now? We'll have to move through the building fast and neutralize anyone putting up a fight."

"Good job I brought these." Logan flapped open his jacket to reveal a pocket stuffed with plastic ties. "I use them for my runner beans."

Hans fetched his Beretta, holster and magazines from the rear of the jeep. He briefly considered the bulletproof vest borrowed from the embassy, but dismissed it, since it would slow him down and impede his agility.

"You know what the mayor looks like, right?" he asked Logan.

"Yeah, weasel-faced runt with a pointy beard. Comes in the bar now and again with that idiot of a bodyguard."

Half an hour and two unanswered calls later, Enrique still hadn't showed.

"Right, we can't afford to leave it any longer. We'll go without him. You drive, Eddy."

Hans hugged Penny and hopped in the passenger seat of the BMW. "Remember, I'll try and keep you updated, but if you haven't heard anything in three hours, get on the phone to Karen."

"Will do, Hans, and take—"

The BMW's wheels spinning on the gravel drowned her words.

As Logan pulled onto the main road, Hans' phone rang.

"Enrique!"

"Hans, I'm so sorry. I went off the road in the Porsche. I'm in the hospital with a broken foot and suspected concussion."

"We've got to go ahead with the plan."

"Yes, you must. I'll keep my phone on in case there's anything I can do."

"Thanks, Enrique."

Logan powered along the coast road, overtaking everything in his path. At the turn inland, he swung the wheel violently to the right and then quickly left, balancing the performance car perfectly to take the corner sideways in a screech of tires without slowing.

"South London School of Driving," he shouted above the rally noise, sensing Hans' surprise.

Hans ordered him to stop the car a quarter mile from the fortress and hide it off the road. From here they would move on foot, aiming to reach the building unnoticed to maintain the element of surprise. They clipped on their radios and earpieces.

With the American leading the way, they jogged up the hillside using the dead ground and scrub as cover, managing to get within twenty yards of the fort's impressive entrance tunnel without spotting a soul. Hans put his finger to his lips and gestured for Logan to stay where he was, maneuvering into position for a scan of the building.

The place looked dead – bizarrely reassuring yet a little unnerving. Hans was about to suggest Logan sprint for the archway while he covered him when something struck him as odd. A garbage can sat halfway along the tunnel, placed against the stonework on the left-hand side. It took Hans a second to figure what was out of place – there was no garbage collection this far from the city.

Hans turned to crawl back to Logan . . . and his heart stopped.

Logan was up and running for the portal.

Hans' initial reaction was to go for the walkie-talkie, but there was not enough time, so he rose to his knees and yelled, "Eddy! No—"

The sniper's bullet glanced off Hans' skull, and he crashed facefirst, unconscious, onto the rocky ground before the shot rang out. Inside the entranceway Logan stopped, confused, and turned to run back. With a greeny-yellow flash, the explosion rocked the hillside, blowing him out of the tunnel like wadding from one of the castle's antique cannons.

83

Hans came around tied to a chair in a dimly lit chamber deep in the bowels of the castle. Head thumping, throat parched, and blinking in the gloom, he felt a thick cake of congealed blood mixed with volcanic grit cracking around his left eye and temple.

Gonzales sat behind a simple desk with Hans' and Logan's weapons and cell phones piled on top of it. His butler, Fernando, leant against the wall behind him, giggling softly like a lunatic.

"Senhor Larsson," the mayor hissed as he sat there snakelike. "So nice to have your company again."

"Commandante Three-Eighty," Hans rasped, spitting out dirt.

"I see you have done your homework," said the mayor with the air of a victor, clearly reveling in a plan come good. "Then you must know who this is." He turned to his butler.

"I expect you're going to enlighten me."

Hans stared into the mayor's eyes yet took in everything in the room. The motionless mass on the floor was Logan, Hans figuring he was dead.

"Allow me to introduce you to Sargento Chavez." He turned to acknowledge the butler, who grunted. "As my most loyal man in Central America, he was better known as El Chacal. Tell me, do you know much Nicaraguan folklore, Senhor Larsson?"

"I'm a huge fan."

"Then you will know El Chacal, "the Jackal," is a fearsome creature that lives in the woods, a beast half-man, half-wolf-dog. Sometimes his clothes are made of twigs and leaves and his face the color of the forest, so he remains invisible. Other times he wanders naked along the footpaths in search of the next child to kill. El Chacal is said to stare into his victims' souls as he strangles them to death. Can you see why Sargento Chavez earned this reputation, Senhor Larsson? Can you imagine the unspeakable acts we got away with down there? Can you imagine the unspeakable acts he has committed against your daughter?"

Hans felt an enormous urge to try to rip free from the chair but knew this was not his time.

"What do you want?" he asked.

"What makes you think I want something?" the mayor preened.

"Because if you didn't I would be dead now."

"Ha-ha! Senhor Hans, once again you have it wrong. It is not what *I* want from *you*, it is what I want *done* to you."

He looked to his sergeant, and they chuckled like old hands.

A faint groan came from Logan's motionless body.

" . . . and to our playboy friend here." Gonzales picked an aging revolver off the desk and waved it limply at the two of them.

Hans recognized it as a Colt M1911, standard US military issue before the smaller-caliber Beretta M9 replaced it, a pistol the CIA shipped in its thousands to the Contras.

At the thought of the agency, Hans decided to play his trump card.

"You know I have informed the CIA of your involvement in the Trade, Gonzales. Their agent on the island will be filing a report and initiating a full-scale investigation."

"You are correct, Hans!" boomed a familiar voice from the back of the room. "You *have* informed the CIA." Enrique stepped out of the shadows and placed a hand on his fellow American's shoulder. "But I shall not be filing a report, and there certainly won't be any investigation – full-scale or otherwise."

"Enrique," Hans muttered, shaking his head and looking down at the floor.

"I gather you know the third member of our team quite well." Gonzales smirked. "In Nicaragua we called him 'the Boy.' When the CIA said they are sending a 'junior' field agent to coordinate my platoon, we all laughed. 'Junior'? we say, because in Spanish 'junior' means 'little rich boy.' So we nickname him 'the Boy.'" He looked at Enrique, the fondness evident in his reticent eyes.

"The little rich boy who made you a fortune exporting cocaine!" Enrique reminded the former rebel commander.

The three Hispanics guffawed like reunited veterans the world over.

"Actually, Hans," Enrique continued, "the only investigation will be the one conducted by our, erhum, 'friends' in the police here on the islands, who naturally will find nothing. Your daughter is going to a sex gang in Europe, and we simply cannot have her big hero father hunting us down for the rest of our lives. So this is why" – he held up Hans' and Eddy's cell phones – "I have sent a text from Mr. Logan's phone to yours inviting you and Penny for an afternoon out on his boat. And" – he waggled Hans' phone – "you have texted back in agreement. Of course, after I have gone to the villa and had a little fun with Penny before I kill her, we will put all your dead bodies in the cabin of Mr. Logan's boat, along with the English girl, and then sink it far out in the channel, where it will never be found, except by the sharks."

Another round of laughter ensued, the former resistance fighters in their element as a team.

"There's one little glitch in your plan," Hans interrupted them. "I'm assuming it was you tailing me on Mindelo the night you killed the Fulani."

"Ah!" Enrique beamed. "Would we be talking about the fingerprints from that bitch's house you sent to your lab *and* a certain rental car agreement? Listen to this."

He played a voice mail on Hans' phone.

Orion, it's Muttley. Look, Odysseus and I have been trying to get hold of you. The fingerprints belong to Enrique Ramos, your CIA friend, and the car was rented in his name, too . . .

"So what is with the code names – er, Orion?" Enrique mocked.

"Why, worried you're in over your head?"

"Just curious. Besides, I have sent your 'Muttley' this text." He scrolled through the list on Hans' cell. "Ah, yes, I wrote, 'Cancel this. CIA contact here informs me he interviewed the Fulani woman on the night in question as per agency protocol.'"

Hans' blood boiled. The CIA man had the upper hand, explaining both his renting of the hire car and his fingerprints on the glass.

Enrique reached into his inside pocket and pulled out an identical walkie-talkie to the one he'd issued Hans at the embassy along with the pistol, spotting scope and bulletproof vest. Holding it in front of Hans' face, "All the embassy's field radios operate on the same set of frequencies." He chuckled. "I also took the liberty of fitting a tracking device into yours."

"Hence how you followed me to the Fulani's house and warned Logan I was breaking into his boat."

"And how I laughed from my 'hospital' bed listening as you bozos crept toward La Laguna this afternoon, and I was already here with a garbage can primed full of Semtex and a sniper rifle aimed at your head. I would have killed you if I'd adjusted a little more for the wind."

"The same Semtex and US military-issued detonator you used to blow up the *Rosa Negra*." Hans scowled.

"And to think you didn't suspect a thing." Enrique held his hands up and grinned like a court jester.

"Actually, that's where you're wrong." Hans had one final card up his sleeve. "I suspected you all along, and I have already made a report to my friends with the 'code names,' as you joke, detailing as much."

"I'm . . . not so sure I believe you, Hans," said Enrique, feeling sure of himself. "I can't see how I could have given anything away."

"Nothing . . . at . . . all?" Hans played up the moment, seizing the opportunity to jump in the driving seat. "First off, how come you never suggested I file a missing persons report, which would have got the CIA involved in Jessica's disappearance under the US Trafficking Victims Act? That would have been the logical thing for you to have done."

Enrique gave a nonchalant shrug.

"Then there was the meeting in Karen's office when you agreed to help us *off* the record with the investigation into Logan. I said I appreciated your time. Do you remember what you replied?"

"I have no idea, but I'm sure you will remind me."

"You said, 'Four people are dead, Hans. I'll make time.'"

"And?"

"How could you have known? The news stations reported Alvarez and his two crew members as injured – and perhaps your sources told you they were dead – but I never mentioned meeting the Fulani to anyone other than Penny and Karen. I knew there and then you had to be involved in the Trade. If I disappear, then the information in my report is enough for my friends with the code names to spend their vast resources tracking you down."

Enrique kept quiet, knowing better than to incriminate himself while figuring out if Hans was bluffing.

Of course, Hans *was* bluffing. He had thought it strange, a little *niggling*, when Enrique came up with the number "four" in that conversation, but he'd put it down to a genuine mistake resulting from conflicting news reports surrounding the *Rosa Negra*'s sinking.

"You know, the Chinese have a saying – 'Never enter a

big game without the backing of a big player.'" Hans made his closing gambit. "You need to know I have that big player. In fact, I have a bigger player than you or your small-time agency buddies could ever imagine."

"Thank you for the lesson in Chinese psychology, Hans." Enrique remained nonplussed. "But you of all people must know that to strike a bargain you need to have something to offer. If what you're telling me is true and I let you go free with your daughter and Mr. Logan, then I go to jail for the rest of my life. And if I kill all of you as planned and your 'big players' catch me, I go to jail for the rest of my life. But what if you are lying? We kill you all and Penny and dispose of your bodies. Then we all remain free men – for the rest of our lives. And Hans" – Enrique brought his face close – "I think you *are* lying."

The mayor looked at his butler. Both frowned, hoping Enrique was right.

"Okay! Enough talk," Enrique barked in Spanish. "I am going to the villa. When you have done what you need to do, bring their bodies and the Davenport girl's to Logan's house in *his* car." He looked to Fernando. "Wrap them in plastic to make sure there is no blood, and wear gloves to drive. I will meet you at his place and have Logan's boat ready. I'll call our speedboat guy and arrange a meet offshore to bring us back." He removed the BMW's key from Logan's key ring and threw it to Fernando Chavez.

"And what about the American brat and the Malian woman?" the mayor asked.

"You bring them in your car. After we sink Logan's boat and the speedboat drops us to shore, he will take the two of them north to the Canaries."

Logan groaned and began to writhe on the floor. The traffickers had cuffed his wrists and ankles using his own plastic ties.

Enrique stared into space for a moment, going over all the loose ends in his mind. Then he threw Hans a mocking two-fingered salute, picked up the sniper rifle and left the room.

84

Hans' heartbeat stepped up as he envisaged the heinous acts Enrique would subject Penny to before he killed her. He wondered why the CIA man hadn't executed him and Logan there and then. He didn't have to wait long for an answer.

"Fetch the *señorita*," Gonzales ordered his former sergeant, "and be quick."

Fernando disappeared and returned seconds later with Umchima. Hans recognized her immediately as the manager of the orphanage in Gambia, the woman he and Penny had followed to the beachfront restaurant the previous day.

She eyed him with disdain.

"Forgive me if I'm tired of formal introductions, Senhor Larsson," said the mayor, yawning. "But Miss Brenda here is taking your sweet little Jessica to a safe house in the Canary Islands as a precaution while we dispose of your bodies. From there a very nice man will deliver her to a gang of terribly sick people in Europe. They have paid good money to abuse her, which they will probably do for a couple of years, after which they will cut her throat and burn her pathetic worn-out body in an incinerator."

"Then 'Miss Brenda' and I have unfinished business."

Hans glared right through the mayor's callous eyes.

"Oh! Perhaps I didn't explain." Gonzales pointed his pistol in the air and cocked it. "If Miss Brenda wishes to involve herself in our little secret, then she must prove herself first."

Umchima looked at the mayor, her flared pupils and nostrils radiating gleeful enthusiasm.

"Brenda, kill them and then the Davenport girl," he snapped.

"Certainly, Videl." Umchima took the Colt and leveled it at Hans' face.

They looked each other in the eye . . .

Hans winked.

Umchima turned and shot the mayor in the head, his brains splattering across the whitewashed stonework.

Fernando's eyes widened as he registered the look of surprise still etched on his slumped boss's face.

Umchima shot him twice in the gut and then dispatched him with a shot to the temple.

"Special Agent Trudy Bansker, CIA," she announced, pulling out a switchblade and cutting Hans free.

"That figures." Hans chuckled and shook the blood back into his hands.

With no time to explain, he grabbed his M9 off the table and holstered it, then picked up his cell phone and took the BMW key from the dead butler's hand.

"Can you take care of Logan and the girls?"

"Go!" the special agent replied.

Hans tore up a flight of stairs and, rather than waste time looking for an exit door, threw up a sash window and climbed out into the courtyard, where one of the traffickers had parked Logan's BMW. Hans jumped into the driver's seat, feeling thankful he was getting into the vehicle alive.

Wheels spinning, Hans flung the rear of the car around and shot through the entrance tunnel. Enrique had three or four minutes on him, but Porsche or no Porsche, Hans knew who the better driver was. He picked up his cell phone and dialed Penny.

Her voice mail kicked in.

"Penny," Hans spoke calmly. "Enrique is coming to kill you. Get out of the villa! Do *not* take the jeep. Take Karen's boat and go around the point. Don't waste time carrying the motor down to the water. Just row out and stay close to the rocks, because he's got a rifle."

Hans threw the phone into the center console and concentrated on the road. Arriving at the junction onto the highway, he slid the car around, taking the right fork faster than Logan did when coming in the other direction, accelerating away leaving a cloud of rubber smoke. He focused on his breathing and reined in his adrenaline-fueled mind, preventing himself from driving too fast around the sharp bends and slowing the speed his surroundings flew past at by half.

Passing car after car, Hans stayed on the left side of the road, only pulling back across when a corner loomed or a vehicle came in the other direction. He reckoned he'd significantly closed the gap between him and Enrique, coming over the brow of a hill to see the Porsche stuck behind a truck in the distance. Hans eased off the gas and, steering the car with his knee, cocked the M9 and placed it back in the holster. His plan was to pull up alongside the Porsche and slam it off the road, but as he put his foot to the floor, Enrique blipped past the truck and sped off.

As Hans closed on the truck, the road narrowed, preventing him from passing. He considered flashing his headlights and honking the horn but knew from experience this wound truck drivers up and resulted in them blocking you from overtaking.

Hans pulled back, fighting to remain calm and give the impression of a carefree driver, but as soon as a gap appeared he pulled into the trucker's blind spot, dropped down a gear and floored the BMW.

Closing on the truck's tailgate at a hair-raising speed, Hans pulled out at the last moment and, leaning out of the window to check the route was clear, shot past the goods vehicle before the driver even realized, losing a wing mirror in the process.

With only a few hundred yards to the villa, anxiety kicked in despite Hans' best efforts to control it. There was no way he could catch Enrique. Nor was there time to phone Penny again – it would waste the precious seconds between them. He pulled into Karen's driveway and skidded to a halt in front of the villa, praying Penny had received his message.

Hans leapt from the car and ran toward the terrace, rounding the building to a scene that filled him with horror.

Time slowed down . . .

He saw Penny's terrified expression as she pulled frantically at the oars of Karen's boat, knowing her efforts were in vain.

Enrique stood by the terrace wall, aiming the sniper rifle.

Hans knew from such a close distance, so long as the

CIA agent went for a body shot there was no way he could miss. He sprinted across the flagstones and dived through the air . . . as the shot rang out.

The high-velocity slug smashed into Penny's chest, the shock wave rippling through her body with such force her arms flung outwards, snapping one of the oars, and she slumped in the bow.

Hans slammed into Enrique's outstretched figure, knocking the rifle from his hands, the two of them flying over the terrace wall and plummeting into the sea. As Enrique panicked and began flailing for the surface, Hans felt a primordial surge of hatred from deep within. Enrique may well have been top dog when it came to trafficking children, but, in Navy SEAL territory now, he was about to pay dearly for his crimes.

From his Basic Underwater Demolition/SEAL, "BUD/S" training, Hans knew Enrique had broken the first rule of survival – do not panic! By struggling, he was using up the air in his lungs four times faster than Hans, who was in his element.

Although the M9 could fire underwater, Hans wouldn't risk drawing it and losing a hold around Enrique's waist, opting to continue powering downwards with determined kicks. It was payback time for what he had done to all those terrified kids – moreover, the price for messing with Jessica Kerry Larsson.

Enrique was not about to give up. He stopped his bid for the surface and attempted to draw a knife from a sheath strapped to his calf. Hans sensed his adversary curl into a ball and in the lessened visibility could make out a chrome pommel protruding from the Nicaraguan's pant leg.

As Enrique arched his body in an attempt to unsheathe his blade, Hans used all his strength three times to shake him away from it – albeit unsuccessfully, for the next thing Hans felt was jarring pain, Enrique thrusting the knife over his head and sinking its razor-sharp point into Hans' shoulder blade.

Unperturbed, the former Navy SEAL pulled his head out of the way and let the CIA man stab into his bone, knowing the knife tip missed his vital organs.

Hans continued kicking downwards until they contacted the sand. In utter desperation Enrique changed tack and shoved the knife through one of the wrists Hans had wrapped around his waist.

Hans' mind screamed at him to lose his hold, but instead he placed his other hand over the knife pommel and thrust it in further – right into Enrique's stomach, the shock forcing him to take an involuntary breath.

For what seemed an age, the Nicaraguan writhed in death throes before his body finally went limp. Hans grimaced and yanked out the stiletto, letting it drop to the seabed. Then he spun the dead CIA agent around and, gripping him by his lapels, stared into a face contorted by fear – eyes bulging and tongue poking out. In that moment Enrique's vanity, wealth and reputation meant nothing. Hans thrust the lifeless clown away and began swimming underwater in the direction of the boat.

Adrenaline from the fight waned as the crushing reality of Penny's death replaced it. Hans couldn't believe that after everything she'd sacrificed for him and Jessie, after everything had come right, he was recovering the body of his partner and unborn baby. A wailing anger built up inside, and as Hans burst to the surface he screamed, "*Noooooo*! *Ahhhhh, noooooooooooooo!*"

Crying like a child, he swam the last few yards to where the skiff's cheerful bob belied a scene he couldn't bear to witness. Throwing a bloody arm around the gunwale, Hans was about to haul himself on board when he heard movement.

"Jeez, Hans! Does it always hurt this much when you're wearing one of these?" She tried to pull open the Velcro flap on the bulletproof vest –

"Oh, Penn—"

– and collapsed into unconsciousness.

85

Hans sat reading a newspaper in a private room in Praia's Agostinho Neto Hospital as Penny and Jessica slept soundly in the breeze of a gently whirring cooling fan. On a table were get-well cards, birthday cards, flowers and gifts from Hans, the Davenports and the nurses on the ward. Phipps guarded the door, and Clayton sat in a rental car watching the main entrance, both armed with 9 mm automatics, a convenience afforded to them by the Concern's symp in immigration. Hans wouldn't relinquish his Beretta to Karen until they were safely on board the Learjet the next day. The remaining traffickers in the mayor's syndicate would likely go to ground following the events at La Laguna, but he would leave nothing to chance.

Penny's examination and X-ray showed two cracked ribs and severe bruising following the shooting. Jessica had a slight fever from opiate withdrawal and ugly bruises all over her body from the butler's beatings. She made Hans proud, shrugging off her experience and expressing only concern for Holly's welfare. Hans knew the full extent of her abuse had yet to manifest, but they would deal with that as a family when it did. It seemed crazy to imagine, but they had come through a lot worse.

Hans had the lasting visible scarring. Fortunately, the

bullet Enrique fired at him up at the castle only grazed his skull, but enough to leave a four-inch-long jagged cut on the opposite side of his head to the damage sustained from the gangrene. His wrist bandaged, he watched his girls sleeping, his wounds not an issue.

The three of them could have departed Cape Verde the previous evening, since the Learjet had arrived with a highly skilled surgeon and medic from the Concern on board, but speaking to Muttley, Hans requested Eddy Logan flew stateside with them when the surgeon deemed his condition stable enough. Eddy lost two fingers and his right ear in the explosion. He also broke his collarbone and left femur, punctured both eardrums and experienced significant internal bleeding. Yet despite Logan's fragile state, the surgeon felt he would be better off taking the six-hour flight in the fully equipped Learjet to reach the Ross Medical Center in Boston rather than remaining in the island's humble hospital risking secondary infections and medical inefficiency.

Logan's former partner, Krystal, paid a tearful visit to the Agostinho Neto, the staff directing her to Hans when she asked them for information on what had happened. Hans was up front about Eddy's involvement in the rescue operation, stressing his selflessness in volunteering to protect the islands' orphans. He told Krystal to go to Logan's villa and pack a bag for him and collect his passport, then do the same herself, explaining there was just enough space for her on the Learjet, and he would take care of her expenses while Eddy recovered in the US.

Holly Davenport was in a room a few doors down. She'd come through her ordeal physically unscathed, the mental trauma not yet known due to the drowsiness induced by the drugs she'd ingested. The doctors had put her on a two-week reduction regime to lessen the withdrawal symptoms. For Mike and his wife it was nothing less than a miracle to have their little girl back, a miracle for which they owed Hans Larsson. Mike had apologized for notifying the police of their conversation about Eddy Logan, which had resulted in the police raid. Hans assured Mike it actually went in their favor – helping him to eliminate Eddy from his investigation and acquire his assistance in the rescue.

The mayor's and his butler's deaths made the front page of *Expresso das Ilhas*, but with no mention of Enrique Ramos' demise. From Hans' limited knowledge of Spanish, he could work out the gist of the Portuguese text, enough to know the Cape Verdean authorities had declared the incident a "botched robbery." Hans smiled and looked forward to hearing what Karen had to say about the cover-up.

He didn't have to wait long. Phipps knocked on the door and whispered, "Yo, Larsson, you got company," in his usual gruff tone.

86

Karen entered the room accompanied by Special Agent Trudy Bansker, bearing gifts and flowers for Penny and Jessica and a twelve-pack of ice-cold Strela.

"Thought you could do with a beer," Karen whispered, setting the gifts down and giving Hans a long hug. "How're they doing?"

"Considering everything that's taken place since *Future* sank, I'd say they – *we* – are doing okay." He turned to acknowledge Agent Bansker. "And that's thanks to this woman."

Bansker stepped forward, beaming, no longer clad in drab attire suggestive of an orphanage manager from the African outback but a pair of figure-hugging black jeans, blue-satin heels and a short-cut leather jacket.

"Ha, I gotta whole team thing going on behind me!" she was quick to remind him.

They shook hands and hugged politely.

"I'd love to hear about it," said Hans. "There's a visitors' room down the hall. How about we take a couple of beers and give these guys some peace?"

With a lot to discuss, Brenda and Karen happily agreed. Hans patted Phipps on the shoulder and led the two women along the corridor.

In the visitors' room they found a few simple gray

office-type tables with overflowing ashtrays, and a glass-fronted counter displaying curled-up sandwiches, cartons of juice and a selection of demented flies. A bored, obese woman sat behind the counter, charged with serving up instant coffee and tea – at her own pace – from a steaming urn.

"So," Hans began as they cracked open beers, "how did Trudy Bansker end up hunting down child traffickers on Cape Verde?"

"Actually, I have a question for you first, Hans. How did you know I wouldn't shoot you back there at the castle?"

"I was watching you down on the seafront the day before – at the restaurant, following a tip-off from the police. I saw you go to the restroom and swap SIM cards – it's not as if 'Brenda Umchima' would have any reason to do that, so I figured you had to be law enforcement."

"To cut a long story short, Hans, the real Brenda Umchima was a government official in Mali. She fled the country after her American mother and Mozambican father were murdered at the start of the Tuareg uprising and entered the States on her US passport. Because of the political unease in the region, she got flagged by the CIA. I've worked for the agency in West Africa for the last ten years and have a working knowledge of the region and its languages. As well as my mixed parentage, it made me a good candidate for a classified investigation the agency was instigating. My handler was John Kellan, deputy head of the organization. I reported only to him and his trusted inner circle on the project – Operation Marianas."

"Into people trafficking on Cape Verde." Hans nodded

thoughtfully, noting the CIA's ironic use of geography, the Marianas island group being on the same latitude as Cape Verde but on the opposite side of the planet.

"With a particular focus on a CIA agent here they felt had gone bad."

"Enrique Ramos," Hans murmured.

"Correct." Bansker took a sip of beer.

"How come Ramos came under suspicion?" asked Karen.

"Every two years CIA agents come under scrutiny from the directorate in a process called 'the Sweep' – bank accounts, liaisons, personal issues, choice to stay in positions, everything."

"And Ramos appeared to have an unhealthy interest – or interests – in Cape Verde," Hans proffered.

"Cape Verde is what's known in agency circles as a 'dumpster' – a draft an agent might take to further their career, but not for more than a couple of years. Yet this guy had been here for ten."

"So he had to be getting something more out of it," Karen mused.

"Most agents can't wait to get back stateside and tackle some nitty-gritty homeland crime. The longer an agent stays outside the zone, especially if he has no family tying him to the area, the more likely it is that he's developed connections – good or bad. It was increasingly obvious Ramos was living above his means – contrary to what the public might think, agents don't drive vintage Porsches – but his investments were untraceable."

"And Nicaragua?" said Hans. "Enrique as the US' man down there, helping Gonzales smuggle cocaine and turning a blind eye to his abuse and murder of kids. Was that flagged up in this sweep?"

"It's no secret to the agency that Ramos and the mayor had relations going back to the Contra affair, but there's no evidence of these guys being partners in crime today and linking them to the trafficking."

"So what did?" Hans asked.

"It was actually what *didn't*. Enrique was using his insider privileges – like accessing trafficking syndicates through the database – to help the mayor make connections. But he was also using his position and knowledge to compromise antitrafficking operations conducted in the region. The agency and Interpol have spent millions trying to infiltrate the gangs in the last few years, only for the operations to fall on their ass each time – suspects going missing, Internet forums suddenly shutting down, factories using child labor emptying overnight . . ."

"So in the end everything pointed to him," said Karen. "Ramos was the only official here that could have known about the operations."

"Yes, but we still didn't have any proof. That's where I came in. For operational security, it was imperative I work alone and without agency backup."

"Men in dark suits and Ray-Bans wandering around the island would have soon got back to Ramos or the mayor," said Hans.

"They'd be more subtle than that, but you get the point," said Bansker. "I had to enter the country unarmed and couldn't even meet a fixer here to pick up a weapon. We broke just about every national and international law by carrying out the mission without the

Cape Verdean government's permission. Any chance of plausible denial went out the window when I blew the mayor's brains out and ended up with a casualty and two kids on my hands."

"Fortunately, our two governments are 'cooperative,'" said Karen, making air quotes.

"We came up with the cover story of Brenda Umchima fleeing to Gambia as an asylum seeker, and then we set up the bogus orphanage – at least we set up a website and staff for it." Bansker smiled.

"Staff?" Karen raised an eyebrow.

"If you ring the number on the website, you'll speak to the orphanage's delightful but rather inept secretary, Isatou, and hear raucous children in the background—"

"And in reality Isatou is a CIA agent in a room in Langley with a soundtrack playing in the background." Karen raised an eyebrow.

"In Silver Spring actually."

They all smiled.

Bansker opened another can of beer, and Hans and Karen could see she had already told them far more than her remit dictated.

"Will you stay with the agency?" Hans asked.

"From what I can see, from my limited time with it, the agency's basically a legitimized crime bureau covering for the sick ills of the ruling elite." She shrugged. "John Kellan is a good man, but he's out there on a limb surrounded by hyenas."

Hans and Karen flicked eyes at each other – this woman wasn't stupid or brainwashed by the machine. Having spent years in West Africa, she had witnessed the reality of international food programs, economic sanctions and puppet governance and wasn't about to buy the party line.

Karen casually gripped her neckline with two fingers.

Hans tapped an innocuous fingertip against the strap of his watch – twice.

"The reason Operation Marinas was set in motion," Bansker continued, "wasn't about doing the right thing to protect innocent children. It was that one of the main traffickers was a US government official, and the repercussions for the country's reputation if they'd gotten exposed didn't bear thinking about. Times have changed. Corporate fraud and Internet crime are the new black or orange or whatever – stuff operated remotely and later easily denied. To conduct such old-school rackets as human trafficking – like drug running – is asking for trouble."

"Wait." Karen raised a ruby-red fingernail. "I thought you said there were ops into trafficking here even before Enrique became a suspect."

"He's not the only bad egg in the box. About five years back an investigation by the FBI found approximately a sixth of foreign adoptions in the US were shams, and that most of them had been expedited by a single official – who conveniently shot herself in the head the day the feds went to arrest her."

"Are you saying that someone higher up the chain had their claws into her?" Karen's nail pressed into her beer can.

"Someone was abusing their power to coerce her into letting these adoptions go ahead, and when it all hit the fan they pulled her plug."

"And do you know this person?" Hans asked.

"I'm too small a fish for that kinda intel. But from what I gather, no one in the agency ever managed to find out. I think they were hoping Enrique Ramos would tell us – with a little 'gentle' persuasion."

"I guess I put paid to that option." Hans downed his beer and looked up at the huge whirring ceiling fan as he recalled his and Ramos' last meet.

"So Mr. Big is still out there," said Karen.

"Not just out there, but bigger than we thought." Bansker took an envelope from her bag, removed a photograph and slapped it down on the table. "This was left at my hotel reception."

The picture, taken in the States, featured a boy of about eight years old dressed in school uniform clambering into a smart sedan outside school gates. On it someone had scribbled in red ink "He's next!"

"My son, Jake," Bansker confirmed without emotion.

"Whoa!" Karen leant forward to examine the photograph. "Can you get it tested for DNA and prints?"

"I can, but if this person's smart enough to deliver the threat in less than twenty-four hours after the mayor's and Ramos' deaths, it ain't gonna lead anywhere."

Sitting there bending the tab on his beer back and forward, Hans kept silent. He knew Enrique and Gonzales were by no means the top of the food chain – with the mayor's Illuminati connections, this thing went *much* higher. However, he'd planned to leave the island with Penny and Jessica and put this behind them – for the time being at least – perhaps buying that RV and traveling the Good Ol' US of A for a while. The fact the men responsible for the heinous crimes committed against his child were still out there and active put something of a damper on things.

After a time he piped up, "Karen, as US ambassador, how are things since yesterday?"

Karen took a deep breath and exhaled slowly. "*Was* US ambassador, Hans. I resigned this morning. Have you read the paper?"

"You mean the police putting the shootings at La Laguna down to a botched burglary? No mention of Enrique's demise or the trafficking ring?"

"I spoke with Chief Inspector Amado and my seniors back in Washington. I can accept that an open investigation into child trafficking would be bad for tourism in these impoverished parts, and that to broadcast a US intelligence operation would cause all sorts of questions and make the traffickers go to ground—"

"But you sense a cover-up."

"It stinks, Hans, and I won't be party to it. Why initiate a CIA op if they're not going to see it through?"

"Because," said Bansker, "John Kellan, the director, conducted this op completely off the books, put his career on the line to preserve its integrity. But now that it's out in the open" – she tapped the photograph with a blue-painted nail matching her shoes – "you can bet our friend here is pulling the strings."

87

When Brenda and Karen left, Hans stayed in the dreary cafeteria and downed another beer. Irrespective of whoever else was involved in the trafficking, he had decided to leave it all behind and return to the States to spend time with Penny and Jessica, but something bugged him, and he couldn't put his finger on it.

After a visit to Eddy Logan, who lay semicomatose with Krystal holding his hand, Hans returned to Penny and Jessica's room and, following a quick chat with Phipps, crept inside and picked up the daypack containing his high-tech camera. He snapped a few pictures of his sleeping girls, then pressed a button to review them on the Canon's display screen. The camera was in gallery mode, showing the most recent photos in a psychedelic grid.

One of the thumbnails was the shot Hans took, using the self-timer, of him, Penny and Gonzales at La Laguna. He smiled, remembering the pedestal displaying a Soviet-made RPG head he'd rested the camera on. The Soviets had backed the Sandinista government in Nicaragua and supplied such weapons to their troops. The mayor must have taken the missile as a memento. The connection with the area also explained Gonzales' use of Latin American Spanish.

Feeling morbid curiosity, Hans navigated to the thumbnail and enlarged it to fill the screen – *Ahhh!*

That was what bugged him!

There was a photograph on the mayor's wall right behind his fancy desk where they'd stood either side for the shot – four men in combat fatigues kneeling in a line holding M16 rifles. When setting up the camera, Hans had spotted it immediately, purposely shielding his interest from the mayor and focusing the lens on the picture instead, intending to use the Canon's high-pixel clarity to enlarge it later.

Hans ejected the camera's memory card and powered up his notebook. After saving the photographs to the hard drive, he opened FlickerView, double-clicked the shot in question and then zoomed in on the four combatants.

A twenty-three-year-old Enrique knelt next to Gonzales – Commandante 380 – both wearing olive-green foraging caps and the intoxicated grin of war. Alongside them, Fernando stared dead ahead, a vacant expression on his dumb face.

"Hans, is that you?" Penny stirred.

"Right here, honey." He set the notebook down and went to her side. "How is it?"

"Feels like I've been shot – ouch!" She grimaced.

"That's *prob*ably because you have." Hans kissed her forehead. "Can I get you anything?"

"Some new ribs would be good." Penny eased herself onto an elbow. "What are you looking at?"

"See for yourself." Hans lifted the notebook. "Do you remember the picture I took of us with the mayor in his office?"

"Uh-huh."

"I spotted this photo on his wall, taken in Nicaragua during the civil war."

Penny craned at the shot. "Enrique . . . Gonzales . . . his butler."

"And this fourth guy." Hans tapped the screen.

Penny stared for a few seconds. "Well, definitely not Latino. I'm guessing American – *CIA*?"

"Howard Baxter." Hans nodded. "The guy who got my team drowned in Sierra Leone."

"The same guy who blocked Muttley's request for US Navy assistance when *Future* went down?"

"Yeah, and I'm pretty certain he had Kerry and JJ killed too."

"And do you think he's linked to the Trade?"

"Look at the photo, Penny. Don't all roads lead to Rome?"

"Yeah, of course," Penny muttered, knowing where this particular road led before she'd even seen the picture. "You're going to kill him, aren't you?"

"Penny, I—"

As Hans spoke, Jessica emerged from slumber.

"Papa," she murmured, rolling to face them.

"Sweet pea, I thought you were gonna sleep forever!"

"No, I'm fine." She gave a stoic shrug.

"You've been Daddy's brave girl, hey?"

"Ah! I told that man you were gonna come and kick his ass."

"Oh, you did, did you?" Hans glanced at Penny as they fought not to laugh.

"Yeah, I told Holly too. She was a bit scared – she's just a little kid. She didn't even know where America is –

she called us Mercans."

"So, you're feeling fine." Hans grinned.

"Snoozin's for losing, Papa."

Penny stretched out a hand, and Jessica grabbed it. "I love you, sweet pea."

"I love you too, Penny. Can we go back to Portland now?"

"Hey!" said Hans. "We can all go back to Portland tomorrow. But do you know what?"

"What, Papa?"

"There's someone who wants to say hi!"

Jessica's face froze in fear. "Wh-wh-who, Papa?"

Hans reached into his daypack. "It's this little guy," he said, waggling the culprit in front of her.

"Bear!" she screamed, taking her buddy into her arms.

Chris Thrall is a former Royal Marines Commando and author of the bestselling crystal meth memoir *Eating Smoke*. A qualified pilot and skydiver, with a degree in youth work, Chris has backpacked throughout all seven continents, worked with street children in Mozambique, driven aid workers from Norway to India and back by coach, and scuba dived with leopard seals in Antarctica. He lives in Plymouth, England, and plans to continue adventuring, charity work and writing.

www.christhrall.com

www.twitter.com/ChrisThrall

www.facebook.com/ christhrallauthor

Acknowledgments

To my Jenny for your encouragement and unconditional support. My loyal Eating Smoke readers, many of whom said, "Chris, you write it, we'll read it." My awesome delta team of Mike "Rosco" Ross, Carole Poke, Patrick Burke, Nikki Davenport, Sian Forsythe, Nikki Densham, Fiona Jackson, Kenneth Fossaluzza and Marc Spender for volunteering to read the manuscript and feeding back with invaluable observations and advice. Andy Screen at Golden Rivet your amazing artwork and dedication has brought the Hans Larsson series to life. Marcus Trower, for polishing the final draft and being a great editor to work with. Thank you.

Books by Chris Thrall

The Hans Larsson series

1 - The Drift

2 - The Trade

Non fiction

Eating Smoke: One Man's Descent into Crystal Meth Psychosis in Hong Kong's Triad Heartland

Printed in Great Britain
by Amazon

21502225R00215